THE YELLOW DIAMOND

MICHELLE GRAHAME

authorHOUSE

AuthorHouse™ UK
1663 Liberty Drive
Bloomington, IN 47403 USA
www.authorhouse.co.uk
Phone: UK TFN: 0800 0148641 (Toll Free inside the UK)
*   UK Local: (02) 0369 56322 (+44 20 3695 6322 from outside the UK)*

Published by AuthorHouse 08/24/2022

ISBN: 978-1-7283-7479-6 (sc)
ISBN: 978-1-7283-7480-2 (hc)
ISBN: 978-1-7283-7481-9 (e)

BY THE SAME AUTHOR

Love Will Have to Wait
Lord of Hades
Rhapsody in Black

Dedication

In Loving memory of Frank

ABOUT THE AUTHOR

Michelle Grahame lives in Northwest Kent, and enjoys visits from her family, reading and taking part in local activities. "I love creating characters and plots for my novels." Says Michelle. As an avid collector, she likes attending boot and antique fairs, where a random purchase can become an inspiration for her writing. A qualified Art Historian and lecturer, now retired, she has had many opportunities to engage with people who share her interest. The YELLOW DIAMOMD, and its sequel, STAPLEWOOD PARK, are her first historical novels.

If you enjoyed **The Yellow Diamond**, I would love to hear from you. www.michellegrahame.co.uk

CHAPTER 1

T he Marquis of Coverdale, leaning against the mantelpiece of his mother's withdrawing room, was not attired for a morning call, but dressed for riding. He caught a glimpse of his stock in the over-mantel looking-glass, and rearranged a crease before saying: 'Well, Mama?'

The Dowager Marchioness, seated by the fire, looked up from her needlework. 'I wanted to see you, Justin.'

His Lordship raised a dark eyebrow. 'I rather gathered that, from the note I received, just as I was about to set off for the park, and here I am, always the obedient son.'

'Well, you see, dear—'

But any explanation his mother was about to give was cut short by a discreet tap on the door. The butler entered, bearing a silver salver, which he presented to her ladyship, who took the single card, read it, and passed it to her son.

'The persons you have been expecting have arrived, M'lady. Do you wish me to show them up?'

'Yes, Clarkson, immediately, and then bring refreshments, coffee, madeira wine, and some pastries, that sort of thing.' She waved a languid hand.

'Very good, M'lady.'

The butler withdrew, and the marquis took the opportunity to examine the card, a simple one bearing the printed name: Sir Piers Abbot, Abbots

Court, Somerset." Written below, in ink, was the legend, "Miss Abbot and 'Mrs Fletcher."

Moments later, three people were ushered into the room. tall lady dressed in plain green merino, relieved only by narrow bands of lace at the neck and cuffs, and a much younger lady, barely out of the schoolroom, whose sprigged muslin dress, paled into insignificance in the shadow of her outstanding beauty: large cornflower-blue eyes and rosebud lips, and tip-tilted nose, set in a heart-shaped face, framed with blonde ringlets. The third member of the trio was a young man, with blond hair, and fashionably clad, but clearly not London-tailored. He was visibly leaning on an ivory-handled ebony cane; his face was pale and his expression drawn.

'Oh, my dear children, and Mrs Fletcher, too, welcome, welcome indeed. I hope your journey wasn't too trying.' She was looking anxiously at the young man and held out her arms.

The girl rushed forward. 'Oh God-mamma, how kind of you to ask us here.' She clasped the old lady's hand with both of hers.

This was the first clue that the marquis had gleaned of what was going on, but his mother soon provided more information. 'Justin, dear, this lovely child is my god-daughter, Rosalie, and may I introduce Sir Piers Abbot?'

The Marquis held out his hand, and the young man came forward rather stiffly to shake it. 'How do you do, My Lord? I am very pleased to meet you.' He bowed.

'Your servant, Sir Piers,' replied the Marquis, still somewhat bewildered by the turn of events.

'Mrs Fletcher, I am so glad you were able to find the time to come. May I introduce you to my son, the Marquis of Coverdale? Justin, this lady is the guardian of these two young people.'

The marquis raised a dark eyebrow; the lady seemed very young to be a guardian, besides it being unusual for any woman to be in that position anyway, but he smiled his welcome as Amanda Fletcher bobbed a curtsey. Her next utterance took him by surprise completely.

'It was so kind of Lady Coverdale to suggest that you might be able to help me out of the little difficulty I find myself in. I expect it has all been explained to you—'

Keeping a straight face, he replied. 'not precisely, Mrs Fletcher,' skewering his mother with a lance-like glare, which she studiously avoided. She was spared a reply by a footman arriving with a tray of drinks and pastries.

Looking meaningfully at her son, the marchioness said: 'perhaps you would like to take Mrs Fletcher to the book-room, where she can explain matters in more detail, while I talk to these dear children.'

'An excellent idea, Mama.'

'Thank you, Alfred, have some refreshments sent to the book-room at once.'

'Yes, M'lady.' He set he tray on a small table and withdrew.

The marquis turned to the lady in question, who was wearing a quizzical expression, tinged, with a touch of amusement.

'Allow me to escort you, Ma'am.'

Once settled in the large book-lined room, furnished with reading-desks, easy chairs, and a pair of large globes, Amanda Fletcher felt it should be she, who opened the conversation.

'How much does "not precisely" mean, concerning my problem, My Lord?'

Justin gave a little half-smile. 'I imagine from that remark, Mrs Fletcher, you realise I know nothing at all. In fact, your very existence was unknown to me before you stepped into my mother's drawing room. The other two, I suppose, I have been vaguely aware of before. I'm afraid my mother has either been extremely forgetful, which is unlikely, or deliberately kept me in the dark, for reasons of her own.'

Before she could reply, another footman arrived. Justin immediately took the tray and dismissed the servant. Placing the tray on a nearby table, he turned to ask Amanda what her preference was.

'Coffee, My Lord, if you please.'

Once comfortably seated, Justin began, 'Perhaps we may now try to unravel your …er …difficulty, Mrs Fletcher,' he said, with an encouraging smile.

After a short pause, while Amanda gathered her thoughts, she began. 'It is primarily a financial problem, Lord Coverdale,' then realising he might think she was short of money, she went on hastily, 'our mother has just told you that I am the legal guardian of those two young people upstairs, and therefore am in control of their finances until they come of age. While in Somerset, there is no difficulty, but now that I …we …are in Town, there is. I shall need to draw on money for all kinds of expenses, especially for Rosalie's debut.' She stopped, feeling she was rattling on.

Justin looked puzzled, and said, 'I don't think I understand the problem.'

'That is because you are a man, My Lord. You may not be aware that women are not permitted to have account at London bank, and it would be impossible to apply to my fellow trustee, a solicitor in Taunton, to send money by post, so I need to be able to set up banking facilities. I have brought a banker's order, drawn on the trustee account. Your mother wrote to me saying you could help.'

'Did she, indeed?'

'Yes.'

'Well, she was right. Of course, I can. I will speak to my secretary as soon as possible, and it can be fixed in no time. You have enough for your needs at the moment?'

Amanda couldn't help a little sigh of relief. 'Oh, yes, quite sufficient, but not enough to last the whole Season.' She put down her cup and rose to go. 'Thank you so much, Lord Coverdale, for offering to help; it has taken a lot of worry from my mind.'

'Please,' begged the marquis, 'won't you stay a little while longer and tell me what else is still on your mind. Let me pour you another cup, Mrs Fletcher.'

Amanda wondered why he thought she had other worries, but nevertheless, sank back in her chair and accepted a second cup of coffee.

'I don't know what made you think I have further concerns, but you are right.' She looked up and saw kindness in his unusual golden eyes.

'I believe if someone says they've been relieved of a lot of worries, it probably means there are more, or perhaps it is because you have the guardianship of two young people, when, if you will excuse me saying so, I imagine you are barely older than them, yourself. If you don't consider it an impertinent question. How did it come about?'

Amanda was going to tell him more about Sir Piers and Rosalie but had not expected to do so, so soon. 'No, My Lord, it is not impertinent at all. It came about because my late husband, Agnew Fletcher, was their guardian, and when he died two and a half years ago, he arranged with the other trustee I think I mentioned him, a Mr Smallbody, of Taunton, that they should become my wards on his death.'

Justin nodded. 'And that arrangement suited you?'

'Yes, Agnew had been a residentiary canon at Wells Cathedral, and we had a house in the cathedral close, which of course I had to leave when he died, so going to live at Abbots Court was very convenient for me, as well as being able to oversee Piers and Rosalie, who were nineteen and fifteen at the time, although I had known them from the time Agnew became their guardian.' She took another sip of coffee, and her hand trembled a little as she replaced it in the saucer, nervous about what she was going to say next. 'I know, Sir, that you are a man to be trusted, and ...'

'Indeed, Mrs Fletcher,' the marquis interrupted, 'and how did you come by such information? If it is true.'

'Oh, I know it is true, My Lord, I have friends not in high places, or of high rank, but of great intelligence and in positions of trust in the interests of this country.' She saw surprise in Justin's expression. 'And,' she went on, 'I have read as much about you as I could find;; it's quite a lot. Marquis of Coverdale, Earl St. Maure, Viscount Fairfield. MA, JP, and deputy lieutenant of the County of Essex.'

Justin was a little taken aback; 'Why all this research into my personal life?' he queried.

'Because what I am going to tell you now may be of vital importance to Piers and Rosalie, and perhaps to me too. I'm sorry, I have to think, and I do it better standing up.'

Amanda rose to her feet, but signalled to his lordship stay seated, then began to walk up and down the centre of the long library, unwittingly giving Justin an opportunity to observe her in more detail than he had hitherto been afforded.

Her dress, he noted, although drab in colour, was of the finest material, and so well-made that it flowed around her long legs as she strode up and down the room. She wore a widow's cap of fine lavender lace, but it could not entirely conceal an abundance of auburn hair that was doing its best to escape from its confinement. Her high-bosomed figure was supple, but her shoulders were, perhaps, a little broader than the current fashion dictated. Her air of deep concentration could not disguise her fine, brown eyes or

5

attractive features. He liked what he saw. Amanda Fletcher was clearly a woman out of the ordinary, and he was keen to hear what she had to say, even although it probably meant getting involved, perhaps in something he would rather not.

The lady resumed her seat. 'I must first explain how Sir Percy left his money in his will. The estate of Abbots Court and its income, became wholly owned by Piers, and when he reaches the age of twenty-five, he will have the bulk of Sir Percy's considerable wealth, and I will be relieved of the burden of administering it, together with Mr Smallbody, of course.'

'That seems quite straightforward, does it not?' Justin commented.

'Yes, it is, but it is Rosalie's inheritance that is giving me a real problem. Her father left a relatively small portion of his estate to his daughter and put it in trust for her lifetime, so no would-be fortune hunter could play fast and loose with it. Something I must say I approve of. I don't think it is right that a woman's husband can take his wife's money when she marries, but that's beside the point. It's the law, unfortunately.'

Justin thought for a moment. 'Miss Rosalie is a very pretty girl, but now she is about to embark on her first Season, with only her face to recommend her to possible suitors, no dowry, is that the problem?'

'Oh, indeed no. Rosalie *has* a dowry. Excuse me a moment.'

To his surprise, Amanda stood up again and turned her back to him, He saw her hands detach something at the back of her neck, and when she faced him again and held out her hand, her palm was almost completely covered with the most amazing jewel he had ever seen. An enormous pear-shaped, brilliant-yellow gem glowed and sparkled on Amanda's hand. Justin was rarely lost for words, but the sheer size and magnificence of the jewel fairly took his breath away.

Amanda was the first to speak. 'Rosalie's dowry,' she said.

CHAPTER 2

'God in Heaven!' The marquis finally found his voice. '*What is that?*'

'Just what it appears to be, My Lord.' Amanda turned her hand so the jewel's facets threw off living sparks of sunlight. 'It is a flawless 63 carat, or thereabouts, very rare, yellow diamond.'

'May I?' Justin extended his hand towards the jewel.

'Certainly, please do.' Without touching Amanda's hand, he took the jewel by the thin velvet ribbon, from which it had been suspended round her neck, and held it up to the light. The midday spring sun shone through it, casting a shower of fiery sparks of light into every corner of the room as it slowly revolved.

'I have never seen anything like this, *ever,*' Lord Coverdale remarked, 'and I have seen a good many high-quality gems in my life.'

Amanda knew what he said was true; even she had heard of the famous Coverdale emeralds. 'It has a name. When Mr Smallbody gave it to me, it was accompanied by a piece of paper with words written on it in a foreign language and script. He said he had no idea what it meant and had never tried to find out, but I knew someone who could. He told me it translated as *"The Light of the Sun."*

Justin was about to speak when a light tap was heard on the door. He stuffed the jewel into his pocket before saying, 'Come in.'

The butler entered. 'M'lord, her ladyship has asked me to say that a light nuncheon has been laid out in the small dining room, should you wish to partake.'

'Thank you, Clarkson, you may take the coffee tray, and that will be all.' The moment the servant withdrew, the marquis pulled the jewel out of his pocket and handed it back to Amanda. 'You must know I have a lot of questions.'

Resuming her seat and placing the diamond on the small table situated between them, she said, 'Yes, please ask them. I will answer if I can.'

'First and foremost,' the marquis began, resuming his own seat, 'why are you wearing a king's ransom round your neck? Surely that is very dangerous?'

'It's certainly very uncomfortable.' She smiled. 'I haven't been able to take it off for three days, but as for danger, I couldn't think of a safer place.'

Or a more desirable one, Justin thought, then pushing the thought away, he said, 'Surely some sort of safe …?'

'Yes, we do have one at the Court, but I couldn't leave it there when I was going to be away for several months. You see, it was in Mr Smallbody' s care until just before Christmas, when, at one of our monthly meetings, he took it out of a secret drawer in his desk, explaining that he was no longer the person to be in charge of it, as ill health was forcing him to retire. So, there was I, obliged to be its keeper.' She glanced at the jewel, and it seemed to her to glower back at her, menacingly.

'Yes,' Justin replied, 'I can see that makes some sort of sense.' He was not accustomed to many women of his acquaintance making sense. 'My second question is, how did it come into the family's possession in the first place?'

'The short answer to that is, I don't know, and neither does Mr Smallbody. But I do know some facts from which deductions can be made.'

'Tell me; the nuncheon can wait. I can't.' The Marquis leant forward and touched the diamond with the tip of his forefinger. 'What tales you could tell, if you could only speak. Sorry, Mrs Fletcher, please continue.'

'Sir Percy was a second son and, at a young age, joined the Honourable East India Company and went out there to make his fortune …'

'Which it seems he did,' interrupted the marquis. 'Sorry—'

'…While there,' Amanda went on, 'he made the acquaintance of my husband, then newly ordained, and who, without a curacy or living, was some sort of chaplain to the HEIC. Agnew was obliged to leave India after only a short time, due to ill health, but later, when he came to the cathedral, he renewed his friendship with Sir Percy, who by then had unexpectedly inherited the estate, and the title, on the death of his brother. That is all I really know. Sir Percy died in 1810, the year after I married Agnew.'

'Hmm,' Justin reflected, 'not much to go on, but at least it explains how this,' he indicated the jewel, 'got to England. Now I must ask my third question, although I expect I already know the answer. You want me to keep the thing safe, do you not?'

Amanda took a deep breath. 'In a word, yes.'

'Well, I will, and I think I know just the hiding place for it.' He stood up, went over to one of the book-cases, and stretched up, tall enough, without recourse to the library steps, to run his finger along the second-to-top shelf. He plucked a thick, leather-covered volume from the shelf and brought it over to Amanda. 'Take a look.'

She read the title on the spine, *Reflections on the Human Condition*, and raised questioning eyebrows.

'Inside.'

The first pages of text looked normal, then she saw that most of the centre of the book had been cut away, making a space about three inches square.

'Your king's ransom will be quite safe in there, I think.' Justin picked up the jewel and handed it to her. He was right; with its ribbon coiled round, it fitted snugly into the box-like space. She closed the book. The marquis returned it to the shelf.

'Now, I hope that relieves your mind, Mrs Fletcher. No one will ever look for it there, and anyway,' he added, 'hardly anyone uses this room, except me.' The thanks he was expecting were not forthcoming. It was his lordship's turn to sigh. 'I suppose from your silence I can deduce that I have not satisfied you,' he said with a slight edge to his voice. 'Is there something else you're not telling me?'

'I ... I fear there may be danger connected to the diamond. The last thing I want is to bring it to your mother's house.'

'Danger? How could that be? Only you and I know where it is, and the only other person who knows of its existence is your Mr Smallbody. Those two upstairs don't know, do they?'

'No, they do not, but someone does.' She drew a small piece of paper from a pocket concealed in the folds of her dress, and handed it to the marquis.

He unfolded the note and read the few words written there: 'Sir Piers Abbot, *The Light of the Sun* is not legally yours. It should be returned to its rightful owner.' The writing was as clear as the statement.

'Whew!' exclaimed the marquis. 'Who sent you this?'

'I've no idea, but it isn't the first one. I received, or rather, one came just before Christmas, but that one was addressed to Mr Percy Abbot, and the one in your hand, just a few days ago. Both were slipped under the front door at the Court, but no one was seen doing so. And fortunately, they fell into my hands before either Piers or Rosalie could see them.'

'Well, Mrs Fletcher, you are quite right; the jewel should not remain in this house. I will take it upon myself to keep it safe, I promise you.'

'I don't know how to thank—'

'Then don't. I think it's time you went to partake of that cold nuncheon that awaits you.

'You are not coming?'

'No, I want to think about all you have told me and decide how best to go on.' He opened the door for her. 'You'll find a footman to show you the way to the small dining room. My mother has an abundance of them. She can never remember their names, so calls them either James or Alfred.' He called over one of the two who were standing in the hall. 'Show Mrs Fletcher to the small dining room.'

'Yes, M'lord. ; at once, M'lord.'

To the other footman, whose light-brown complexion was a contrast to his pristine powdered wig, he said, 'Tell them to bring my horse round,' and added, 'What is your name?'

'Henry, M'lord…but her ladyship usually calls me James.'

Justin smiled.

CHAPTER 3

It was three days before Amanda saw the marquis again, and apart from the relief of no longer having to carry the diamond around, her mind was occupied with all the plans that Lady Coverdale had been initiating for Rosalie's entry into polite society. Her ladyship's own modiste was summoned to assess her god-daughter's wardrobe, which she considered quite inadequate for a London season, and Madame Celeste was delighted to have a lovely young lady to clothe in the latest fashion. Amanda was very firm that the dresses should be of the finest quality, but of a style and material proper for a girl of Rosalie's age.

Rosalie, herself, was delighted at first at the thought of a new wardrobe, but soon got bored with standing on a stool and being tugged and pinned into half-made clothes.

The spring weather had turned fickle, with heavy showers, but on a suitably warm afternoon, Lady Coverdale decided to take a carriage ride in Hyde Park.

'Amanda, my dear, please be ready to leave at four o'clock. The fashionable world will be there then, and it is an ideal opportunity to make them aware of my protégée, and generate invitations to the season's events. Rosalie is a very pretty, well-behaved girl; I know she will take.'

Soon after their arrival, she discussed Rosalie's debut with Amanda. 'The season has barely begun,' she said, 'and I believe it would be best to introduce your ward quietly at first, simple dinners with a little dancing, or music afterwards, and perhaps games of lottery tickets with other young people. Do you not agree?'

Amanda felt she had to agree, no matter what was proposed, but she was delighted with the marchioness's suggestion. 'I believe Rosalie would much prefer to be introduced in that way. She is a confident girl, and quick to learn, but inexperienced in the ways of polite society.'

'I find her very prettily mannered, and of course her antecedents are impeccable,' Lady Coverdale said, smiling. 'I believe society will take to her very quickly.'

'If I may make a suggestion, Lady Coverdale, Rosalie was at Mrs Pritchett's Academy for Young Ladies, in Bath, with a Lady Sophia Carstairs, and they became great friends; they've corresponded since leaving the establishment, and I know the family is in town. Would it be possible for them—?'

'Of course, my dear, I know Lady Carstairs quite well. I will call.'

Amanda smiled. One thing she knew for certain: with a marchioness for a sponsor, every door in the polite world would be opened wide. But there was still one worry, if Rosalie was set to become a successful debutante. She could not say the same for Piers. He spent most of his time in the billiard room, appeared for meals on time, played piquet or backgammon with Rosalie or Amanda in the evening, but there was no male company for him in the house. Lord Benedict St Maure, Lord0 marquis's younger brother, had his own suite of rooms in the house, but Amanda wasn't even sure if he was in residence, and his name was never mentioned in any conversation with the marchioness. Could she impose on his lordship's goodwill once again, this time to advise her concerning Piers? She was about to find out.

Lady Coverdale's carriage was equipped with every comfort, from good springs to well-padded seats and fur rugs against any possibility of catching cold. Not long after they entered the park, the marquis and two of his friends, who were enjoying a canter, slowed down when the carriage approached.

'I say, Coverdale,' the younger of the three, riding a twitchy chestnut, exclaimed. 'Who is that absolute stunner, sitting beside your mother?'

For a moment, Justin saw only Mrs Fletcher but then realised that his young companion was obviously referring to the undoubtedly lovely Miss Abbot. He smiled across at the third member of his party, an older man, wearing regimentals and riding a handsome grey, as if to say, Ah, these young people.

And then said exactly what was hoped for: 'I'll introduce you, Dorsett; she is my mother's god-daughter.'

The three riders drew up beside the now stationary carriage.

'Mother, may introduce my friends, both of whom you are already acquainted with, to your party?' Receiving assent, he went on, 'Colonel Fortescue and Mr Hubert Dorsett, Mrs Fletcher and Miss Abbot and Sir Piers Abbot.'

With pleasantries exchanged all round, the three riders turned and walked beside the carriage.

Hubert rode on the side where the Abbots were sitting. He couldn't take his eyes off Rosalie but seemed unable to string two words together, then turning to Piers, he exclaimed, 'Oh, I say, didn't we go to the same school? I seem to remember a little squirt of that name, in the same house.' He laughed. 'I expect you can give as good as you got now, eh?' Piers gave a noncommittal smile. 'Now you're in town, I must introduce you to some fellows, talk over old mischiefs, don'cher know, get up to some new ones, eh? What say? By the way, glad you've recovered from that fall; heard about it from another chap who was out that day.' He turned to the marchioness. 'Your Ladyship, may I have your permission to call?'

The worried look on Amanda's face during this exchange did not go unnoticed by Lord Coverdale.

Meanwhile, Colonel Fortescue, who had been engaging the marchioness in conversation, suddenly struck his forehead with his fist. 'Of course. Fletcher. I didn't make the connection at first. You *are* the talented Mrs Fletcher, aren't you?'

For a moment, Amanda looked embarrassed, and the rest of the company slightly surprised at this unexpected pronouncement.

'Dr Pargeter told me all about you, showed me some of your work, said it was second to none.'

Amanda gathered herself together and said, 'I fear the good doctor is prone to exaggeration. Do you know him well?'

Before he answered her question, the Colonel drew out his pocket watch and, having ascertained the time, said, 'I'm afraid duty calls.'

He saluted and took his farewells, cantering off in the direction of Gloucester Gate. Mr Dorsett, finding his mare difficult to control, was forced to follow suit.

Meanwhile, the marquis had been observing closely and listening to all that was being said with great interest. He had at least discovered something that could explain the stiffness of gait he had observed in Sir Piers' movement at their first meeting. A recent hunting accident might well be the cause, but Colonel Fortescue's remarks to Amanda remained an intriguing mystery. With his big bay gelding perfectly under control, he brought the horse close to Mrs Fletcher's side of the carriage.

After exchanging civilities, he said, 'This is not really the time or place for business discussions, but I thought you would like to know that I am now in a position to solve your banking problem and would like the opportunity to explain what I have achieved, I hope to your satisfaction. Would it be convenient to call upon you tomorrow morning?'

Amanda looked towards her hostess for confirmation. 'Is that agreeable to you, Lady Coverdale?'

'Of course, my dear; it is Justin's house, although he prefers not to live there. He is welcome at any time. Shall we say eleven o'clock? I would a word with you too, Justin, after you complete your business with Mrs Fletcher.'

'At your service, as always, Mama. Till tomorrow, then.'

He saluted with his whip and cantered away.

The following morning, Amanda was admitted to the library by one of the many footmen; she scanned the shelves for any books of interest, while she awaited the arrival of Lord Coverdale. She had taken extra care with her appearance. Well, why not, she told herself. She was going to meet a very attractive man, who probably not only didn't care what she wore, but probably wouldn't even notice. That's why not. She was quite wrong on both counts.

The marquis entered just as the bracket clock chimed eleven. Amanda dropped a curtsey, and the he bowed, greeting her warmly. 'I have some papers for you to sign, and then you should have no more money worries. Let me explain; shall we sit?'

'By all means,' said Amanda. 'I hope I did not put you to a lot of trouble.'

'Not at all; it was easily accomplished. All you have to do is sign this document and this letter, permitting my man of business to pay any bills you or your wards may incur, and to advance you cash, as and when you require. The money will be drawn on an account at Hoare's bank, transferred from Taunton.' He handed the letters to Amanda. 'Perhaps you would like to go over to the writing desk and peruse them before signing.

'I am quite sure everything is in order,' she replied, 'but as a guardian, one cannot be too careful. I do not wish to appear rude, but I'm sure you understand.'

'Yes, of course. You are right to take financial matters seriously.'

As Amanda was reading, he took the opportunity to admire her. Her blue dress was of a lighter material than the green one of a few days before, and the lower neckline, although partially concealed by a white fichu, was very attractive. He just wished she would give up that widow's cap and let her auburn hair show its full beauty. She was, in every way, like no other woman he had ever met.

With the letters signed and sealed, and tucked away in his lordship's pocket, Amanda expressed her gratitude for his trouble and made to leave.

'Please,' said the marquis, 'won't you stay a little while? I have taken the liberty to order some coffee and sherry wine, if you prefer, to celebrate the conclusion of our business. And I still haven't told you what measures I have taken to protect certain property that you have put under my protection.'

As he spoke, a light tap on the door announced the arrival of the refreshments, and Amanda took her seat again.

'On consideration, I believed that the book was better than a safe; I simply put it on a shelf among other books in my study; I do not have a book room in Mount Street. I hope that meets with your approval.'

'Of course, Marquis; I am just relieved that it is no longer in this house.'

'You have had no further anonymous notes regarding the jewel?'

'No, and I hope none has arrived at Abbots Court, either.'

'Now, about your other concern.' Justin took a sip of his wine and waited for the inevitable denial.

'I don't have any more concerns—"

'Yes, you do. You are worried about Piers. I know you are.'

'All right, I admit that I am, but I can hardly see what you can do about it, My Lord.'

'Well, I certainly can't unless I know what it is; from what Mr Dorsett said, your ward has had an accident. Perhaps you could begin by telling me about it.'

'Yes, a fall while hunting, a very bad one, at least the fall itself was not a hard one, but the horse rolled on him.'

'That can indeed be very dangerous,' the Justin commented. 'Was he far from home?'

'Yes, he was out with the Beaufort, some fifty miles away.'

'He must be a good rider; the Duke of Beaufort doesn't let just anybody ride to his hounds. Was Piers taken to Badminton after the fall?'

'I wish he *had* been, but it was considered too far away; they had drawn some ten miles from the house. Piers was taken to a local farmhouse, and I'm afraid that was the start of the problem he has now. If you have pencil and paper, I can show you.'

'In the desk drawer.'

They both went to the *bureau plat* that stood at one end of the room, and Amanda took a seat. The marquis stood behind to look over her shoulder, as she quickly and accurately sketched the lower half of a skeleton.

'These large bones form a circle, the pelvis, and give the strength the hip bones need to support the legs. Unfortunately, Piers' pelvis was disjointed at the centre, and the large bones on either side were both broken.'

Justin leaned forward to look at the drawing more closely. 'That's a terrible injury. When did this happen?'

'At the end of last year's hunting season.'

'And he is still not recovered?'

'No, and the sad thing is, he never will be, not completely, that is. Let me explain.' Amanda took another sheet of paper and drew a diagram of a pelvis in larger scale. 'Here,' she pointed to the right side, below the hip socket, 'the break was quite clean and has healed well, but on the other side, the break was higher up and more complicated, and the bones have not knitted together in alignment.'

'What does that mean for Piers?' asked the marquis.

'Sadly, it means that his left leg will always seem to be shorter than his right.'

'By how much?'

'About an inch. I know that doesn't seem much, but if you try walking with only one boot on, you will find that it causes a very definite limp. Piers is very self-conscious about it.'

'Could it not be corrected in some way?'

'Well, we tried having a special boot made by the local bootmaker, but it was very clumsy, and he said it was very uncomfortable, and so he refused to wear it, and what with that, and not being able to ride for at least another six months, he is at the moment a very frustrated young man.'

The marquis gave Amanda a look of concern. 'Is he in pain?'

'Not so much now, but being laid up for so long has caused all his muscles to weaken; he needs exercise to build them up again, but it is quite difficult to find the right sort of exercise in the country. The roads and lanes are rough and full of holes, and we cannot risk him having another fall. So, it is difficult to know what is for the best.'

'You say that being in the farmhouse for so long was the cause of his present disability. Why is that?'

'With an injury of this sort, it is essential that the patient is kept as still as possible for a long time, eight weeks or so, to try and prevent damage to the internal organs, and this the local doctor and the farmer's wife achieved extremely well, but Piers' legs should have been splinted together and properly aligned right from the beginning. By the time we got him home, the bones were partly set; it was too late.'

'What a pity we have no way of seeing into a body when anything like this happens,' the remarked. 'Nevertheless, I'm sure a better job with a boot or shoe can be done in London. Will you let me look into it, Mrs Fletcher?'

Amanda sighed. 'Yes, I suppose so, but it's yet another imposition on your time.'

'I'll let you into a little secret. Since Waterloo, although I wasn't in the army, I had certain duties that kept me busy throughout Bonaparte's regime, and—'

'Yes, I know,' she interrupted.

'How do you know?' thundered Justin, startled into anger.

'Oh, Sir, do not worry; I have no idea what you did, only that you were employed on politically sensitive missions.'

More curious than cross now, Justin asked, 'who told you? No, don't answer that. I have no doubt that it was the illustrious Dr Amyas Pargeter, D.Phil., DLitt., FRS, etc.? I got my secretary to look him up after his name was mentioned by Colonel Fortescue.'

'Yes, when I knew we were coming here, I got him to look you up too.' They both laughed.

'Well, solving problems of one sort or another was what I did, and now I don't.'

'Don't what?'

'Have any problems to solve; well, not many, that is until you came along. You have given me something different to think about. Perhaps you could trace the outline of one of Piers' boots, the one that needs adapting, and send it round to Mount Street.' He smiled. 'There are plenty of underemployed footmen in this house.'

The clock struck midday, giving Amanda a reason for not taking up any more of the marquis's time. 'Goodness me,' she exclaimed. 'I promised Rosalie we would go shopping. Please excuse me.' She whisked out of the room before either Justin or a footman could reach the door to open it for her.

CHAPTER 4

Amanda had quickly done the marquis's bidding and despatched a footman to Mount Street with the required sketch of Piers' shoe. Then Amanda and Rosalie spent an enchanting afternoon shopping. Both agreed that neither Bath nor Wells, and certainly not Taunton, could offer anything like the quantity and variety of goods so temptingly on display in places like the Pantheon Bazaar, or Burlington Arcade. Purchases of fans, fine kid gloves, knots of coloured ribbon, and spangled scarves quickly followed one upon another. Having loaded their maid with boxes and packages, and sent her back to Berkeley Square, Rosalie couldn't resist a final purchase of a pair of silver and paste-set buckles for evening shoes for Piers.

'I do not think he will want to do much dancing,' Amanda said. 'It's as much as anyone can do to get him out of the house, 'but I've got a plan, and I need you to help with it.'

'I'll do anything that will help him to feel better. It is sad to see him so despondent.'

'I know you would, Rosalie. Well, I think dancing would be an excellent kind of exercise for him. Especially as it takes place on a flat surface; taking exercise in the country can always risk a fall. Now, the quadrilles and cotillions that are danced at society balls are not like the country dances in provincial assemblies, and then there's the waltz, which is quite the thing these days.'

'How do you propose to get Piers to agree to this?'

'Just as you would do anything for him, I'm sure he would do this for you.'

'Do what, Amanda?'

'I know you are a very good dancer, Rosalie, but I'm sure it wouldn't do you any harm to have a bit more practice before you present your skills to the *Ton*. I shall ask your godmother to recommend a dancing master; he can come to the house and give you both private lessons. Then if it's a success, perhaps your friend from school can be persuaded to join you. What do you think?'

They had reached the door of Coverdale House and went inside; after a footman took their cloaks, Rosalie said. 'But what about Piers' limp? He's very self-conscious about it. He won't believe he can dance.'

'I've got a plan for that, too, but I shall not arrange anything else until I see how that works out; it should only be a few more days.'

Rosalie laughed. 'Is there anything in this world that you don't have a plan for?'

After a brief visit upstairs to pay his respects to his mama, the marquiswalked thoughtfully back to his own spacious apartments in Mount Street and discovered, to his surprise, that Amanda had already fulfilled her task. A folded and sealed note awaited him on a silver salver in the hall. He was about to break it open when he noticed that the seal had a small crest imprinted on it. A superficial glance showed him that it depicted a hand holding a star.

Mmmm, he said to himself. *This lady gets more interesting by the minute.*

On reaching his study, he carefully cut round the seal without damaging it, examining it with his quizzing-glass. Now he could see that the hand with the star was emerging from a viscount's coronet. He laid it to one side and unfolded the page of foolscap paper. On it were drawn two outlines, one marked 'Shoe' and the other 'Boot,' in extremely neat capital letters. There was no other writing on the page.

Justin refolded the paper and placed it in his pocket, then sat, contemplating the image on the seal. It certainly was not one he recognised, but his books on heraldry and genealogy were in the library in the Berkeley

Square house; research into it would have to wait. He had other more pressing matters to attend to. He called for his curricle, match greys, and tiger, to be readied immediately.

Halfway along Pall Mall, Justin could see a ruckus was occurring in the centre of the road. A rider was trying to control his horse, which was pirouetting, caracoling, half-rearing, and endeavouring to discompose its rider in every possible way. On drawing closer, the marquis recognised young Hubert Dorsett and the chestnut mare he was riding in the park. To give Hubert credit, he was trying to do the right thing: not hauling on the reins or sawing at the horse's mouth, instead attempting to lower the horse's head, but to no avail.

The situation was not being improved by a crowd of onlookers and impatient drivers shouting out catcalls and contrary advice. But there was an imminent danger: either the horse would decide to bolt, probably leaving a trail of destruction behind it in the crowded street, or it would rear up and fall over backwards, severely injuring or even killing its young rider.

'Hold their heads,' the marquis ordered his tiger, as he jumped from the driving seat and walked slowly towards the frightened horse.

The crowd, sensing that here was a person ready to take charge, quietened down. Before long, by means of gentle persuasion, quiet words, and a strong hand, he was able to lead the horse farther down the street and away from the crowd.

'If I were you,' he said to a grateful, but shamefaced Hubert, 'I would send this horse back to Middlewich Hall and purchase another, more suited to town conditions, and less likely to audition for Astley's Equestrian Circus in a public road. Meanwhile, I suggest you go to the park and gently ride some of the nervous energy out of this one.'

'Thank you, My Lord, thank you for coming to my rescue, most grateful,' Hubert mumbled.

'Not a problem, and I congratulate you on keeping your seat in such difficult circumstances. If this little episode gets you ragged in the clubs, you can be sure that no one heard it from my lips.' The marquis was about to let go of the reins when he added, 'By the way, Hubert, other than riding, have you any other sporting skills?'

'Well, My Lord, I'm not much good at boxing, but I fence a bit.'

'Excellent. I may have something you can help me with. Will you call on me at Mount Street, let us say four o'clock?'

Justin walked back to his curricle, now drawn to the side of the road, and resumed his journey to Jermyn Street.

Hubert Dorsett's father was, in some sort, a distant cousin of the marchioness. He had a pleasant country house in Warwickshire and not much money until he married an heiress from the north who, it had to be said, had strong connections with trade, although he hoped that any disadvantage this might have to his son would be overcome by his connection to the noble family of Coverdale. He had therefore appealed to Lady Coverdale for her good offices for Hubert, and that lady had immediately passed on the request to Justin.

As he waited for young Mr Dorsett to arrive, Coverdale reflected with a wry smile that his mother was very good at offering his services to others without any reference to himself. However, in this instance, Hubert Dorsett may well prove to be just the person to instigate the plan that was forming in his mind. Promptly at four o'clock, the young man was shown into his study.

Hubert was understandably nervous, unable to imagine how he could be of service to such an elevated personage Although their relationship to the Coverdales was frequently mentioned at home, he knew it to be tenuous and only by marriage. He bowed deeply and murmured, 'My Lord.'

'Good you could come, Hubert,' Justin said. 'Please be seated.' He moved over to a decanter-laden side table. 'Brandy? Wine?'

Feeling a little in need of fortification, Hubert said nervously, 'A little brandy, if you please, Sir.'

The marquis poured a small glass and handed it to Hubert. 'I think you'll find this to your taste.' He took the armchair on the other side of the fireplace. 'I hope your horse suffered no ill effects from this morning's little contretemps.'

'Oh, no, My Lord, right as rain, but I have decided to take your advice and acquire a more suitable mount for town conditions.'

'Good man. Now, about why I have asked you to come here.' He explained his intentions to Hubert and the part he wished the young man to play; he finished by saying, 'I am sure I can rely on your discretion. This meeting never took place.'

'No, indeed sir, not a word; upon my honour, My Lord.'

'Just one more thing. I am aware that in some circles, antecedents, such as your mother's, are looked down upon, but I know that probably in my lifetime, and certainly in yours, trade and industry will be the lifeblood of this country. Be proud to be part of it.'

CHAPTER 5

Amanda, Rosalie, and Piers had been at Berkeley Square for nearly a week. They had driven out in the park with the marchioness on several occasions and met important members of polite society, including Princess Esterhazy and Lady Jersey, who were pleased to send vouchers for Almack's, that exclusive club, ruled with a rod of iron by the patronesses. Young bucks and fortune hunters were drawn to pay their respects, paying extravagant compliments to Rosalie's beauty. She, however, was not overly impressed; having been the toast of assemblies in Bath and Taunton, she recognised empty flattery for what it was.

Now she was getting ready for her first real foray into society. Not a grand ball, but an evening party with music and dancing and a buffet supper.

'Keep still, Miss Rosalie,' the maid she shared with Amanda scolded, as she did up a row of tiny buttons at the back of her young mistress's jonquil silk dress. 'I won't have time to do your hair properly if you wriggle so.'

However, with her blonde hair arranged in a simple style and ornamented with a turquoise-studded comb, and a recently purchased spangled scarf draped across her elbows, Wilkins declared herself satisfied, and Rosalie presented herself in Amanda's boudoir in plenty of time.

'My dear, you look lovely; you will be greatly admired. Now, Lady Coverdale wishes to see you in her salon, before we go.'

'I wish …' began Rosalie, looking at her guardian. 'I wish—'

'What do you wish?' Amanda placed a white shawl round her shoulders, partly covering her grey silk dress.

'That you would wear something more colourful; you are still young, and not my mother. You should be having more fun, too.'

'I am a widow, Rosalie, and I must dress accordingly. Now we must go down.'

Looking every inch, the marchioness she was, Lady Coverdale, in rich purple velvet with a demi-train and magnificent diamond necklace, came forward and addressed Rosalie, echoing Amanda's words. 'You look lovely, my dear.' She held out a flat leather case. 'Here is a little something for my beautiful god-daughter.'

Rosalie stepped forward and dropped a curtsey, taking the box.

'Oh, look, Amanda!' she exclaimed. Nestling on cream velvet was a charming double string of pearls. 'Oh, thank you, Godmama. Thank you. Amanda, will you help me put them on?'

'There.' The pearls glowed on Rosalie's creamy skin and emphasised the slenderness of her neck,

'Just as I thought, my dear,' Lady Coverdale announced. 'They are perfect for you. Now, I can hear the coach arriving, but what a pity, Amanda, that you could not persuade Piers to join us.'

Amanda was disappointed too, and not only because he wouldn't come, which was not really unexpected, but because she had had high hopes of the marquis being able to do something to help, and she had not heard anything of him for several days.

The party was being held in the Grosvenor Square mansion of Earl Carstairs. An informal gathering of about thirty couples, together with chaperones of the young girls, it would commence with a musical evening which combined performances by talented amateurs and a quartet of professional players. This would be followed by supper and end with dancing.

Rosalie was a very accomplished musician, both on the pianoforte and on her favourite instrument, the harp. Amanda knew that she missed being able to play at Coverdale house, as she had done every day at Abbots Court. She also knew that some of the playing they were being subjected to was far inferior to her ward's talents. She noticed many glances being cast in Rosalie's direction by envious young men, who, as soon as the performances were over, eagerly sought introductions from their hostess.

Piers was engaged in his usual pursuit of billiards when the butler entered the room and said in measured tones, 'Sir, the Marquis of Coverdale begs the pleasure of your company in the book room.'

To say that he was surprised was more than an understatement. Piers had barely spoken a word to the marquis since his arrival in Berkeley Square, although Amanda had spoken of him on more than one occasion, and he had a sneaking suspicion that she liked him quite a lot.

A footman leaped from his chair to open the door as they approached, and Clarkson announced, 'Sir Piers, My Lord.'

Justinsaw that Piers was very like a masculine version of his sister. Taller, of course, but with equally good proportions and the same golden blond hair, although at the moment he lacked the bloom of good health that Rosalie displayed. Drinks had already been brought in, but Piers declined.

'Later, perhaps,' said Justin, settling into an armchair and crossing his long legs. 'I've asked you here because Mrs Fletcher is very concerned about you and—'

'B...B..But, she had no right ...' Piers stammered, blushing to the roots of his hair.

'Yes, she has,' the marquis stated firmly. 'She is your guardian, and your welfare, and that of your sister, is very much her concern, so just listen to me. She has told me all about your horrible accident and the consequences you have suffered and are still suffering. She has described to me in detail, with diagrams, exactly what your injuries were ...'

Piers smiled. 'Yes, she would.'

'... and the effect they are having on your ability to move with freedom. I told her I would give some thought to the problem, and I have come up with something that may be of help, but to be honest, until you try it, I have no idea if it will work, or if you will accept it.' The marquis picked up an object that had been lying on a table by his side. 'I see you are wearing pantaloons and shoes. Would you be so kind as to remove your left shoe?'

Piers was so amazed by the turn of events that he meekly did as Justin asked and handed over his shoe. Justin examined it and then placed the object into it, making sure the fit was a good one, and handed it back to the astonished young man. 'Put it back on and see how it feels. Go on, stand up, try walking about the room.'

Piers did as he was told and immediately realised that, although his shoe felt a bit cramped, he no longer had a lopsided gait. He was lost for words.

'I had only one of these made,' Justin said, 'just to see how it goes and how you feel about it. I believe you will see that it is quite unnoticeable to anyone else.'

Piers came and sat down, taking off his shoe and examining the insert that the marquis had fitted. He saw that it was made of fine polished leather, sloping in height from about one inch at the heel to the thinness of an inner sole at the toe.

At last, he found his voice. 'My Lord, this ... this is wonderful. How did it come about, sir?'

'A little connivance between your guardian and me, and the handiwork of a first-class bootmaker. I realise that some adjustments may be necessary in the future, but for tonight, it will have to serve. You'd better get your man to dress you in quick-sharp time. We are going to a party. No, do not argue, Piers; it is not up for discussion.' The marquis sounded severe, but he was smiling.

Once suitably dressed and sitting beside Justin in his luxuriously appointed town coach, Piers' nerves got the better of him. 'They won't be expecting me. I don't think I should...'

'On the contrary, it is me they will not be expecting. I have not been invited. It will be up to you to convince the hostess that the friend you have brought along is a suitable person to mix with polite society.'

This remark so amused Piers that he forgot his misgivings, and the short drive was soon over.

The Marquis of Coverdale and Sir Piers Abbot made their appearance at Lady Carstairs's party just after the supper interval had begun. Their entrance had all the panache and surprise that the marquis expected it would. They made their obeisances to a delighted hostess and to Lady Coverdale, who were seated together with Mrs Fletcher, enjoying thin slices of ham and glasses of ratafia, and were invited to join them.

Justin declined gracefully and said, 'I see Miss Rosalie sitting over there.' He indicated a table where lively conversation was taking place. 'I believe young Piers here would find himself in more entertaining company if he were to join them. For myself, madam, I am sure your husband has organised a card room for those of us too old for dancing.'

His mother poked her son in the ribs with her fan. 'Don't be a tease, Justin, but I suppose you'd better run along, that is if your old bones will allow such rapid movement.'

'Go on, Sir Piers, join your sister,' the marquis said, adding, 'Enjoy yourself, and don't drink too much.'

Amanda later recalled that she could have been knocked down by a feather. Not only had Lord Coverdale managed to get Piers to come to the party, but he somehow improved the uneven gait he was so embarrassed about, to the point where it was barely noticeable. She could hardly wait to find out how he had managed it. Then she realised, disappointingly, that unless the marquis wished to tell her about it himself, she would have no opportunity to do so. Etiquette forbade her to call on him.

The company which Piers joined consisted of his sister, two of the Carstairs daughters, Hubert Dorsett, and another young man, dressed in regimentals and introduced as Robert Fortescue.

'I believe I had the honour meeting a relative of yours in the park, the other day,' said Piers.

'My father, Colonel Fortescue, no doubt.'

'Riding a magnificent grey?' said Piers.

Robert smiled. 'Yes, that would be Dominus, carried him all through Waterloo without a scratch.'

'Amazing,' exclaimed Piers, 'but then blood will out, when it comes to stamina.'

'Oh, enough of this horse-talk, Piers,' exclaimed Rosalie.

'Ladies, shall we go to the retiring room and get ready for the dancing?' suggested Sophia Carstairs.

With the women gone, Hubert found just the opening he had hoped for. 'I need to buy a new horse, one more accustomed to town conditions. Not a slug, of course,' he added quickly. 'Either of you two fellows up to join me at Tattersalls tomorrow, see what's going? Fortescue? Sir Piers?'

'Sorry, Dorsett,' the young officer said immediately, 'on duty all this week.'

'How about you, Sir Piers?'

'Glad to, but drop the "Sir," please, Dorsett. Never been to Tattersalls;

new in town, see?' Piers added, 'That chestnut mare you were riding in the park looked rather hot to handle; needs a bit more schooling, I should think, but first-class blood and bone.'

The arrangements were duly made for Hubert to pick Piers up the next morning. Then Fortesque suggested that the three of them repair to the card room before the ladies returned, but Hubert, who did not want to miss the chance of asking the lovely Rosalie to be his partner for the first dance, declined. When the three ladies returned, the two Carstairs girls were disappointed, but Hubert knew that Fortescue's liking for cards meant that Piers would not have to explain why he did not dance.

The tables had all been removed, and dancing was well under way when the marquis returned to the room. He made straight for where his mother was sitting and took the seat vacated by Lady Carstairs, which was next to Amanda's.

'How on earth did you manage it?' Amanda exclaimed.

'Manage what, Justin?' His mother enquired.

'To get Piers to come to the party, of course. Neither his sister nor I were able to,' said Amanda.

'A little gentle persuasion, and the promise that there would be a card room.' He turned to Amanda and said, *sotto voce,* '… and the resources of a very good shoemaker. Will you not have a dance with me, Mrs Fletcher? Don't tell me you're a widow or too old to dance.'

'Well, My Lord, perhaps propriety would allow one of the country dances, but for one thing,' she replied, with a wicked twinkle in her eyes.

'And what might that be?'

'That such vigorous exercise at your age might precipitate your gout.'

Justin leant down and whispered in her ear, which made her smile, and then he led her onto the dance floor.

During the dance, which gave intermittent opportunities for speech, he explained to her all he had put in train for Piers' rehabilitation.

'I have every trust in my mother's cousin, Hubert Dorsett, carrying out my orders, and Piers will soon be racketing about town, as every young man should be.' He saw Amanda's look of alarm. 'Don't worry, Hubert will look after him, and I hope Piers will be able to prevent that headstrong horseman from buying a showy stepper, with only three sound legs and gone in the wind.'

CHAPTER 6

The following week was one of indifferent weather, unsuitable for carriage drives or walks in the park, but under the auspices of Hubert Dorsett, Piers discovered that fencing was just the sort of exercise that appealed to him. And because he was the sort of young man who didn't believe in half measures, he was determined to do it well. Just as Amanda had hoped, his spirits improved, and he began to make friends and was put up for membership of the best clubs, with Coverdale as sponsor.

Rosalie, on the other hand, felt the absence of music in her life hard to bear. Certainly, the music room at Coverdale House was well equipped with instruments, but the pianoforte, although a good one, was sadly out of tune, and the harp too large for her petite figure.

Noticing one evening that she was in the doldrums, her godmother asked, 'What is the matter, child? Are you not well?'

'Oh, no, Godmamma, I am in very good health; it's just …' She didn't know what to say.

'I want you to be happy, Rosalie. Do not be afraid to tell me if something is troubling you. Have you spoken to Mrs Fletcher?'

'Yes, but she doesn't feel that … that it's not her place to …'

'You are a pretty, well-behaved girl, Rosalie, and I am sure that Amanda Fletcher has had a lot to do with that, since your mother died when you were quite young. Please tell her that she can speak to me on any head concerning the welfare of her wards.'

'Thank you, Godmamma. Do you wish me to read to you from Miss Austen's charming novel?' Rosalie picked up a copy of *Sense and Sensibility*.

A few days later, a piano-tuner came to the house, and the instrument was returned to working order. Rosalie could frequently be heard playing it, but Amanda knew that her ward still missed her harp. It was not a large instrument and could probably be brought up from Somerset without too much difficulty, but she had no idea how to go about it. Another problem for the marquis? But then she had not seen him since the dance.

This was to be put right the very next day, when he called at Coverdale House to find Amanda and Rosalie on the doorstep, about to go out. Amanda was escorting her ward to visit her school friend in Grosvenor Square.

'I have a better plan, 'suggested the marquis. 'Suppose we take Miss Rosalie to her destination, then you and I, Mrs Fletcher, shall be able to drive to the park, or anywhere you would like to go.'

'Oh, yes, Amanda,' cried Rosalie, 'please let's do that. I have never ridden in a curricle before.'

Forestalling Amanda's possible dissent, he told his tiger to hold his magnificent match-bays, and jumped down, handing Rosalie onto the vehicle.

'Oh, very well,' Amanda was forced to agree agr, then addressed the marquis. 'Would you mind waiting for a few minutes, while I fetch something, Sir?'

'I am entirely at your command, Madam.'

Only minutes later, she was back outside, carrying a leather document case. The short distance to Grosvenor Square was quickly accomplished, and Rosalie deposited with her friends. With more room on the seat, the marquis was able to observe that his travelling companion was wearing a dark-blue half-coat and paler blue dress over a petticoat trimmed with several blue flounces and a bonnet trimmed with matching feathers. He couldn't refrain from making a complimentary remark.

'Yes, Sir, I've decided to be little more adventurous in my dress of late. Rosalie says she is tired of seeing me look, as she puts it, like a boring dowager!'

'My dear Mrs Fletcher, you could never look boring, even if you were wearing a coal-sack.'

Before she could reply to this remark, the marquis whipped up his horses, and they set off at a spanking trot. 'Have you any idea where you would like to go, Mrs Fletcher?' he asked, smiling. 'I am at your disposal.'

'Yes, but I do not know if it will be too far. I have not been able to ascertain from a map.'

'If it's Gretna Green, I'm afraid that I shall have to make alternative travelling arrangements. A curricle and a pair, however well-bred, would find that journey too long.'

Knowing that he was teasing, she replied with a straight face, 'Thought we'd start with the Royal Botanic Gardens at Kew.'

'An excellent plan. Have you a particular reason to go there?'

Amanda pointed to the leather case. 'I have some work which should have been delivered some time ago. I could have trusted to the mail, but as I knew I was going to come to London, I thought I could deliver it in person.'

'Now that really intrigues me,' said the marquis. 'What sort of work does a lady like you undertake?'

'I don't know what you mean by "like me," but if you are implying that women shouldn't work, then your house wouldn't be cleaned, your food cooked, or your laundry done, and, I may add, other pleasures catered for. I work, Lord Coverdale, because otherwise I would have no income.'

'But …' began Justin.

'There are no buts. I admit that I am fortunate in being able to live at Abbots Court and having all my day-to-day needs cared for. I also am permitted, under the conditions of my guardianship, to defray any extra expenses that involve Piers and Rosalie. For myself, I have what the canon left me and my work.'

The marquis slowed his horses to a walk. 'I had no intention of belittling you, Mrs Fletcher. I apologise.'

'No, I should be the one to apologise. I should keep my opinions to myself.'

'Not at all; you are quite right. There is no doubt that this is a society where women often get a raw deal. Now, are you going to keep me guessing about your work? If you are, goodness knows what my imagination might infer.'

'Well then, I'd better tell you, had I not?' Amanda went on, 'You'll probably think it's really rather dull, but I enjoy it very much, and they pay me for it. Oh, look, I do believe we are passing Mr Turner's house. Is that not so, Marquis?'

'I haven't the slightest idea, and you are just being deliberately provocative. Tell me what is it that you do, or I will leave you at the roadside.'

Amanda laughed. 'I believe you would too. Very well then, since it so important to you. I am a botanical illustrator. I am currently employed to draw and press examples of the flora of Somerset. I have in that case my work of the past four months. And before you get the idea that I sit at an easel painting dainty watercolour flower pictures, that is not what I do.'

'I would never associate the word "dainty" with you, Mrs Fletcher, and that is a compliment, I assure you. Now, please enlarge on the work that you do.'

'First of all, I have to describe where I found the plant and what sort of soil and terrain it is growing in, then carefully dig it up. All known plants have several names: common names, local names, and scientific names, which are always in Latin, although that is not really in my remit. Then I have to draw the plant, all of it: root, leaf, stem, flower, seed, whole, and dissected. When I have completed that, I then have to press it, so that the specimen can be preserved and kept at Kew. I get paid for every one that I do.'

His lordshiplet out a 'whew!' of surprise and admiration. 'Will you show me your work when we get to Kew?' he asked. 'That should be in about twenty minutes.'

'Yes, if you wish. Now you can tell me how you managed to get Piers to leave the billiard room?'

'Just as I said, gentle persuasion and a skilled bootmaker, and some help from a relative, who I was able to give slight service to.'

'Would that be Mr Dorsett?'

'Quite possibly, but I would be glad if you kept that information to yourself; although I am responsible for the footwear, everything else is due to Hubert.'

'My lips are sealed, My Lord.'

The marquis glanced at her profile. 'Except in this one matter, I prefer them otherwise.'

Amanda made no reply.

On their arrival at the gardens, their names were announced. The director, Mr William Aiton, was summoned from his office, and he insisted on providing refreshment. He engaged his illustrious visitor in conversation, while Amanda went to deposit her work with the archive department's botanist and explain that temporarily, she would be unable to continue until the London season was over. By the look on his face, she could see what he thought of any season that didn't include the study of botany; nevertheless, he was pleased with the work she had done so far.

Following the visit, they strolled in the gardens, enjoying the newly greened trees and spring flowers gilding the grass. They visited William Chambers' famous Pagoda, the tallest structure in London, but decided there wasn't time to climb to the top.

'Coming here with you, sir, I believe has raised my credit,' said Amanda. 'I have never met the director before. He will know who I am from now on.' She smiled. 'But I think he had seen my name, and as I sign my drawings A. Fletcher, he was probably quite surprised to discover that I'm a woman.'

'Well, Mrs Fletcher, you are certainly a woman who always surprises *me*. Tell me how you get about when you are obtaining specimens for your work. Do you ride?'

'No, Sir, I drive. I drive because the tools I need to carry would make riding impractical.'

'Yes, I can see that; so what do you drive?'

'A donkey.'

Justin let out a hoot of laughter. 'A donkey? I do not believe it.'

'You should, because it's true. He's a very nice donkey, called Duncan, much easier to tether at the roadside, or in a field, than a horse; besides, he is cheaper to care for. I can't allow the trust to pay for work I do for myself. Surely you can understand that?'

Her answer subdued the marquis, as well as giving him food for thought.

CHAPTER 7

On the drive back, Amanda asked her noble coachman how he occupied his time. 'After all, it's only fair that I should know something about you, don't you think?'

'I'm never fair,' he quipped. 'Nevertheless, I will tell you. I take my seat in the House of Lords; before that, I was a member of the Commons, until my father died. I have an estate to look after in Essex, and in the past, I have had various dealings on behalf of the government, which I cannot tell you about, but not so much since the end of the war. Otherwise, I follow the pursuits generally considered *de rigueur* by the society I live in. Does that satisfy you?'

'You very well know, sir, that it does not,' Amanda said a little primly, 'but I shall not pursue the matter.' She concentrated on observing the passing scenery.

After a short period of silence, the marquis said: 'tell me about Abbots Court, Mrs Fletcher, unless, of course you have decided that any further conversation with me is pointless.'

Amanda took note of the teasing tone in his voice but decided to ignore it.

'From its name, you will gather it was once closely connected to an abbey. After the Dissolution, this was pulled down and the land granted to the present family, who built themselves a house, using materials from the abbey. Externally, it is little changed since the sixteenth century. Inside, it has been redesigned by various generations, with differing degrees of success and convenience.'

'What is the estate like?'

'Not large, about two thousand acres, mixed farm and woodland, a small park, and a village. It's very pretty, and the land is good.'

'It sounds delightful. And Sir Piers is fond of it?' the marquis queried.

'Yes, very, he takes great pride in looking after it, and we have a good steward, who is taking care of it while we are away.'

'That is very good to hear, and now that you are talking to me again, what task have you in mind for me to perform today?'

'I don't know what you mean, My Lord.'

'Yes, you do, or you wouldn't call me "My Lord" in that haughty tone of voice.'

'Oh, all right then, it's about Rosalie.'

'Being difficult, is she?'

'Not at all. Everyone gets the wrong idea about Rosalie; just because she's so pretty, they think she must be empty-headed. Well, I can tell you she is not. She's an intelligent girl, with a great deal more to her than her looks.'

'So?' The horse broke into a canter because Justin wasn't giving full attention to his driving; once back in control, he repeated, 'So?'

'She is very musical; I mean really good, and your mother has very kindly had the pianoforte put back into tune for her, but she pines for her harp, which is her main instrument.'

'Is there not a harp in the music room, also?'

'Yes, there is, but not only is it far too big for Rosalie, but, according to her, it's in a sorry state and would need to go to a harp-maker to be restored.'

'I'm not surprised; my mother is not at all musical, although my father enjoyed concerts, and he had a good singing voice. But the really musical one in the family is my brother Benedict … but then, of course … What was it you wanted me to do, Mrs Fletcher?'

Amanda noted the marquis's immediate switch of subject away from his brother, and much as she would have liked to know more, she didn't ask.

'I just wondered if it would be possible to have Rosalie's harp sent up to London from Somerset? I can pay for it; it's just that I don't know how to go about it, and I thought—'

'As usual, you thought right. I shall put my secretary onto it at once; he will arrange everything, but it may take several days. It could take a week, even.'

They had reached the edge of the town, and the increased traffic and noise from the cobbles drowned Amanda's expressions of gratitude.

When they arrived at Coverdale House, Justin excused himself from coming in, but thanked Amanda for a very pleasant day, adding, 'and if I may say so, an instructive one, although, alas, I never did get to see your work.' His last remark as he climbed back into the carriage: 'Miss Rosalie's harp will be on its way in no time.'

The week that saw the arrival of Rosalie's harp also saw her first visit to the prestigious Almack's Assembly. It was also Amanda's first time, but she was determined to play only the part of chaperone. It was going to be Rosalie's chance to shine in a large assemblage of the cream of London society. She was meticulously briefed on how to behave and, more importantly, how not to behave, at the prestigious venue. Only to dance with partners who had been properly introduced, and certainly not to waltz with any man who was not personally approved by one or more of the patronesses. Piers was persuaded to come, somewhat against his will, but agreed on hearing that there would be a card room, and also by Lady Sophia, who had joined them in the dancing class and who swore that she would never speak to him again if he didn't dance at least once with her.

Rosalie was dressed to perfection; her blonde locks were arranged on the crown of her head, and a few curls allowed to fall gracefully onto her forehead, threaded through with a pink ribbon on which had been sewn tiny pink rosebuds. Her dress, white silk with an overdress of the finest muslin, puff sleeves, and a not-too-daring décolletage. The muslin was caught up at intervals round the lower edge, with more pink rosebuds, to display several flounces of blond lace.

'You look exceptionally lovely tonight, my dear,' said the marchioness, as the three ladies and Piers awaited the town coach. Amanda's dress was of Pomona green satin, trimmed at elbows and scalloped neckline with Brussels lace. Her hair was styled in a discreet chignon, kept in place by an amber comb; pearl and amber earrings were her only jewels. On the way to the assembly, she wondered if the marquis would put in an appearance and realised that she was beginning to hope that he would do so, rather more than she ought.

Piers fulfilled his obligations to his sister and to Lady Sophia, putting into practice what they had learnt from the dancing master, before slipping away to the card room with Hubert. Rosalie was undoubtedly becoming the belle of the ball, and less well-endowed spinsters cast envious eyes but could find no criticism to levy.

Eleven o'clock was the latest time that anyone was admitted to the Assembly, a rule rigorously enforced by the patronesses, and by twenty to eleven, there was no sign of Lord Coverdale.

'It really is too bad of Justin,' his mother grumbled to her friends. 'He said he would come. I suppose he's forgotten.'

But his lordshiphad not forgotten. His arrival was announced a few minutes after his mother spoke, and he immediately made his way over to her, making his bows to the ladies. His mother tapped him on the hand with her fan.

'Leaving it a bit late, my son. The ladies will have their cards filled by now.'

The marquis just smiled.

It was the first time Amanda had seen him in full evening dress, knee-breeches, swallowtail coat, shadow striped waistcoat, and exquisitely tied cravat, looking both elegant and distinguished by his very restraint. Yet that restraint marked him out above those gentlemen who had chosen brighter colours and more flamboyant accessories. Her heart felt as though it was putting in an extra beat, as he came and sat beside her on the seat recently vacated by Rosalie.

'How are you enjoying your first visit to Almack's, Mrs Fletcher? A fine display of high society, is it not?'

'I am enjoying watching Rosalie having such a good time; she barely has time to catch her breath before she is claimed by another beau.'

'Ah, yes, Rosalie, indeed, but I asked how *you* were liking it.'

'It is undoubtedly a colourful spectacle, but I have to admit that I find a meadow full of wildflowers more interesting.'

Before the marquis could comment, Piers came up to them. 'Sir, I cannot thank you enough for what you have done to help me …'

The Justin raised his hand. 'No thanks are necessary; say no more about it.'

'I have actually been on the dance floor, just to do my duty, of course.'

The marquis kept a straight face. 'Of course, what young man wouldn't want to do his duty, when it means having a pretty girl in his arms? Now I can see that Lady Sophia is sitting on that couch over there, looking as though the one thing in the world she would like, is a glass of lemonade. Why don't you provide it for her, and put one over on the eager young men surrounding her?' He turned to Amanda again. 'May I beg the honour of the next dance, Mrs Fletcher?'

Amanda shook her head. 'I thank you, Sir, but this evening is for Rosalie. I prefer the position of duenna.'

'Very well; another time, perhaps.' He sounded disappointed. 'When you have another task for me to perform. I understand from my secretary that Rosalie's harp arrived safely. I must come and hear her play sometime.'

He stood up, bowed, and drifted across to a group of people at the far side of the room.

Amanda felt awful, of all the things in the world she wanted was to dance with Lord Coverdale, and now she had offended him. But worse was to come. The lady sitting beside her, an intimate of his mother's, turned to her and said, 'Mrs Fletcher, do you see that lady the marquis is talking to?'

Amanda looked across the ballroom. 'Do you mean the lady in crimson, covered in assorted gemstones?'

'Yes, she is the only child of General Sir Mathias Prideau; he owns the estate next to Coverdale. He has been very ill, and Honoria has only just returned to town.'

Amanda wondered why she was being treated to this apparently random information.

The Honourable Mrs Dearing, an incurable gossip, went on, 'I shouldn't really be telling you this.' She leant closer and fluttered her fan in front of her face. 'But Honoria and the marquis are unofficially betrothed.' She twittered on, failing to notice the shocked look on Amanda's face. 'Well, not quite betrothed, you understand, but everyone expected it at the end of the last season, and then the general became ill, before any announcement could be made, and I wondered, since you are living at

Berkeley Square, if you might have heard something…' She laid a hopeful hand on Amanda's glove.

Barely able to speak, Amanda swallowed, and managed to say, 'Mrs Dearing, I am not one of the family; matters of that kind would never be vouchsafed to me.'

'No, no, of course not, but one never knows; things slip out sometimes, don't they?' She looked across at the marquis. 'He's so good-looking and such a presence. I'm sure you agree, Mrs Fletcher.'

Amanda was glad she was sitting down when she was told of Lord Coverdale's intended engagement, as she was sure the news would have made her go weak at the knees. Fortunately, further conversation with the insatiable gossip was forestalled with the return of Rosalie to the protection of her duenna.

On the way back to Coverdale House, the marchioness fell asleep. Rosalie chattered on about her dance partners, mostly that they were boring but danced well, or the other way round. Piers talked about a forthcoming visit to the Daffy Club, but Amanda was noticeably silent. She was analysing the reaction she had had to Mrs Dearing's surprising information. Finally deciding that it was its unexpectedness that was the cause of the physical symptoms she had experienced, nothing more personal. After all, had she not said to the marquis, only a few days before, that she hardly knew him at all? He had had no reason to discuss his private life with her, and nor had he done so. Perhaps it had been foolish of her to think that a man of his rank and wealth, and at the age of thirty-two, would not have been seriously thinking of the succession to his title and estates. He had been helpful and interested in her work, and there was no doubt that she would have to call on his good offices, if a more permanent place for the diamond was to be found, but she was determined that there there would be no more carriage drives.

CHAPTER 8

L ife at Coverdale House went on smoothly. Amanda's time was fully occupied, since Rosalie's popularity resulted in invitations to routs, balls, Venetian breakfasts, and the opera. This last was also attended by the marquis, but he was seated at the opposite side of the box to her, and she was careful to see that they only exchanged pleasantries.

For Justin, however, life was proving difficult. The return of Honoria Prideau to London was causing him considerable anxiety. He had not proposed marriage to her, and her precipitate departure from town last season had postponed any occasion at which to do so. It would be a good match; she was from a suitable family, he had known her socially for many years, and she would ultimately inherit an estate that would bring many benefits to his own.

She had pleasant features, was well educated within the confines of what passed for female education of the day, and had a rather poor taste in clothes, which he was sure could be improved with an experienced lady's maid, but above all, Honoria bored him, and they seemed to have little in common He used to think this did not matter much; after all, she would be occupied with running the house and being a society hostess, as well as furnishing him with an heir, several spares and perhaps a pretty daughter he could spoil. But with the arrival of a certain Mrs Amanda Fletcher into his life, his view on lifelong partnerships was beginning to change.

He was troubled because Honoria rightly had expectations. He had paid her court during the previous season, and everyone knew it. There would be no shame to him, perhaps a little censorious gossip, if he didn't follow through with a proposal, but her reputation could be severely damaged in the eyes of *the ton*. Furthermore, she had already had three seasons without attracting a suitor, so failure this time would be an extra humiliation.

For almost the first time in his life, Justin didn't know what to do. Much as he would have liked to talk to someone about his problem, there was no one he could discuss such personal matters concerning his feelings about one, let alone, two women. Discussing it with his mother was out of the question, although at one time, he could have told Benedict, but, sadly, not now. He felt very alone.

If Amanda had concerns about her feelings for Justin, they were instantly put out of her mind with the arrival of a letter from Taunton. It was brought on a silver salver by Clarkson, when she and Rosalie were at breakfast. Breaking the seal, Amanda read the contents with mounting anxiety.

Rosalie saw her guardian go pale and grip the paper, till her knuckles turned white.

'What is it, Amanda? What has happened? You look terrible.'

'I am afraid it is very bad news, my dear. We must all return to Somerset at once. I must beg to see Lady Coverdale immediately, or at least as soon as she is prepared to see me.'

The marchioness did not keep early hours and always broke her fast in her bedchamber.

'But what has happened, Amanda?' Rosalie demanded.

'Mr Smallbody has died. This letter is from Mr Brewster, his partner.'

The significance of this was lost on Rosalie; she had rarely seen him and was only vaguely aware of his function in her life. But to Amanda, he had been the administrative mainstay of the guardianship, responsible for the accounts, payment of bills, and running the general practicalities of the trust. Now some other arrangement would have to be made, and with all due speed. Return to Abbots Court was essential.

'I don't see why we've got to go home.' Rosalie sounded peeved. 'It's not as though he was a relative or anything, and it's probably too late for the funeral.'

'Rosalie! That's no way to speak.'

'Sorry, Amanda. Nevertheless, it's true,' the girl murmured.

Amanda could understand her chagrin. The season was reaching its height, the weather had been splendid, and all sorts of interesting activities had been planned. If they left, Rosalie would miss many of them; naturally she was aggrieved.

Amanda sent a message to Lady Coverdale, begging for an audience at her earliest convenience, and the answer came back, that she would receive Mrs Fletcher in her boudoir immediately.

Lady Coverdale was *en deshabille,* reclining on a daybed, sipping chocolate. 'What is so urgent, my dear? What has happened?'

'I have received a letter from Taunton, telling me that my fellow trustee has died; there is business there I must attend to immediately, so we must depart as soon as convenient, My Lady.'

'I see, although I don't understand that sort of thing myself. I leave everything to Justin.'

For a moment, Amanda wished she could "leave everything to Justin", but then pushed the thought away.

'I shall make arrangements right away. We may be ready to leave tomorrow and be in Somerset in two days from now.'

'Do Piers and Rosalie have to go too? I have grown very fond of the dear children. They will both be very disappointed.'

'Of course, Piers must come, but …' Amanda thought for a moment and then added, 'I don't suppose it is really necessary for Rosalie to accompany us.'

'Well then, that's settled; she can stay here. How long do you expect to be away?'

'Maybe ten days; I do not think it will take longer, but Rosalie has a rather full diary of events. Who is to chaperone her?'

'I will be going to some of them, and I can arrange for other mothers to look after her when I am not there. Do not concern yourself on that head, Mrs Fletcher.'

'Oh, Lady Coverdale, that is so kind of you. Rosalie will be delighted. I'm afraid I left her close to tears.'

'Well, go and dry them for her, and tell Clarkson to arrange an express to be sent to warn your household of your coming; you do not want to arrive in a house draped in holland Covers.'

'Yes, your ladyship; I will do that.' Amanda smiled; the idea that the marchioness arrived anywhere without every comfort being already installed, let alone still in dust sheets, was an impossible one.

Piers, who had planned to sleep till noon, was not pleased to be aroused so early, but when Amanda had explained the situation to him, he fully understood. He set about sending messages to his friends that he had been unexpectedly called out of Town but had every hope of returning within two weeks. Clarkson proved to be a tower of strength, making all the arrangements for their journey and the overnight stay on the way.

They set off at ten the following morning; footmen hoisted bags and trunks onto the roof and placed baskets of food and bottles of drink inside the post-chaise and four that had been hired for the journey. Piers, his man Grooby, and a maid assigned to look after Amanda.

Rosalie saw them off at the door. She was a little tearful and apprehensive, but Amanda assured her she would be fine. The marchioness, and her own faithful maid, Wilkins, would look after her. Moments later, the post-boys set the carriage in motion; they were off.

They spent the night at the well-appointed coaching inn on the Bath road and left in plenty of time to reach their destination by the afternoon. During this last part of the journey, Amanda asked Piers how he was enjoying life in Town.

'Very well; capital, in fact. Dorsett and his friends are great company, and I feel much stronger than I did. Before I came, I thought I would never be able to do anything properly again, but now, I know that is not so.'

Amanda leant forward and put a hand on his knee. 'I'm so glad, so very, very glad. I was quite worried about you; you seemed so depressed.'

'And what about you, Amanda, are you enjoying the visit?'

'Of course; who wouldn't? A beautiful house, every need catered for, an amenable hostess; how could I not?'

'What about the most eligible bachelor in town, that you've been dashing about with?' Piers gave a wicked grin.

'Really, Piers. I have not been dashing about with anyone.'

'Well, you were seen in his curricle, and I understand it is a very rare occurrence, seeing the noble marquis driving anywhere with a woman of quality, who isn't either his mother or sister, on board.'

'He drove me to the Royal Botanic Gardens at Kew, so I could deliver my latest work to them; that is all.'

'I'd lay a monkey they were surprised to see you in such exalted company.'

Privately, she agreed with him but certainly wasn't going to say so. His next remark did surprise her, though.

'Do you miss Abbots Court? It's so lovely at this time of year.'

Amanda thought for a moment before replying. She knew that during his long convalescence, Piers had been much in the company of Elizabeth Armitage, the rector's daughter, who, with Rosalie, had spent much time by his bedside, entertaining him, but it was not a connection she wanted to encourage. The invitation to visit London had been very fortuitous.

'Well?' he repeated. 'Do you?'

'Of course, I do, not least because I am missing nearly the whole summer season to collect plants.'

'Town is fun. But you know, Amanda, I think I'm really a country person, at heart.'

Amanda hoped it was the countryside he had a passion for and not Lizzie Armitage.

They arrived at Abbots Court in the late afternoon, to see the house bathed in the westering sun, the grey stone, which could look forbidding in bad weather, radiating a welcoming warmth, and the diamond-pane windows sparkling like their namesakes. When they had left, the short drive that led up to the house was still in the sparse grip of winter, and they were returning in full greenness of early summer.

Around the lawn, the ancient oak, cedar, and lime trees were casting long shadows, their leaves dappling the grass in a constantly moving mosaic. Amanda realised that coming home after a long absence, reinforced everything she loved about the Court, even although it wasn't really her home. She looked at Piers and could see from his expression that he felt the same.

As soon as they entered, Amanda could see what good advice she had been given by the marchioness. Everything had been organised in advance of their arrival. Mrs Ford, the housekeeper, greeted them with the announcement that refreshments would be ready in the drawing room presently, and that dinner would be served at their convenience. Then she drew Amanda's attention to a letter awaiting her arrival.

The rooms at Abbots Court were much smaller than those at Coverdale House but, to Amanda's taste, much more comfortable. She loved the velvet cushion-covered seats in the window embrasures, the painted Chinese wallpaper, the Dutch marquetry cabinets, and above all the wide fireplace, flanked with rich carvings and headed by the coat of arms, unlit now in summer's warmth, but delightful to sit beside, in high-backed chairs, in winter.

She sat down, enjoying the pleasure of familiar things, while she waited for Piers to come in and considered how much about the trust she should tell him, now that Mr Smallbody was no longer there to arrange financial matters. Of one thing she was certain: She would say nothing about the diamond. The fewer people who knew about it, the better, and there was already the worry that someone else did know about it. She was relieved that no more alarming notes had been waiting for her on the hall table, as she feared might be the case.

The letter she *had* received was from the remaining partner in the firm of Smallbody and Brewster, asking for her to arrange a meeting at her earliest convenience.

When Piers joined her, Amanda said, 'We will have to go to Taunton as soon as it can be arranged, probably the day after tomorrow, Piers. I think it would be best if you send one of the grooms with a message to the lawyer, to that effect. Would you do that soon?'

'Of course I will, and that will give me a day to look around the estate and find out what might need doing. I noticed that some railings near the lodge has come down; probably the wind, I expect.'

Amanda hadn't noticed, but she recognised Piers' keen eye for every aspect of the land which was under his care. She wasn't so keen on his next utterance.

'And I must go and visit Miss Armitage, show her how well I've got on since we left. I know she'll be really pleased to see that my limp is all but gone. Thanks to your marquis—'

'He's not *my* marquis,' Amanda interrupted. 'I've already told you that.'

'Anyway, he's a jolly good fellow. You know he got his bootmaker to fit all my footwear with that clever insert, and I've had my own lasts made, so in future, all my shoes and boots will fit. None of this would have happened without him.'

'Yes, I'm very grateful to him for that too, but now we must talk about what we should say to Mr Brewster. As of now, I am the sole trustee of your and Rosalie's estate, I mean, the money he left in trust for you and Rosalie. I must have someone else to help me look after it.'

'Why can't you do it, Amanda?'

'Because the law makes it very difficult, if not impossible, for a woman to handle large sums of money; if it were my money, as a widow, I could, but since it is not, I may not.'

'That's stupid. I know you could do it perfectly well.'

'That's as may be, Piers, but as things stand, I can't.'

'Can't I do it?'

'Not until you are twenty-five.'

'So what are you going to do?'

'When we meet Mr Brewster, I shall want you to observe carefully, so you can give me your opinion. I know practically nothing about him, but someone has to look after the financial side of things.'

'What about Coverdale? I'm sure he would be perfect for the task.'

For a moment, Amanda revelled in the idea; as Piers said, tJustin would indeed be perfect.

Instead, she retorted sharply, 'Don't be ridiculous, Piers. He is barely a friend, let alone a relative.'

'He's been a very good friend to me.'

'That is altogether different.'

'There is one thing. Can you tell how much money my father left? It's all right; I'll understand if you can't, Amanda.

Amanda thought for a moment, Piers was a steady young man, not academic, and so far, showing no tendency to profligacy. Perhaps knowing how much he was due before he came into possession of it would, on the whole, do him no harm. She drew in a deep breath. 'In excess of one hundred thousand pounds.'

After their meeting with the solicitor, Amanda, as she said she would, asked Piers for his opinion of Mr Brewster.

'Well, Amanda, we don't know him well, as yet. Do you know what Mr Smallbody thought of him? I think that could be important, don't you?'

'A very sensible remark, Piers.'

'Mr Brewster had been his junior partner for twenty years or more, so I suppose he must have been satisfied with his character.'

'I still think the marquis would make an ideal trustee, though.'

'Well, he can't be, so there is no more to be said on that point.' Amanda looked at the carefully wrapped parcel that was placed between them. 'I see you went shopping while I was away. Have you bought anything interesting?'

'It is a book, a present for Lizzie, Miss Armitage, I mean. There will be plenty of time to give it to her when we get back. You could drop me off at the rectory on our way home, Amanda.'

Amanda frowned. 'Do you think you ought to be giving presents to young ladies, Piers? Gifts can be very significant—'

Piers cut her short. 'Amanda,' he said sharply, 'I owe Lizzie far more than a book. You had to run the estate as well as look after the house while I was laid low. Lizzie, and Rosalie, too, were the only ones who understood how I was feeling. It was they who stayed with me through the worst times, made me eat and drink when all I wanted to do was cry. Yes, I know, men aren't supposed to, but she was the one who always bore the brunt of my bad temper. I can assure you that a book is but poor recompense for all the hours she stayed by my bedside.'

Amanda was completely taken aback and said nothing for several seconds. Then, she said, 'Oh, Piers, I had no idea; you never said, Lizzie never said, nor Rosalie, either.'

'I know, I never told you. You had enough on your plate.'

'But the nurse I hired, didn't she …?'

'Not much; she sat beside the fire, knitting, when no one else was there and occasionally straightened my pillow. But it was Grooby and Lizzie who did all the hard work, changing the bed-linen, which always took ages because it was so painful for me. And it had to be done frequently, because I sweated with fever. And yes, she even helped Grooby wash me. So now you know all.'

Amanda realised that she did indeed know all, not least how much Piers was turning into a really confident and thoughtful young man, with very definite views of his own.

'I will drop you off at the rectory, Piers.'

CHAPTER 9

At first, Rosalie felt the loss, if only temporary, of Amanda and her brother, although the time was soon filled with numerous activities. She had known Wilkins, the personal maid she shared with Amanda, since she was a child, and there was no need for strict formality between them, so she could share some of her thoughts with someone other than her godmother, of whom she was still rather in awe.

As well as enjoying many social occasions, she was also preparing for a musical soirée that Lady Coverdale was giving in a fortnight's time. Rosalie took her music very seriously and was determined to give of her very best. the best, and this required as much practice as she could fit in. Since shopping expeditions with friends and reading to the marchioness took time during the day, she found that the best time was early in the morning.

Her bedchamber was in a different part of the house from the music room, so she would creep down, perfectly respectable, but not fully gowned, to practice on the pianoforte and harp before breakfast. After she had been doing this for several mornings, something a little strange happened. A piece she had not played the day before, nor was she going to play at the concert, was sitting on the piano's music stand. The first time, she dismissed it as something she had forgotten to put away, or perhaps it had fallen on the floor, and a maid had picked it up, but when it happened again the next day, and again the day after, she knew someone must be playing tricks. The piece was a Mozart sonata, which she was quite familiar with, so she decided to play it. The next day, there was a different piece ready for her to play.

In an effort to find out, she asked Wilkins, 'Is there anyone else living in the house, besides the family and the staff?'

'I couldn't really say, Miss Rosalie; it's a big house, but I believe I know all the female staff. We all have our rooms in the attics, and the footmen all sleep in the basement. I am not familiar with them; they eat at a separate table in the servant's hall.'

'You haven't heard of anyone else, then?'

'No, Miss Rosalie,' she paused and then went on, "cept—no, I don't know.'

'Go on, Wilkins, tell me.'

'Well, Miss Rosalie, I once overheard someone they referred to as the sergeant, mentioned, and a Captain Benedict, but I don't know who he is, and the person who it said it stopped talking as soon as they saw me.'

'Can you remember exactly what they said?'

'Not really, something about "taking something up to the sergeant, I wasn't really listening, although perhaps they thought I was.'

'You didn't ask?' Rosalie sounded disappointed; she always wanted to know things and usually wasn't afraid to ask.

'It isn't my place to ask.'

'No, I suppose not.'

'Why do you want to know, Miss Rosalie?'

'Now who's asking?' Rosalie replied with a laugh.

'Sorry, Miss.'

'I just think someone may be listening to me practise, that's all.'

Now Miss Wilkins became concerned; after all, she had been left, at least in part, in charge of Miss Rosalie's welfare.

'Have you seen anyone? Has anyone approached you?'

'No, no, nothing like that, I assure you; don't worry. Perhaps it's just someone who likes music. What can be wrong with that?'

But the following morning, something really strange occurred. There was certainly a different piece of music on the stand, but this time it was not printed, but a handwritten manuscript. It wasn't very long, about two and a half pages, but beautifully written, with every musical annotation meticulously scripted.

Rosalie studied the arrangement carefully before trying it, absorbing the melodic line. It was no easy piece, and whoever wrote it knew what they were doing. It was an exciting mystery. It was not until she had played it three times that she acquired the confidence to give the piece full rein.

She was concentrating so hard, she didn't hear a door closing quietly, but there was a definite whiff of cigar smoke in the air, when she had finished. For some reason, she felt unable to continue with the pianoforte, so turned to her harp, instead. Later, on reflection, she decided that it must be one of the servants, one with strong musical tendencies, who had left the manuscript. She decided to say nothing more to Wilkins or anyone else; it was her little secret.

Rosalie's social engagements for the next few days meant that she was too tired to practise early in the morning, but although she managed an hour or two during the day, no more musical mysteries occurred. It was both a relief and a disappointment. The real pleasure of the day was a letter from Amanda, saying they would be leaving Somerset by the end of the week.

The next day, there was another surprise. Not only were several more pages of manuscript waiting for her on the piano, but the first two pages had been slightly modified to accommodate her small hands, which had previously proved difficult for some of the bass chords.

There were also a few words written at the top of the page: 'I"hope you will find this easier", but no signature. She played the music again, and again, when she had finished, there was the faintest smell of tobacco smoke.

Should I write back? Rosalie wondered. Finally, she decided to just write 'Thank you' beside the message.

One more day of practice brought the concluding pages of the piece. She played it in full and loved it. Although it was relatively short, six pages in all, it was full interesting phrases and subtle key changes. The inherent melancholy in the piece made her feel sad that it was finished, but there was one more surprise. Below the last line, it had been given a name: "Sonatina for Rosalie".

Who could have written it? Why were they so secretive? How did he (or she, know her name? Questions to which she had no answer and no one to ask.

CHAPTER 10

The marquis opened a bureau drawer, carefully lifted out the wax seal he had cut from Amanda's note, and examined it once again with his magnifying glass. It intrigued him just as much as it had the first time, and it was still a mystery. The only way he could answer the questions in his mind was to go to Berkeley Square and consult the books on heraldry and genealogy there; it might give him an opportunity to see Mrs Fletcher again, and find out more. However, he was doomed to disappointment on that head. As soon as he enquired after her, his mother informed him that Amanda had returned to Somerset with Piers.

'May I be told the reason for the visit?' he asked. 'It's rather sudden, and in the middle of the season, too, is it not?'

'Amanda, Mrs Fletcher, did not tell me much, only to say that a Mr Small or somebody had died, and it was imperative that she return at once. Rosalie is still here.'

'I see.' And Justin did indeed, see. The sudden death of the other trustee must have been a great shock to Amanda and clearly demanded her immediate return.

'They will be coming back as soon as she has completed whatever business they have in Somerset.'

'I'm glad to hear that, Mama Their presence in this house seems to have livened it up considerably.' He took his leave and went downstairs to the library, thinking about this extra burden that had now been thrown on Amanda's shoulders. He smiled; well, they were probably broad enough.

A trawl through De Brett's Peerage produced nothing significant, and the book on heraldry confirmed that the coronet on the crest was indeed that of a viscount. All of which he already knew. He shut the book with a bang and stalked towards the door, which was opened by a footman as soon as he touched the handle. This always annoyed him. Why was his mother so keen on having footmen standing about all over the place? He scowled, then, thinking the poor man might think he was in the wrong; he looked at the man again and smiled.

'I have seen you before,' he said, but I have forgotten your name.'

'Yes, M'lord. her ladyship calls me Alfred, M'lord.,' and then added, with the slightest of smiles, 'or sometimes, James.'

Yes, thought Justin, as he retrieved his hat, gloves and tasselled cane from yet another footman, she probably does. 'But what do you call yourself?'

'Henry, M'lord.'

'Of course, now I remember.' Justin strolled towards the front door, which the hall porter was already holding open. He sighed; he really didn't like all this ceremony and couldn't understand why his mother insisted on it. He hesitated on the top step, undecided where to go next. A bit of company at his club might help to dispel his blue mood, so he set off on foot for St James's. Just as he reached the steps of his club, Colonel Fortesque was emerging.

This was a fortuitous meeting. Remembering their last outing in the park, when the colonel had mentioned Mrs Fletcher's name in conjunction with a certain Dr Pargeter, the Justinimmediately thought he might be the one to furnish him with more information.

'Ah, Fortesque, just the man I wanted to see. Can you spare me a few minutes of your time?'

'Certainly, Coverdale, I am in no particular hurry. Am I to believe you came here specifically to find me?'

The marquis laughed, urging the military man back through the portals of the club. 'No, I can't say I did. I came looking for some company, but meeting you may serve my purpose even better.'

'Always glad to oblige, Sir. Always glad to oblige. What can I do for you?'

'Let's go somewhere more private; one of the reading rooms may be empty at this time of day. Can I order you a drink?'

'No, I thank you. I am on duty in about an hour, doesn't look good for the soldiery to find one smelling of brandy, what? But you go ahead, Coverdale.'

Justin ordered himself a brandy from a club servant, and the two of them entered a small room at the rear of the building, furnished with leather chairs and with a table on which the day's newspapers were spread out, and another with periodicals.

The drink arrived, and Colonel Fortesque said, 'Now Coverdale, what can I do for you?'

'What can you tell me about a Dr Amyas Pargeter? You mentioned him in connection with Mrs Fletcher, who, as you know is staying with my mother, along with her two wards.'

'I'm afraid I cannot tell you much. He is more an acquaintance of my father, being more or less the same age, but I do know he is highly regarded in a number of different fields.'

'Such as?'

'He is an Oxford man, an Emeritus professor of natural sciences, philosophy, and God knows what else, but he is also a professor and practising surgeon at St Bartholomew's Hospital. Is that of any help?'

'Not really, but it confirms that his admiration for Mrs Fletcher's work, about which I now have some knowledge, must be at the highest level. A surgeon, you say?' The colonel nodded. 'I wonder,' mused the marquis.

'You wonder what? I don't see what you are driving at, Coverdale.'

'I'm sorry, am I being evasive?' The Colonel nodded again. 'The matter I am curious about is one of great delicacy, and I'm not sure if I should pursue it at all.'

'I can keep my mouth shut,' Fortesque replied, a little sharply.

'My dear fellow, of course you can; I did not mean to imply … I mean, it is my own conscience that is troubling me.'

'It is to do with the lady, then?'

Justin took a sip of his brandy. 'Yes, I suppose it is. I have never met anyone like her in my life, and I cannot contain my curiosity.'

'Well, I'm afraid I'm not going to be of much help. I really do not know Mrs Fletcher. All I know is that Dr Pargeter holds her in high regard, but you knew that already. I'm sorry, Coverdale.'

'Ah, well,' the marquis said, sighing, 'but perhaps you could tell me something about this? I know you have made a study of such things.' He pulled the paper containing the wax seal from his pocket and passed it to the Colonel.

Fortesque took the seal over to the light and examined it closely. 'I've seen it before, somewhere, but I can't … Oh, yes, I can …'

'Yes?' Coverdale leaned forward.

'At least a bit. The hand holding a star, or mullet, is not unique; several families have it, but I know one that does…did, is an extinct viscountcy. That's all I can tell you, sorry.'

Disappointed, Justin held out his hand for the seal and replaced in his waistcoat pocket. 'Thank you, Fortesque, for your time; not a word about this conversation to anyone.'

'Of course not, but I must say, Coverdale, your name is being bandied about the clubs in connection with a certain Miss Prideau; bets are being taken.'

'Yes, I *do* know, but unfortunately, there is nothing I can do about that. It is up to Miss Prideau to deny any such rumour. Any word from me would seriously damage her reputation, and that is the last thing I want to do.'

'Of course not; no honourable man would.'

The Colonel took his leave and, the marquis stayed on, finishing his drink and pondering on his next move in his investigation into Amanda Fletcher's past. Eventually, he went into the card room and exchanged pleasantries with a few friends, but decided not to make up a four at whist, and after a short while, he left the club and hailed a passing hackney cab. 'St. Bartholomew's Hospital, driver.'

The cab drove into the City and deposited the marquis outside the arched entrance. From there, he strolled into the courtyard and toward what looked like the main door. A porter opened it at his approach. Inside, another uniformed man was sitting behind a desk.

'Can I be of service, Sir?' he enquired.

'I rather wanted to see Dr Pargeter, if he is available.'

'Who shall I say is …?' His lordship presented his card. 'Certainly, My Lord; at once, My Lord. Please, My Lord, will you come this way?' The desk clerk led the Marquis upstairs to the famous Great Hall. 'If Your Lordship would wait here, I will inform Dr Pargeter of your presence. I am afraid it may take a little while; Dr Pargeter is sometimes not easy to find, My Lord.'

'That is quite all right; I shall spend the time looking round the magnificent hall.'

Having looked at portraits of the great and the good in the medical profession, his eye was caught by a large gold urn-shaped cup, situated on a high shelf. The inscription on the socle was in French and too small to make out, but he could distinctly read the name, 'Pargeter,' in larger letters.

About twenty minutes later, a tall, spare man, close to seventy years of age, entered the hall and held out his hand.

'Please accept my apologies for keeping you waiting, Lord Coverdale. I was just finishing a tutorial when your message arrived.'

'Not at all; I have been looking at all the famous medical and scientific men who have grace this hall, and that handsome gold cup with your name on it.'

The Doctor waved a deprecating hand. 'A very generous gift, but more suited to this room than to my study. I do not believe we have met, My Lord, but of course I am aware that you speak in the House of Lords, and before in the Commons, when you were an MP. What brings you here, and more specifically, to see me? Not a matter of your health, I hope.'

'No, I'm glad to say, nothing of that sort,' the Marquis assured the older man. 'I know we have never met, but I have heard a great deal about you in the last few weeks, and we have a mutual acquaintance.'

'And who might that be?'

'A Mrs Fletcher, a most redoubtable lady.'

'Indeed, she is. Whatever you have come to see me about, let us retire to my quarters, where we can talk in more comfort.'

The Doctor's study was warm and furnished with dark, leather-upholstered furniture, not dissimilar to the club Justinhad just left. It was lined with books, and every available surface was covered in papers, some spilling onto the floor. A large table held various instruments including a microscope, and several jars containing unidentifiable, at least to the marquis, preserved specimens.

'Please, take a seat,' said the Doctor, followed by 'ah,' as he quickly removed a pile of papers and books from the only other chair. 'Now, My Lord, with what may I be of assistance?'

'First, I had better tell you my connection with the Abbots. My mother, Marchioness of Coverdale, is godmother to Miss Rosalie Abbot, and as you no doubt know, Mrs Fletcher is guardian to her and her brother, Sir Piers.'

'Yes,' the Doctor said, nodding, 'I have had occasion to meet them both; delightful young people.'

'All three have been staying with my mother, in order to give Miss Abbot her first season in London. I recently had the pleasure of driving Mrs Fletcher to the Royal Botanical Gardens at Kew, where she delivered some of her latest work. Your name was mentioned.'

The Doctor maintained a neutral expression. The marquis felt all this was getting him nowhere. Time to try a different tack if he was ever going to find out what he wanted to know.

'I found out this morning that Mrs Fletcher and Sir Piers had returned to Somerset, because a Mr Smallbody had died …'

'Oh, dear,' the Doctor exclaimed, finally showing some interest. 'How very unfortunate. Poor Amanda; she will have to cope with the guardianship all alone, now.'

Justin had a brilliant idea, which he knew in reality was a bit of sophistry, but it was worth a try.

'When she arrived in London, Mrs Fletcher asked me to make funds from the trust available through my bank, all authorised by Mr Smallbody, and I wondered if she had any other male relative who could help, now that he is no more.'

'Yes, I see. Things could become awkward for her, but I'm afraid there is no one else. Her father died some years ago. He had been a student of mine at Oxford, a brilliant man; very sad, such a waste, as indeed had her husband been, but at different times, of course.'

No useful information there, then, the Justin thought, and tried a different tack.

'Mrs Fletcher drew part of a skeleton for me; did she use the one I see over there as a model?' He pointed to one in the corner of the room, hung from a gibbet-like stand.

'Probably,' the Doctor replied a little cagily, 'but if it was known she came here to work for me, it would be considered very strange in the polite world, so we do not speak of it outside the hospital, but why would she be drawing skeletons for you, My Lord?'

'Mrs Fletcher was explaining to me the exact nature of the injuries that Sir Piers sustained as a result of his fall. She was worried that his limp was preventing him from joining in the activities that young men should be experiencing on their first visit to London.'

'Yes, it is very unfortunate, but I was abroad at the time of the accident, and by the time I returned, the damage had been done, and I could not put it right.' The Doctor sighed. 'Perhaps one day, we will be able to perform long and delicate operations without causing the patient incalculable pain. Were you able to help the young man at all?'

'Only to the extent that I got my bootmaker to adjust Sir Piers' shoes, thus rendering his gait more even, and introducing him to a young cousin, who encourages him to be more sociable.'

'That is good news, sir, but I am afraid the damage is permanent and may well cause him problems in later life.'

The realised he had the opening he wanted, and fished the seal from his pocket, once again.

'When Mrs Fletcher furnished me with an outline of Sir Piers' shoe, to give to the bootmaker, she sealed the note with this. Can you tell me anything about this, Sir?' He held it out.

The Doctor hooked a pair of steel-rimmed spectacles round his ears and looked at the seal, handing it back almost immediately. His next remark took the marquis completely by surprise.

'Do you have a river or a lake at your country seat, Lord Coverdale?' he asked.

'Yeees,' Justin replied slowly, unable to understand the significance of the question.

'Do you go fishing? You know, that thing that you do with a line with a lure and a hook at the end, which you dangle in the water, hoping an innocent passing fish will be deceived into thinking it's dinner?'

The marquis was silent for a moment but then burst out laughing and shaking his head; finally he said, 'I think I'm the one that has been caught, hook, line, and sinker, am I not, Dr Pargeter? Was I so transparent?'

'Well, after forty years of listening to students' excuses, I am a master at seeing through to the truth, and I might even tell you about the seal, if you can assure me that Mrs Fletcher will be well protected on her journey back to London. There is a lot of unrest in the country just now ... one never knows.'

'Doctor, I think you're disseminating now. I believe you are concerned about something Mrs Fletcher might be bringing back with her. Is that not so?'

The Doctor looked surprised. 'You know about it, then?'

'I not only know about it, sir, but I have it in my safekeeping.'

'Canon Fletcher told me about it, but I have never seen it. Is it as magnificent as I believe it to be?'

'It is the most amazing jewel I have ever seen. It must be one of the rarest and most valuable in the whole world. Mrs Fletcher brought it up from Abbots Court, because she did not want to leave it in an empty house. Nor did she want it to stay in Berkeley Square, so she asked me to look after it for her.'

'That means only you, me, and Mrs Fletcher know of its existence; that must ensure some degree of safety.'

'If that were true, I would agree,' said the marquis seriously, 'but I fear it is not. Mrs Fletcher received two notes, delivered by an unknown hand, claiming that the diamond, they called by its name, *The Light of the Sun*", did not belong to the Abbots and should be given back. There was no indication to whom it should be given, and as far as I know, no further notes have been received, but it is a worry.'

'A worry, indeed, but I'm sure you will keep a discreet eye open for any further developments, and as you have now shown me that you have Mrs Fletcher's trust, and to stop you asking any more questions, I will tell you whose crest it is on that seal.'

'If you're sure, sir. I don't want to pry.'

'Yes, you do, and yes, I am. It is the crest of a now extinct viscountcy that was held by Mrs Fletcher's grandfather, on her mother's side. However, I do not feel at liberty to say more, and that will have to satisfy your curiosity. The lady herself should be the one to tell you more, if she wants to.' The doctor rose and held out his hand. 'I am very pleased to have met you, Lord Coverdale. I trust you to keep the welfare of the Abbots and Mrs Fletcher in mind, but now, if you forgive me, I have a lecture to give. The porter will show you out.'

Justin left with a great deal to think about, but he was extremely pleased to know that in Dr Pargeter, Amanda Fletcher had a very good friend indeed.

CHAPTER 11

Amanda and Piers returned to Berkeley Square five days before the musical soirée was to take place. Rosalie was ecstatic to have them both back again, and although she had been longing to tell Amanda about the mysterious occurrences in the music room, she now felt strangely reluctant to do so, it somehow seemed like a sort of betrayal of the unknown composer. But the next afternoon, when they were seated in the boudoir, a comfortable room between their two bedchambers, and after Amanda had regaled her with all the news from Abbots Court, the right moment came.

'Now, Rosalie, how are your preparations for the concert going?' her guardian enquired. 'Have you had enough time to practice, with all your other engagements keeping you so busy?'

'Oh, yes. I generally practice early in the morning, when Godmamma is still in her rooms. There's no one to disturb, or to disturb me, then.'

'And it's going well? I'm sure it is; I don't really need to ask.' Amanda smiled. 'But what about the programme? Is it decided yet?'

'Godmama has arranged for me to visit Signor Amonetti, the leader of the Amonetti Quartet, who are also playing at the soirée. He will decide which pieces I will play on the pianoforte. I have been practising several. I expect he wants to audition me.' Rosalie grinned. 'I suspect he doesn't want his famous quartet to play in the company of a complete duffer.'

'He needn't worry on that score. I don't suppose he has ever played with an amateur as good as you are, my dear. What about the harp pieces?'

'Those I can choose entirely on my own, but there is one thing, though. I don't know if I should say anything.'

'You can tell me, Rosalie. You can always confide in me; you know that.'

Rosalie decided to tell Amanda most of the truth. She fidgeted with a knot of ribbons on her dress before beginning, 'I found a handwritten composition in the music room. It's a lovely melody, quite short, but full of feeling and beautifully composed. Do you think I could play it at the soirée? I'd really like to. I played it for Signor Amonetti; he thought it was very good and said I could play it if I wanted to.'

'There's no hint as to who composed it?' Queried Amanda.

'No, none at all.' Rosalie was adamant.

'Well, I can't see any harm would come. People who write music usually want someone to play it, just as writers want people to read their books. I think you should do just as you like.'

Rosalie was thankful that Amanda was not musical enough to want to see the score. The dedication, 'A Sonatina for Rosalie,' would certainly engender some awkward questions.

For the evening of the soirée, the music room was to be a blaze of light surrounding the dais, where the players were to perform. Three-branched candelabra were set on the pianoforte, and torchères bore more candelabra for the quartet. Every wall sconce had candles that reflected their light in the mirrors. Numerous gilded chairs had been set in the body of the room, which faded back into darkness, so that the audience would be focused on the performers.

The Broadwood and Sons rosewood grand piano had been tuned again, especially for the occasion, and Rosalie spent some time in the morning tuning her harp, which she always did herself, and was then persuaded to rest in the afternoon, to be at her best for the evening. As well as the concert, there would be a long interval with a lavish supper, offering a variety of dishes to suit all tastes, and copious quantities of champagne, wine, mild punch, and lemonade. For those with a lesser taste for music, a card room provided alternative entertainment, although it was considered bad form to venture into it before the interval. A dinner for a few selected friends and relations, which included the marquis, took place at seven o'clock. Amanda and Rosalie ate upstairs to give them plenty of time to dress, and the music was scheduled to begin at 8.30.

The Amonetti Quartet opened the concert with music by Beethoven, then Rosalie, resplendent in white spangled satin, and with a coronet of white roses in her upswept hair, took her place on the dais. Her rendering of a Mozart sonata drew much applause from an appreciative audience. She was followed by Amonetti, who played several solo virtuoso pieces on the violin, and the first part of the evening's entertainment concluded with one of Rosalie's études for the harp, engendering more enthusiastic applause. She and Amanda did not join the supper party, rather resting and enjoying light refreshment in the small dining room. The marquis joined them, his face wreathed in smiles. 'My mother wishes to say how pleased she is,' he said. 'The evening is going splendidly. Congratulations to you both, and especially to you, Miss Rosalie. I really had no idea how good you were.'

Rosalie said, 'Thank you, Sir,' in a small voice, and Amanda added, 'I would hardly have suggested that Rosalie play, if it were otherwise, Marquis.' Her tone indicated a mild reproach.

'I'm sorry. Of course you wouldn't. I'm looking forward to the next part of the concert, but I can't stay now. I still have a host's duties to perform.'

The second half of the soirée followed much the same pattern, but ended with the Amonetti Quartet playing Schubert's *String Quartet No 10*. There was much applause and calls for encores. Signor Amonetti obliged with another virtuoso violin piece, and when the room had quietened down, he stepped forward. And then he said in Italian-accented English, 'My Lords, ladies and gentlemen, I would like to say sank you to my protégée, Signorina Rosalie, and ask her to play a very beautiful piece, one that she has already played for me; alas, the composer is unknown.'

Rosalie, who had been seated beside her harp, came forward to the piano; she had played the music so many times, she did not require the score. The piano, surrounded by a new set of candles, replaced during the interval, made seeing the far end of the room, dark by contrast, difficult, but with fewer people in the audience, some having taken advantage of the card room, she thought she could make out the pale face of someone dressed in black, standing in the very farthest corner.

The composition lasted less than two minutes, and when it was over, a member of the audience requested that she play it again. The moment she finished the piece for the second time, she peered into the back of the room, but the man, if it was one, was no longer there. The success of the Marchioness of Coverdale's musical soirée was the talk of town, and those who were there were able to feel superior over those who were not invited.

The next day, Justin called at Coverdale house and asked if it was possible to speak to Amanda. 'I need,' he explained to his mother, 'to discuss if new or different arrangements must be made, now that you have told me that Mr Smallbody has died.'

'I'm sure you do, dear, but I believe she is out walking in Green Park with Rosalie. You can wait here,' a pronouncement that Justin thought very ingenuous, considering it was his house, 'or go and meet them. I do not expect them to be long. Rosalie usually reads to me in the afternoons when I am not at home.'

'Thank you, Mama, I shall wait in the library. I'll inform one of your footmen that I wish to see Mrs Fletcher, on her return.' He had been browsing the books or idly twirling one of the globes for less than fifteen minutes, when a footman opened the door and announced, 'Mrs Fletcher, My Lord.'

Amanda dropped a curtsey. 'You wanted to see me, Sir, and I may say I have been desirous to speak to you.'

'Shall we sit? My gout has been troubling me of late.'

For a moment, Amanda looked shocked, then she noticed the twinkle in the marquis's amber eyes. 'By all means, My Lord, shall I get you a footstool?'

JUstin smiled. 'No, but it is a trifle chilly in here. The fire has dwindled to almost nothing.' He went over to the hearth and poked the smouldering coals to life, adding another couple of lumps. 'There, that should soon do the trick. Now, tell me what you found in Taunton.'

'Mr Small body's partner, will, at least for the time being, take over the financial affairs of the trust, and the money orders to your bank will continue as before. I did not see any reason to change that arrangement.'

'I half-expected you to want to see me sooner. It has been nearly a week since you returned.'

'We've been very busy preparing for the concert. Rosalie has been playing for Signor Amonetti and has had to be escorted to his studio, although he certainly exaggerated a bit by calling her his protégée.'

'Well, I don't suppose it has done either of them any harm,' replied the marquis, crossing his long legs. 'But now that your co-trustee has died, what are your plans? Not that it's any of my business, of course.'

Ignoring this last remark, Amanda answered him, 'Piers and I have talked the matter over, and we decided to leave the appointment of a second trustee in abeyance for the moment. We both agree that Mr Brewster is a competent lawyer, who is well informed about the trust and the disposition of the moneys. We will decide later what to do.'

'Hmm,' said his lordship.

'I know what you are thinking, sir. What if anything happens to me? Who will be in charge then?'

'Precisely, my thought exactly. Would you like me to look into it for you, Mrs Fletcher?'

Amanda sighed. It was what she really would like, but felt ashamed that it would mean putting yet another imposition on obliging host.

He sensed her reluctance. 'Do not worry on my account; my secretary will do all the work. It is, after all, what I pay him handsomely for.'

'In that case, I shall be most grateful for the information.' Amanda smiled.

'I will put it in hand immediately. But there is an altogether different matter I would like to speak to you about.' He rose up to poke the fire again, and this time, the coals burst into a satisfactory blaze. 'That piece of music Rosalie played as an encore; do you happen to know where she found it?'

'I only know she said she found it among other sheet-music in the music room and was very taken by it. Why do you ask?'

'I just thought I had heard it, or something very like it, before, and I was curious, that's all.'

'I see. You could ask her yourself, of course, but I expect you would get the same answer.'

'More than probably.' He rose to his feet. 'Thank you, Mrs Fletcher, for agreeing to see me. Perhaps we could have another drive, once this cold spell is over.'

Amanda said nothing, as she rose and dropped a curtsey. 'At the moment, Marquis, Rosalie is with your mother; if I ask her now, perhaps she can show you the manuscript. Is it important?'

'I don't know; it's interesting.' He opened the door and spoke to the footman. 'My compliments to the marchioness, and convey my wish for Miss Rosalie to join Mrs Fletcher in the library.'

Only a few minutes passed before Rosalie rushed into the room, exclaiming, 'Oh, Amanda, is something wrong?'

'Not at all; his lordship wishes to ask you something, that is all.'

Rosalie, who hadn't seen the marquis leaning on the mantelpiece, whirled round and dropped a curtsey. 'I'm sorry, My Lord, I didn't know you were there.' She curtseyed again.

Justin gave a wry smile. 'You need not be afraid of me, Rosalie; I don't eat beautiful young ladies, you know. Has somebody told you that I do?'

'No ... no, My Lord, it's just that ...'

'Just what?'

'Everyone, well not everyone, of course, but my friends here in town, seem very much in awe of this family, and living here with the the....' Her voice tailed off.

'Look at me, Rosalie, I don't believe you have raised your eyes above the carpet since we first met. I have a face, you know.'

Rosalie raised her head, and the little dimple in her cheek, that was currently driving her male admirers wild, appeared, as she smiled. 'Well, sir, it is rather a long way up.'

'That's better,' the marquis said, smiling back. 'Now I've asked you here to find out about the piece you played, beautifully played, I may say, as an encore at the concert. Mrs Fletcher tells me you found it in the music room. Is that so?'

'Yes, My Lord.'

'Perhaps you could let me see it.'

Amanda joined the conversation. 'It is probably just as you left it, since you haven't been practising today.'

Rosalie knew perfectly well that it was not. She had taken it up to her bedchamber and hidden it in her closet. 'I will fetch it for you, sir.' She went towards the door. 'It will only be a matter of moments.' Very shortly, she returned empty-handed. 'I'm sorry, My Lord, it seems to have disappeared. I know it was on the pianoforte last night.'

The marquis gave her a shrewd look and then said mildly, 'Never mind; I'm sure it will turn up somewhere.'

Rosalie said eagerly, 'I can play the music for you, sir. I have memorised it all; I do not require the music.'

'Thank you, Rosalie, some other time, perhaps. Meanwhile, I must take my leave of you two ladies, if you will excuse me. I have someone else I want to see.' He bowed, and left the room, leaving Amanda puzzled and Rosalie relieved.

'You are a very accomplished dissembler, Rosalie, but unfortunately for you, I have known you long enough not to trust that look of innocence in those cornflower blue eyes. Where is that score?'

Rosalie blushed and lowered her gaze. 'I will tell you, Amanda, I promise, but for the moment, it is someone else's secret, and till I know whose, I can't say. Please don't be cross.'

'I'm not cross, although I admit I am curious, but I also have your safety to consider, so if anything untoward happens, you must tell me at once. At once, do you understand?' Amanda spoke sternly. She was thinking of the yellow diamond and the risk it would always carry to those who possessed it. Nothing would relieve her mind more than not to have the responsibility for it.

Another bit of the 'conundrum of the *secret sonatina*, as Rosalie termed it, literally fell into her lap the next day, as she was reading *Sense and Sensibility* to her godmother. As she turned over a page, a slip of paper fell out, perhaps used as a bookmark by a previous reader, and when she glanced down at it, the few words written there were by a hand she recognised immediately; they were the same as those she had seen on the score of *"A Sonatina for Rosalie"*.

For a moment, she stopped reading, and the marchioness asked, 'What's the matter, child? You've gone quite pale; are you not feeling well?'

'I'm sorry, Godmama, I … I just lost my place for a moment. I am quite well, I assure you.'

Well, perhaps we have had enough for today. Have you got a party tonight?'

'Yes, Piers and I have been invited to a small gathering at the Carstairs's. It is to be their second daughter's first evening party.'

'Run along, now, and enjoy yourself, my dear.'

Rosalie managed to conceal the slip of paper in her hand as she curtseyed to the marchioness and quickly left the room. Once back in her own bedchamber, she took it over to the window to examine it more closely. The words themselves were meaningless, so she retrieved the score from her closet for comparison, and she had not been wrong about the script; the same neat rather spikey letters matched exactly. However, Rosalie's first sense of excitement soon wore off as she realised that the discovery really didn't advance her knowledge of who the anonymous composer could be, and it would not be easy to make enquiries as to who it was without raising suspicions. Perhaps Piers could help. She did not see him often, as he was now fully occupied with new friends, and the functions they did attend together were not the sort where they could converse together privately.

She and Piers were unchaperoned, as the party was a small one, and in the coach conveying them to it, Rosalie said, 'Have you heard of anyone else living in the house, I mean other than ourselves and Godmama? I don't mean the servants, at least I don't think so.'

'Not really, but Grooby once spoke of someone he called the sergeant. I don't know if that's who you mean.'

'I've heard of him too, at least Wilkins has,' Rosalie interrupted excitedly. 'Have you seen him?'

'I'm not sure; I may have. I came out of my room, and a man was standing in the passage. He turned his back to me the moment he caught sight of me.'

'What was he like? Did you see his face?'

'No, it was much too dark anyway, but he was of medium height and rather stocky build. But there was one thing I did notice ...'

'Yes, what? Tell me.'

'I am going to if you stop interrupting, Sis. He wasn't wearing Coverdale livery; of that I am certain.'

'What was he wearing?'

'I couldn't see exactly, but it seemed to be more military in style. I only saw him for a moment, and in a dark passage too. But I suppose he could be this mysterious sergeant.'

'Why didn't you ask someone?'

'None of my business.'

'Men! 'Rosalie said, disgusted, as the carriage arrived in Grosvenor Square.

CHAPTER 12

Amanda was coming down the main staircase, dressed to go out, just as the hall porter opened the door to admit his lordship. 'Ah, Mrs Fletcher, how fortuitous,' Justin said. 'You are just the person I wish to see. Will you take a drive with me? My curricle awaits, and the destination is yours to command.'

This was all spoken before Amanda could say a word, and much as she would like to accept, she felt it would be prudent not to. Her presence beside the marquis in his curricle might set tongues wagging, to the detriment of Miss Prideau.

'Well, Sir …,' she began.

'Please, Mrs Fletcher, I have something I wish to say to you.' His voice held an almost pleading note, as he continued, 'It is really important.'

He had never asked anything of her before, and she certainly owed him a debt of gratitude for all he had done for her and Piers. 'Very well, then, but I do not wish to drive in Hyde Park.'

'Thank you, I am much obliged, Mrs Fletcher. We will drive to St. James's Park and walk by the lake.'

The day was warm, but trees in full leaf shaded the paths, and they walked largely in silence, which puzzled Amanda, as he had specifically said he wished to talk, but when they came to a bench and the marquis suggested they sit, she agreed.

'What I am going to tell you, Mrs Fletcher, I hope most sincerely that you will keep to yourself. You may also think there is no connection to you, but I assure you there is.'

'Before you begin, Lord Coverdale, are you quite sure you want to divulge something that is going to be, I feel, a personal matter, and something that you later regret having done so.'

'I am quite sure, Mrs Fletcher, so shall I begin?'

'Please do.'

'There is someone to whom I am very close; in fact, I have known him all his life. I will tell you a little about his background. It was always his ambition to join the army, but he did not like the idea of buying a commission in some fashionable regiment or having one bought for him. Rather, he wanted a career where expertise resulted in promotion, rather than social standing, and being of a mathematical turn of mind, he went as a cadet to the Military Academy at Woolwich to train as an engineer and artillery officer. He fought in the American War of 1812, with great honour, and was promoted to captain. He returned just in time to command a battery, defending the Chateau de Hougoumont, one of the key points during the battle of Waterloo.'

'I believe everyone has heard of Hougoumont, Marquis, one of the most gallant efforts by defenders in the history of warfare,' Amanda interjected.

'Indeed it was, but here the captain's story becomes confused. I only know that the French finally overran his battery, and only he and a gunnery sergeant survived, although the sergeant was severely wounded by a cuirassier's sabre. The captain, who was unscathed, carried his sergeant for nearly a mile; eventually, he caught a loose horse to help him with his burden, until they reached a field medical station. Exactly how or why the captain survived is something of a mystery, and he, himself, cannot explain it, as part of his memory has been expunged. But I get the feeling that there is something so awful that he fears to remember it.'

Amanda looked at her companion and could see that the story he was telling was distressful.

'Whatever the reason, he resigned his commission and retired, for the most part, to an estate in Kent, left to him by his father, only coming up to town on rare occasions. He seemed to be his usual witty, charming self, with many friends, but on those occasions when we met, he was a changed man. Briefly, and in company, he appeared the same, but I understood him better than most, and I knew he was putting on a front, at great expense to his peace of mind. He never stayed long in company, or indeed in London, preferring his rural retreat. But worse was to come, and it was unfortunate that at the time, I was away in Vienna.'

'Ah, yes,' said Amanda. 'The Congress, of course.'

'Quite so,' Justin agreed. 'What happened next, occurred when a twenty-one-gun salute was being fired in Hyde Park, to mark the occasion of the Princess of Wales's birthday. What followed was told to me by those present at the time. The captain was standing at the front door, preparing to go out, when the salvo began, and whether by mischance or poor discipline, two of the guns fired simultaneously, causing an extra loud report. On hearing it, the captain collapsed on the doorstep and had to be carried back to his bedchamber. This occurred on 7 January last year, and although he recovered his senses quite quickly, he has not left the room since.'

'Not left his room for over a year?' Amanda was shocked.

'No, nor has he spoken a single word to any member of his family. He is looked after by the sergeant whom he saved at Waterloo, and he does speak to him, but not much, I understand. He eats very little and spends most of his time writing music, mostly random notes and phrases, or staring into space, and quite frankly, Mrs Fletcher, I fear for his life.'

Amanda impulsively laid her hand on the marquis's sleeve. 'Oh, Sir, your poor brother!'

'You knew?' He asked, astonished.

'No, I guessed, or at least I put two and two together; it wasn't difficult. I am right, am I not?'

'Unfortunately, yes. Benedict has apartments in the west wing. They are above the music room, which is why … well, that is really why I have told you his history, because I believe you can help.'

'If his family can do nothing, I hardly see what a stranger such as myself can do, surely his … your mother; should she not be the one?'

'As I've already explained, he refuses to see any of us, and anyway, their attitude isn't entirely helpful. My mother believes he will get better on his own and prefers not to think about it, and my sister says he should pull himself together and act like a man. Neither approach is going to work. I know that. But there is one thing that just might. The sergeant has told me that since you and the Abbots have come to stay, and he has heard

Rosalie playing the pianoforte, there has been a change. The sergeant also believes Benedict *has* left his room, possibly on more than one occasion. This would be the first time for sixteen months.'

'That must give you hope of more improvement.'

'Yes, it does, and I think I may have some evidence of it. Do you remember me saying that I thought I had heard the melody of Rosalie's encore piece before?'

'Yes, and I believe the little madam knows more than she is telling about that. To you or to me.'

'So do I,' said the marquis. 'Benedict used to write a lot of music at one time, and although she said, probably truthfully, that she found the score on the piano, I can only suppose that my brother put it there in order for her to find it. Therefore, I am asking you, as her guardian, if you would allow him to be in the music room and listen to her play; if she agrees, that is. He might just begin to improve if …'

'I'm sure she would, but of course she would have to be suitably chaperoned.'

'That could be a problem, if he still doesn't want to see anyone else, but I will speak with the sergeant, and perhaps we can work something out to your satisfaction. He has never been violent, you know.'

As they walked back to where his tiger had been waiting with the horses, the marquis said: 'I believe there are a great many returning soldiers who suffer in the same way as Benedict. They may take to drink or laudanum, to try and take away their anguish of what they have been through, or even worse, be shut away in lunatic asylums because they are considered to be mad. Perhaps such men have seen and experienced so many terrible things on the battlefield, more than their minds can take, and should be treated as wounded too, but since the wounds are invisible, and neither their friends and relatives, nor the medical profession, can understand or treat them, they are left to suffer alone.'

They walked on in silence, Amanda pondering on the thoughts the marquis just voiced. As they reached the gate of the park, where the curricle was awaiting them, she said, 'I believe there is hope for your brother, and he is very lucky to have you to help him, Lord Coverdale.'

'And perhaps you and Rosalie too?' he replied with a hopeful tone in his voice.

'Perhaps.'

Just as he was helping Amanda down from the curricle in Berkeley Square, she said, 'I hope you liked Dr Pargeter, My Lord.'

Justin looked slightly disconcerted. 'He told you of my visit?'

'Yes, he sent me a note, but it did not explain the reason for it, your visit, I mean.' She did not add that the note also said, "I like your Marquis".

The marquis regained his composure. 'To explain that will require another drive in my curricle.' He swept his hat off in farewell and sprang into the driving seat, taking up the reins. 'Let 'em go, Freddie,' he called out to his tiger, who nimbly jumped onto the vehicle as it swept past.

CHAPTER 13

Rosalie slept badly and woke just as dawn was breaking, and since it would soon be midsummer, this was very early indeed. Most of the night, she had been turning over in her head how to transpose the sonatina from the pianoforte to the harp, where she was sure it would sound even lovelier. With ideas buzzing around in her mind, she could not wait to try them out. She quickly pulled a petticoat over her night attire, tied her silk dressing gown tightly round her waist, donned a pair of slippers, and quietly left the room.

There was no one about; not even the maids had risen, and she tiptoed down to the music room. To give herself enough light, she pulled back the pair of heavy damask curtains nearest to her harp. Placing the sheet music on the stand, she gave the harp a quick tune and began to explore the ideas that her restless night had engendered, quite unaware that she had an audience of one. Seated at the very far end of the room and partially hidden by a stack of the gilded chairs that had been previously set out for the concert, a man waited and listened.

Totally focused on her music, and dashing between pianoforte and harp, her concentration was suddenly shattered by a sneeze. She stood, momentarily shocked, then saw a black-clad figure make for a hitherto unnoticed door at the end of the room.

Instinctively knowing she was in the presence of the composer, she called out, 'Don't go,' and rose to take a few steps toward him.

The man hesitated.

'Please stay. I love your music.'

He stayed still.

'Would you like me to play something for you?'

He still didn't move, but Rosalie sensed a slight relaxation in his stance. After short silence, he said, 'Yes. Yes, please.' His voice was deep and slightly hoarse.

'Harp or pianoforte?'

'Harp,' after a pause, again, 'please.'

He took a few steps forward, and as she returned to her instrument, a shaft of light from the rising sun streamed through the only uncontained window, piercing the greyness and illuminating the man's tall figure for a brief moment, before he recoiled into the shadows again, almost as if the sunlight had scared him. Rosalie saw that he was thin, almost to the point of emaciation, with long, dark hair below collar-length, although, in fact, he was wearing neither collar nor cravat, and she caught a fleeting glimpse of a pale, gaunt face and dark eyes. Afraid that he might try to leave again, she began to play her harp and could hear him draw up a chair. After about ten minutes, Rosalie looked for him again, but this time, he really had gone.

The short encounter with her composer made her lose concentration on the work she had come to the music room to do, so she took the sonatina score off the stand and crept back upstairs, just before Jennie entered her bedchamber with hot chocolate. She had a lot to think about as she savoured the sweetness.

The next afternoon, after she had finished reading to the marchioness, and before it was time to dress for dinner, there being no evening entertainments, Rosalie had planned to enjoy an hour or so in the music room, but Amanda waylaid her.

'I wish to talk to you, Rosalie, on a matter that Lord Coverdale has raised with me.' They sat down in the comfortable boudoir. 'You know, Rosalie, how much the he has helped us since we arrived here. I'm talking about the way, the very tactful way, he has helped Piers to reintegrate with society, and with me in certain financial matters that need not concern you. However, what he has asked of us now concerns you very closely.'

Rosalie fidgeted with her sleeve; she had some idea what Amanda was talking about but wasn't sure what was coming next. 'Is it about that music? You know, the piece I played at the soirée?'

'It certainly has to do with that. The marquis believes it was written by his brother, Lord Benedict St Maure.'

'Oh, does he? I think that may be so,' Rosalie replied cagily.

Amanda gave her a shrewd look. 'There's something about this that you're not telling, isn't there? Now is the time to tell me the truth, the whole truth, especially that bit, and nothing but the truth. Come on, Rosalie; I really need to know.'

'Wait a minute, Amanda.' Rosalie got up and disappeared into her bedchamber, emerging with several sheets of music in her hand. 'This is the score for the sonatina, and it is true that I found it in the music room, but it had been put there by the composer himself, especially for me to play. Only one page on the first day, and then others on the next two. I think he must have wanted to see how I got on with the first movement, before he trusted me with the whole thing.'

'How did you know it was a he?'

'I didn't, at least not at first, then a piece of paper fell out of the book I was reading to Godmama, and I could see at once it was the same writing I had seen on the score, definitely an educated hand.'

'That doesn't prove that the music was written by a man, does it?'

'No, but when you were away, I asked Wilkins if there were any other people living in the house, and she said she'd overheard talk of a sergeant and a Captain Benedict.'

'May I see the score, Rosalie?' Amanda held out her hand.

A little reluctantly, Rosalie passed it across, fearful of what her guardian would say when she saw the dedication, and she was right to be.

'Rosalie! This is disgraceful. You should have told me at once, at once, do you hear me? That man had no right to take such liberties; it's very wrong of him.'

Rosalie had never heard Amanda sound so angry; nevertheless, she was determined to stand up for her secret musician. 'How can it be wrong to dedicate a piece of music? Bach did it; Beethoven did too. I was pleased by it; why shouldn't I be? All he wanted was to hear his music performed.'

'And how could he do that?'

'I think he has rooms above the music room, Piers says.'

'Oh, so you've been talking to Piers about it, then?'

'His rooms are in that part of the house, and I asked if he'd ever seen anyone, and he said he might have seen the sergeant; only a back view, that is. What has all this got to do with what the marquis wants us to help him with?'

Amanda drew in a deep breath. 'The marquis's brother, Lord Benedict, has been very ill, so ill he believes his brother might die, but because he now has reason to believe, due to his interest in your music, that he is showing signs of recovery, he wants to know if you will agree to help, subject to my approval.'

'Of course I will. He certainly looks very ill.' Rosalie stopped and blushed to the roots of her hair. 'I mean—'

'Oh, Rosalie, Rosalie.' Amanda shook her head. 'You're still not telling me the whole truth, are you?'

In a small voice, Rosalie replied, 'No, Amanda.'

'So when did you see Lord Benedict?'

'I think he came to the concert, just for a short while. I looked up and saw a figure, dressed in black, at the far end of the room, but after I played my encore, I looked again, and he had gone. I thought it must have been him ... and ...'

'And what?'

'I ... I've spoken to him.'

'You've done what?'

'I spoke to him, in the music room, yesterday.'

'Go on,' Amanda said resignedly. 'Your powers of concealment know no bounds, do they?'

'It was accidental, at first; I mean, I didn't know he was there. It was very early in the morning, and I wanted to try out something on my harp. He was sort of hidden behind some chairs, and I'm sure I would never have seen him if he hadn't sneezed.'

'Then what happened?'

'He wanted to leave, but I asked if he would like me to play something for him, and he said yes. So I did. Then he left. That's all, Amanda; I promise, that's all that happened. Now you know everything.'

Rosalie thought it prudent not to tell Amanda that at the time, she was wearing her nightclothes.

'I'll just have to take your word for that, Rosalie, but what you have told me throws new light on the problem the marquis has already described to me. Tell me what Lord Benedict looks like.'

'He's very tall and very thin, with longish dark hair and a pale face. I only saw him for less than a minute, and anyway, he wasn't very close to me. I do not think he wants to be seen, or heard, for that matter.'

'Well, Rosalie, certainly not by you. I forbid you to practise early in the morning; you will just have to fit it in during the day. I hope you understand what I am saying; it is for your own good.'

For Amanda, Rosalie's description of Lord Benedict's condition fitted that of his brother, as *he* had heard it from the sergeant. But Rosalie had definitely confirmed that Lord Benedict had left his rooms for the first time in sixteen months. The marquis needed to know about this new development as soon as possible, but she was chagrined to realise that she would have to be the one to contact him. However, another, and, this time, very unwelcome occurrence, made the deed imperative.

Returning from a Bond Street shopping expedition, Amanda happened to glance at a salver on the hall table, and upon it was a letter addressed to 'Miss Rosalie.' She picked it up and immediately enquired of the hall porter from whence it had come.

'I am sorry, Madam, I have no information, but it was not delivered by any messenger while I was on duty. I cannot say how it got there, Madam.'

Neither of the two footmen could add anything further. Thrusting the note into the unusual pocket of her dress, she mounted the stairs, angry that perhaps Lord Benedict had written to Rosalie, a breach of decorum she definitely did not approve of, but on reaching her room and unfolding the note, matters took a much graver turn.

The words were few, but alarming: "*Return The Light of the Sun*". It is not yours. I know it is here.

A cold fear gripped her entire being. It was clear that the writer of the first two notes had followed the family to London. What a mercy, Amanda thought, that she had found the note before Rosalie, who would clearly be totally mystified by it, and curious too. Having got over her initial alarm concerning its contents, she examined the note more closely. The paper quality was good, but not the best; the writing was that of an educated hand; even and free from blots; and there had been no implication of any kind of threat, so far, at least. But the tension had been raised by the inclusion of Rosalie's name, a very worrying feature.

There was only one thing for it; she must inform his lordship straight away. In this, she was frustrated, as she remembered that he had gone to Newmarket with his young cousin, Hubert Dorsett, and taken Piers along, too. Something she had approved of at the time but now regretted.

Rosalie's next big engagement was the famous masked ball given on Midsummer's Eve by the Duchess of Alloa. Amanda was in a quandary. Should she forbid Rosalie to go for the sake of her safety? But the girl had been so looking forward to it, designing masks with the Carstairs girls, and having a special ball gown made, a gift from the marchioness, nd anyway, what possible excuse could she make for not going? Should she bundle them all back to Somerset on some urgent family business?

The ball was being held at Alloa House in St James's Square, not at one of the public venues that held masked balls of dubious propriety, and was strictly by invitation only. The rules were that the men had to wear historical costume, but the women wore ball gowns and all wore masks, which were removed at midnight. All this information she had elicited from the marchioness, together with the somewhat surprising news that Lord Coverdale was intending to make an appearance.

'Very unlike him,' his mothers had remarked. 'He usually avoids such occasions like the plague. I wonder why? Perhaps Miss Prideau will be present, although I sometimes question if she is the right one for him.' She looked up, saw Amanda, and realised this was not a proper subject to discuss in front of a non-relative.

Bearing in mind all that the marchioness had said, Amanda decided that no useful purpose could be served by disappointing Rosalie, but if it was at all possible, she should try to speak to the marquis before the ball, to apprise him of the latest development. Amanda was feeling depressed. Problems deemed to be coming at her, one after another, with no immediate solution, or was it, perhaps, the marchioness's mention of Miss Honoria Prideau that was making them harder to bear?

CHAPTER 14

Rosalie did not like disobeying Amanda's command not to use the
music room early in the morning, but she was equally sure that
the fragile contact she had made with Lord Benedict should be
followed up as soon as possible. He had made his first effort to re-join his
family and, perhaps later, society too, and his attempt must not be wasted.
She needed the help of someone else, and there was no doubt in her mind
that the sergeant was the only possible person she could appeal to.

She knew that Lord Benedict's apartments were situated above the
music room, in the West wing, and that he came and went through a door
at the far end of the room. That, she decided, was where her search should
begin. Fully dressed this time, and about half an hour before breakfast
was served, and while Amanda was still with her maid, Rosalie entered
the music room. This time, it was in full daylight, as the servants had
already pulled back the heavy curtains and secured them with tasselled,
gold tie-backs.

It was easy to find the door she was looking for, even although it was
concealed as part of the panelling and only had a tiny gilt knob set into the
gilded dado. She turned the handle, and the door swung open soundlessly;
for a moment, the darkness on the other side blinded her vision, but once
adjusted, she could see she was in a long passage, lit only by a few narrow,
horizontal windows set high up in the wall. Just beyond the door, she could
see a staircase leading up to the next floor. She hesitated, wondering what
to do next.

To mount the stairs and intrude into Lord Benedict's privacy seemed wrong and could cause a setback, but then, so could doing nothing. Her dilemma was solved by the sound of footsteps descending the uncarpeted stairs. Rosalie took a deep breath and advanced toward the sound, almost colliding with a man as they arrived at the foot of the stairs together.

The man instantly turned away from her, muttering, 'I'm sorry, excuse me, madam,' and made to squeeze past her.

Rosalie held her ground. 'Are you the sergeant?'

'What if I am?' was the gruff reply.

'I … I am Rosalie Abbot.' Rosalie had decided to lay her cards on the table at once. 'I need to talk to you about Lord … Be … about the man you look after.'

'Why? You're not out to make trouble, are you? I won't 'ave it.'

His voice was so severe that Rosalie's courage nearly failed her, but she thought of that broken spirit upstairs and carried on. 'No, Sergeant, far from it. I want to help, and I know Lord Benedict has come down to listen to me play, and if music is helping him, then perhaps we could come to some sort of arrangement. Don't you think?'

Throughout, the sergeant kept his back towards her, and she could see that Piers' description had been correct. Then he turned around, and even in the dim light of the passage, Rosalie could see that his left eye was covered with a large patch, but more than that, a livid, puckered scar crossed his forehead and disappeared into grizzling red hair. Below the patch, the scar continued across his cheek, and the upper half of his left ear was missing.

She couldn't prevent a gasp escaping from her throat. 'Oh, you poor man; that must have been terrible for you. I expect it still hurts.'

Surprisingly, the man's stern expression dissolved into a smile, albeit a lopsided one, as the terrible wound had clearly paralysed some of the muscles on the left side of his mouth.

Also a surprise were his next words: 'You'll do, lass … I mean, Miss Rosalie, you'll do.'

'I don't think I know what you mean.'

'I mean, Miss, that if you'd swooned, or turned and fled when you saw my face, you wouldn't be the right woman to 'elp the captain. Now, mebbe, I think you are.'

'I must go now,' said Rosalie. 'It's nearly breakfast time, but tell him I shall be practising at eleven 'o clock. Perhaps you could arrange for some coffee to be brought there and amoretto biscuits, or whatever he likes.'

Without waiting for a reply, Rosalie disappeared back into the music room and arrived in the breakfast room seconds before Amanda made her appearance.

'You haven't been practising, I hope,' she said, walking over to the silver dishes containing an assortment of hot breakfast fare.

'Of course not,' Rosalie replied. 'You told me not to, and I always do as I'm told; you know that, Amanda.'

'Humph,' said that lady, selecting scrambled eggs and grilled mushrooms.

Promptly at eleven o'clock, Rosalie entered the music room; she chose the pianoforte and began playing Mozart's *Rondo Alla Turca*; while doing so, she could smell the aroma of freshly brewed coffee, but because the curtains had been closed again, at the window farthest from her, she could not tell if anyone was drinking it.

But they were. As soon as she finished the piece, a voice from behind the stack of chairs said, 'Would you like some? There are two cups here.'

In a bold effort, Rosalie said, 'Could you bring me one?'

'No.'

'Why not?'

'I don't like the sunlight.'

'If I close the next set of curtains, will you bring it to me?'

'I might.' There was a pause. Rosalie played a few chords while she waited. 'Oh, all right then.'

Rosalie felt she was trying to get a wild animal, a squirrel or a robin, to eat out of her hand and realised she would need at least as much patience to overcome Lord Benedict's fears. She crossed the room and closed the curtains, leaving a tiny sliver of sunlight to escape, then stood beside them, awaiting his next move. The sound of a chair being pushed back and the rattle of a cup on saucer was what she had hoped for. Lord Benedict emerged from his hideaway, carrying the coffee in a shaking hand.

She went forward to take it from him. 'Thank you, Sir.' It took every effort on her part not to let her hand shake too. 'Is there anything you would like me to play? You could come out from behind those chairs, if you like; I don't mind being watched while I play.'

'Where did you learn to play? You must have had very good teachers as well as a great gift.'

'I had a good music master at school, and my guardian arranged for me to study with the organist of Wells Cathedral. Her husband had been a canon there.'

This was progress indeed, thought Rosalie, as she resumed her seat and drank the coffee, placing the empty cup on the closed lid of the piano. She waited while Lord Benedict brought one of the gilded chairs just to the edge of the darkened part of the room. Although in shadow, Rosalie could see that he was much more fully and tidily clad than had been the case at their last encounter. His hair was shorter and better arranged, and although still predominately in black, he now sported a well-tied cravat, and his coat-sleeves showed an inch of white linen cuff.

Well done, sergeant, Rosalie thought. 'Now then, Lord Benedict, have you decided what you would like to hear?' she asked, adding with a smile, 'That is, if I can play it.'

'Yes, but before you do, I do not like being called Lord; I was not born a lord, like my brother was, and I have never felt like one. I am a second son.'

'So what do you like to be called?'

'Captain, Captain Benedict, that is who I am … was. Do you like Bach?' he asked, changing the subject abruptly.

'Yes, but I find him challenging.'

'Good, challenge him for me.'

Rosalie selected a prelude, but Bach always required her greatest concentration, and when she had finished, the captain had gone. Which was just as well, as Amanda entered the room to remind Rosalie it was time for a final fitting for her ballgown.

There was so much Amanda wanted to tell the marquis, but it seemed to her that she was never going to be able to, until they met at the ball, and that was not a good venue for private conversation. The Duke and Duchess's house was one of the grandest in London, and the ballroom one of the largest; even so, it still seemed crowded when the Coverdale party arrived, fashionably, but not outrageously, late.

The scene was a magnificent one. At one end, a small orchestra provided the music, the sides were lined with the ubiquitous gilded ballroom chairs, and vast chandeliers threw sparkling light reflected in long pier-glasses between each window. Garlands of flowers were looped around the walls, and huge vases of exotic blossoms had been placed in every niche, giving off a heavy scent. On one side, the curtains were pulled back to display a garden strung with coloured lanterns, their light thrown into the air by the spray from a dozen fountains. On the floor, the men, dressed in exotic costume from bygone eras, contrasted with the ladies, most of whom (the younger ones, at least) had chosen paler colours, with much gold and crystal ornament, as well as magnificent jewelled necklaces, tiaras, and brooches, worn to show off their wealth (if not always their taste).

The marchioness looked splendid, attired in puce silk, trimmed with Brussels lace, and wearing the Coverdale diadem, on hair piled high and decorated with ostrich plumes. Somehow, with the power of her personality and her high rank, she managed to clear a pathway through the crowd to secure seats for herself and Amanda. Amanda was wearing a bronze half-dress over a central panel of amber silk, embroidered with yellow roses, her hair caught high by a pearl and yellow citrine circlet. It was not a new gown, but the marchioness's modiste had refashioned it in a more modern style, and Amanda was very pleased with the result.

The men were dressed in a large variety of colourful costumes. She could recognise several Charles the Seconds and Henry the Eighths, as well as Francis Drakes, and at least one Julius Caesar, who seemed to be having trouble with his toga. Dandies among the guests, those who sported fancy waistcoats, hight collars, and nipped-in waists, generally loved the occasion; the Corinthians, who favoured superb tailoring and plainer outfits, were always more uncomfortable, but no one refused the Duchess's invitation. Everyone, with one exception, wore masks. The only person in plain evening dress was the Duke of Alloa himself. Nevertheless, he was resplendent in black, with the green ribbon of the Order of the Thistle across his chest; he was, after all, a Scottish duke, and several stars were sewn onto his coat. Rosalie was thrilled and excited by the grandeur of it all, her dress of blue silk, scattered with paste diamonds, which glinted through her fine muslin overdress, echoed the sparkle in her eyes, teasingly seen through the mask.

This ball differed from others she had been to in several ways. There was no formal supper interval, but refreshments of all kinds were available throughout the evening from long tables set up in a large conservatory at the far end of the ballroom, and guests could eat and drink whenever they wanted to. Another aspect was the more free-and-easy attitude to partners; there was less need for formal introductions, and a chaperone could give consent without one. There were several waltzes, instead of just the customary two, and round dances, where men made a circle round the outside, and women in the middle; they danced briefly with whoever was opposite them when the music stopped, then reformed a few minutes later. However, any hint of louche behaviour or appearance of drunkenness was reported to the hosts, by footmen placed around the room, specifically for the purpose, and an invitation would not be forthcoming the next year: a social disgrace that no one wanted to incur.

It wasn't long before Rosalie was claimed by a young man dressed as harlequin, and Piers, wearing the costume of a cavalier, was already dancing with Sophia Carstairs. Amanda was looking round the room to see if the marquis had arrived, and it was not long before his unmistakeable figure, clad as the rakish Captain Morgan, was heading towards her and his mother. After a few words of greeting to his mama, he invited Amanda to take the floor with him. The dance was a waltz, and it was easy for him to whisk her halfway round the floor to where the large French windows had been thrown open, allowing cool air to enter the room and give access to the delightful gardens.

Taking her firmly by the arm, he said: 'You must tell me what has been happening since I've been away, Mrs Fletcher.'

Amanda didn't know where to begin, but she thought he would rather hear about his brother first. 'I believe that Lord Benedict has visited the music room and spoken to Rosalie. In fact, I know it is so, because she told me.'

'That is wonderful news.' The marquissmiled below his mask and then added, 'I hope you think so too, Mrs Fletcher.' Several other couples passed them by, before he said, 'Will you allow her to meet him again?'

'I am fairly sure that she has, although their first meeting occurred very early in the morning, and I forbade her to do that again.' She saw the look of disappointment on the marquis's face and added, 'I mean, when there is no one around.'

'I see, so you have no objections to Rosalie talking to—?'

'Not objections, but reservations. I think he is, or has been, a very sick man, and I must always have Rosalie's best interests at heart.'

The marquis pointed to a seat just vacated by another couple and asked, 'Shall we sit? Or is it too cold, after the heat of the ballroom?'

'No, it's a relief.' They sat, facing towards each other at either end of the ornate stone bench, thoughtfully provided with cushions.

'What more can you tell me?' he asked.

'Well, yesterday, I knew Rosalie was practising, and it was time for her ball gown fitting, so I went to get her, and although she was alone, there was a coffee cup on the piano and another on a chair about two-thirds of the way along the room. I do not think she realised I had seen it, and neither of us said anything, but I believe the only conclusion to draw is that they had coffee together, or at least in the same room.'

'That is progress, indeed. I will come to Berkeley Square tomorrow and speak to the sergeant. If my dear brother is beginning to recover, but it is still early days, I believe any interference on my ... our part could undo the good, Rosalie is achieving. Are you agreeable to letting things take their course for the moment?'

Amanda thought for a while. 'Rosalie is a sensible girl, and I really don't think she is in any danger from Lord Benedict, so yes, I agree, but I will keep a close and, as far as possible, an invisible eye on any developments.'

The marquis made a little gesture towards her, saying, 'I can't thank you enough, Mrs Fletcher. Benedict is very special to me.'

CHAPTER 15

'There is another matter, sir, also concerning Rosalie, that I wish to make you aware of, Marquis.'

'Please do, Mrs Fletcher. You know I am always at your service, if I can be of any help.'

'I intercepted a letter addressed to her; it was lying on the hall table. I thought it might be from a young admirer. She has many, you know—'

'I'm not surprised,' interrupted his lordship.

'But all it said was "Give *back The Light of the Sun*. It does not belong to you."'

'Good God woman! Why didn't you tell me this at once? You know what this means?'

Amanda nodded. 'I'm afraid I do. We have been followed from Somerset. But I could hardly tell you at once, My Lord; you were not at home, and I thought you would like to hear news of your brother first.'

'Very thoughtful, but now that I do know, I will make sure Rosalie is protected, whenever she is outside the house, oh, discreetly, of course. I know the right people for the job, I assure you.'

'I'm sure you do, and I am very grateful. I accept your offer. But there is something strange about all this.'

'What do you mean?' the Marquis queried.

'I mean there has never been any kind of threat implied in any of the notes. It is as if whoever is sending them believes that Rosalie is in possession of the diamond and knows all about it, which, of course, she does not. And give it back to whom?'

'So you think that whoever is sending these notes has, or believes he has, a genuine claim on the jewel?'

'I suppose that's possible,' Amanda said. 'After all, I know nothing of its antecedents. I didn't even know of its existence until after my husband died, and there was no paperwork or history attached to it.'

'I'm sure it originated in India, and as you have said, Sir Percy spent some time there.' The Marquis stood up. 'I think we had better return to the ballroom. I do not want to set tongues wagging, which we might if we stay here any longer.' He smiled. 'A guardian must always be above suspicion.'

'No, of course.' *And especially Miss Prideau's*, thought Amanda, who had caught a glimpse of her in the ballroom. 'I'm very grateful for the time you have given to listening to my concerns,' she said formally.

The marquis looked down at her a little quizzically, as he offered her his arm and escorted her back to Lady Coverdale, who was chatting to Piers, who had not taken part in the round dance that was in progress. He stood up as Amanda approached.

'Only fifteen minutes till we can take off these tiresome masks,' he said, adding, 'and then the card room will be open.'

It was a strict rule at the Alloa ball that cards or other games would not be available until after midnight. Amanda looked at him closely and saw signs of strain about his mouth; she wondered if his hip was giving him trouble after the long journey back from Somerset. If it was, there was nothing she could do or say. She gave her attention to the dancing.

Rosalie was clearly having the time of her life, waltzing or polkaing, with a different partner whenever the music changed. When it stopped, she was between two men, and although she turned towards a man dressed, Amanda thought, as Merlin, it was the other man, wearing a richly embroidered, high-collared coat and a turban, who caught her arm and whirled her away into the crowd. She saw them once more before the music changed again, and the circles reformed, the last time before midnight.

The Duke and Duchess made their way to the platform, and there was a roll of drums from the Highland regiment, which had entertained the guests with pipes and drum music when the orchestra took a rest, the Duke was handed the largest drum, which he banged loudly on the stroke of midnight, as the guests, with much relief, laughter, and, in a few cases, surprise, all removed their masks.

Rosalie came back to Amanda laughing and swinging her mask by one finger. 'That was such fun. I danced with so many different partners, but there wasn't much time to talk, but one of them did say something rather odd.'

Amanda frowned. 'Nothing improper, I hope.'

'No, just odd.'

'Well, what was it?'

'Just before the music changed, he said, almost in my ear, "The Light of the Sun is not yours." What could he have meant?'

Amanda could feel her heart beating like a Highlander drum, but she made a superhuman effort to keep her voice steady, as she said, 'I cannot imagine what he meant. Can you see him in the room now?'

Rosalie's gaze swept the room, but there was no sign of the man in the turban. 'He's not here. Perhaps he's in the supper area, or gone to the card room. A lot of the men have, I think, spoilsports.'

Amanda looked for the marquis, but he was nowhere to be seen, either. There was nothing she could do, except allay any alarm Rosalie might be feeling.

'I shouldn't worry about what the man said. He probably mistook you for someone else; everyone was still masked, remember.'

'Of course, that must be it. I hadn't thought of that.'

Rosalie seemed quite unconcerned, which could not be said of her guardian, for whom the whole evening was turning into somewhat of a nightmare. She was unsure that she had made the right decision concerning Rosalie and Lord Benedict, and now this other worry loomed ever larger. Her talk with the marquis, in the undoubtedly romantic surroundings of the garden, made her desire to be with him more, an impossible dream, of course, emphasised by watching him dance with Miss Prideau, who gave her a vicious glance as they waltzed past.

She had accepted an invitation to take part in one of the country dances by Colonel Fortesque, as they had been introduced in Hyde Park, and his son had become one of Piers' friends, although she was a little surprised when his conversation turned to curiosity about how she had become guardian to the children. Now, all she wanted to do was to go back to Berkeley Square. Fortunately, the marchioness returned from speaking to an acquaintance, with the same idea in mind, and all that remained to do was to find Rosalie and Piers. A footman was despatched to the card room but returned with the information that Sir Piers intended to spend the night with a friend, and Rosalie joined them when the dance was ended, disappointed that they were leaving, but in no way set to argue in front of her godmother.

While they were waiting in the vast hallway for the Coverdale carriage to arrive, Justin joined them to wish his mother good night. Amanda seized the opportunity for a few words with him.

'Ah, Marquis,' she said, pointing to the numerous paintings that adorned the walls, 'perhaps you can tell me which of these portraits is that of the famous Duchess of Alloa, by Lely?'

He took her by the arm and said softly, 'I haven't the faintest idea. What do you want to tell me?'

Delighted, but not surprised, by the speed of his uptake, she answered, 'There has been a development.'

'We had better look at the pictures.' He pointed to one of a lady in a voluminous blue dress. 'What has happened?'

'Rosalie was approached by a man on the dance floor, apparently demanding the return of the diamond. Of course, she knows nothing about it or the notes I received.'

'What did you say to her?'

'I passed it off as a mistake; after all, everyone was still masked at the time. I felt that the more I seemed to be interested, the more curious she would become.'

They moved on to another portrait.

'As far as I can see, Mrs Fletcher, we can do nothing, until whoever is doing this reveals his hand, except to ensure that Rosalie is protected. I have put a very good man to watch the house and follow her whenever she goes out, discreetly, of course, and to report to me if anything suspicious occurs.'

'Amanda, the carriage has arrived,' the marchioness called. 'Your art lesson will have to be postponed.'

Amanda bobbed a curtsey and left the marquis's side.

CHAPTER 16

Rosalie, whose energy was boundless, came down for breakfast at nine o'clock the next morning and was surprised to find that Amanda did not join her, as was normal. However, it gave her an opportunity to hurry through her meal and go in search of the sergeant. Slipping quietly through the music room, she entered the narrow passage by the hidden door, and it was not long before she heard the heavy tread of the sergeant descending the stairs.

She smiled as soon as she saw him. 'I can't stay long, but I've thought of a plan. I do not want the captain to wonder if, or when, I will be practising, so if I leave a message …' She looked round and then pointed to a ledge on the landing. '… there, it will say what time I shall be in the music room. If there is no message, it means I will not have time to play that day, but I will today, eleven o'clock. Put the table and chair a little closer to the pianoforte.'

Barely waiting for him to agree, Rosalie darted back into the music room and met a bleary-eyed Amanda on her way to breakfast. 'You look awful,' she said with more truth than tact.

'I probably do. I didn't sleep well, even though I was tired after the ball.'

'Some coffee will no doubt buck you up. I'm going to the library to see if I can find another book to read to Godmama. We have nearly finished *Sense and Sensibility*.'

'Good luck with that, Rosalie. I doubt if the library contains any novels, let alone modern ones.'

Just before eleven, she entered the music room and adjusted the curtaining according to her plan of gradually letting more and more light into the room. The sergeant had followed her instructions and placed not one, but two, chairs and the table with a silver coffee pot and plate of biscuits about two yards closer to the piano, at which she was seated when she heard the captain arrive. She continued playing for a few minutes and then got up and approached the table.

Punctiliously, the captain rose to greet her. 'Will you pour, or shall I?'

She saw him smile for the first time. It wasn't great as smiles go, but it was progress, nevertheless.

'I think it had better be you, Miss Rosalie; my hand might shake too much.'

Rosalie poured both cups. 'If you shake with only a pot of coffee in your hand, I believe you need to exercise more. The sergeant tells me you haven't left your apartments for a long time.'

The captain didn't reply to that remark, instead asking, 'What do you think of the sergeant?'

'I think he is very fond of you and really wants you to overcome whatever it is that is destroying your life.'

'I did not mean that. I meant, were you not afraid of his terrible disfigurement?'

'No, I wasn't; indeed, I am not. Of course, I was momentarily shocked but certainly not afraid. What is there to be afraid of?'

'Housemaids have fainted at the sight of him, so now he never goes downstairs during the day, but takes his exercise at night.'

'That makes you both prisoners of war in your own country. That is all wrong and very sad.' Rosalie put down her cup. 'Now what would you like me to play?'

'Anything you play is a pleasure for me, even scales and arpeggios.'

As he said it, he was surprised to realise it was true. Rosalie the person was becoming as important to him, if not more so, than Rosalie the musician.

'I think I can find something a little more interesting.' She laughed and began to play a short piece, but as before, when she had finished, he was gone.

The next few days followed a similar pattern, with more conversation and rather less music. On the days she was unable to come to the music room, Rosalie always left a note for the sergeant. After nearly a week, she decided it was time things moved on; she left all but one of the curtains full drawn back, and instead of sitting at the piano, seated herself on one of the chairs, ready for Captain Benedict to arrive. When she saw him, she started to pour the coffee, hoping that he would be too polite to just turn and run. And she was right.

Without remarking on the changed arrangements, he came and sat down. As she pushed the cup towards him, Rosalie wondered if the time was ripe to ask some more personal questions.

Deciding to take an oblique approach, she began, 'How did the sergeant get his wound?'

'Waterloo.'

Wrong question, thought Rosalie; reverting to a safer subject, she asked, 'What would you like me to play, harp or piano?'

'A French cuirassier's sabre. He was my gunnery sergeant, C Battery, Royal Horse Artillery.'

Rosalie had heard from Amanda what little his brother knew about his brother's Waterloo experience, and she knew there was a gap in Lord Benedict's account of what exactly had occurred, and that the missing part may well be the cause of his current state of mind. How to proceed, now that he had mentioned the battle, was a tricky one for Rosalie.

'You and the sergeant have a lot to be grateful to each other for,' she said, hoping it was not the wrong thing again.'

'Why do you say that?'

'Lord Coverdale told my guardian that you saved his life, and now he looks after you, doesn't he?'

'Tell me about your guardian.'

At last, Rosalie was on safe ground. 'She is called Mrs Fletcher and is a widow. When our father died, her husband became our guardian, then he died.'

'You said *our* guardian, who else?'

'My brother, Sir Piers. Hasn't the sergeant told you anything about us?'

'I haven't talked about … things … for some time. Are you fond of your brother, good friends?'

95

'Yes; except for music, we both like the same things. Not that we don't sometimes have our little differences, of course.'

'I like my brother too.'

'Then why don't you let him come and see you?' Rosalie said impulsively.'

'I'd like to hear the harp, today, please.'

Rosalie returned to her instrument, feeling that she had won a battle but was still a long way from winning the war.

For the first time, Captain Benedict stayed until she had finished playing; then he stood up and said, 'Thank you, that was lovely.'

He bowed and left as usual by the concealed door. Rosalie remained seated by her harp, wondering what her next move should be. It was rather like a game of chess with a real person, she thought, instead of wooden pieces, but the wrong move could result in the king leaving the board forever. The only person who might be able to help was the sergeant, but he was not easy to find. Perhaps she might be lucky, if she went to the little landing that led to the captain's apartments, and she was. He was just coming down, carrying a large bundle of some sort of grey material.

'Oh, Sergeant, I'm so pleased to see you. I need your advice.'

For a moment, he stared at her with his remaining eye in disbelief, then realising that she actually meant it, he asked, 'What can I do for you, Miss?'

'First, I want to know if you think Captain Benedict is feeling better, and secondly, do you know of anything that might be of more use? I mean—'

'I knows what you mean, Miss. Do you see this?' He indicated the armful of cloth.

'Yes, what is it?'

'It's from 'is windows, Miss; 'e got me to take 'em down this very morning, while you was playing.'

Rosalie fingered the material; it was thin and gauzy. 'What was it for?'

'To keep the sun out, Miss. 'E couldn't stand the sunlight, until now, an' that's all your doing, Miss. I knows it is. You want my advice? Let the captain decide. 'E'll let you know in his own time.'

Rosalie had to be satisfied with that, as the sergeant stumped off down the narrow stairs.

Amanda had received a letter from Mr Brewster, informing her that he had found a metal deed box belonging to her late husband, at the back of a cupboard in Mr Small body's office. It was locked, and although he had searched the office, no key could be found. He was sending her the box by carrier, and it should arrive within the next few days.

The next day, Clarkson announced its arrival with the solemnity fit for a gift from the Prince Regent and enquired as to where Mrs Fletcher would like it placed.

'Take it up to my room, please Clarkson. I will attend to it later.'

The butler summoned a footman to perform the task. It was some time before Amanda could be released from attending the marchioness's at-home morning, but by twelve o'clock, the last caller had gone, and she was able to slip away upstairs.

The box had been placed on a stool in the centre of the room. Nothing much could be ascertained from the outside, it being wrapped in hessian and thoroughly bound with thin cord, each knot reinforced with red sealing wax. For a moment, Amanda considered trying to untie them all, but impatience overcame her, and getting out her largest sewing scissors, she quickly cut the cord and ripped off the hessian to reveal a black metal box, which measured about eighteen inches by one foot, and had clearly seen better days. On the top, painted in white, was 'Rev. A D Fletcher, Hon. East India Company,' and several indecipherable labels. Despite the dents and scratches, it was indubitably locked. However, as she sat looking at the battered black box, which she knew for certain she had never seen before, impatience was her overriding emotion, and she sent for the housekeeper to arrange for the services of a locksmith.

The sight of her husband's name brought memories flooding back. He had been a kind, gentle man, but their marriage had never been anything but one of convenience. Left alone at twenty by the death of her father, with no home and no relations, her prospects were bleak. Amanda had been earning some money from her botanical work since she was sixteen, but it would never be enough to keep a roof over her head. Dr Pargeter, who was a friend of both her father and Canon Agnew Fletcher, suggested that she might make a suitable wife for a churchman. The canon, recently preferred to a residency at Wells Cathedral, needed a wife to help him undertake the social duties required of him, and so for Amanda, it was a choice of marriage to a man more than twenty years her senior, or look for a job as a governess. She never regretted her choice.

Their marriage did not last long; Agnew died when she was twenty-six, but his greatest legacy to her was the guardianship of the children. It had given her a lovely house to live in and a real purpose in her life, even although the task, especially now, had not been easy.

She sat looking at the battered black box, which she knew for a fact, she had never seen before. With a certain nervous anticipation, she awaited the arrival of the locksmith. The house-keeper announced his arrival, had in no time the box was open and he promised to make new keys.

Amanda's feeling of nervous anticipation soon evaporated, as the box contained little of interest. Some old educational certificates, a record of Agnew's ordination by the Bishop of Rochester, receipts for purchases in India. Amanda looked through them all until she came to the last item, a small parcel, tied with green silk ribbon, and bearing the words, "To whom it may concern", in Agnew Fletcher's handwriting.

She slid the ribbon off, and a small black leather book slipped from her fingers and fell onto the floor. She picked it up and began to read. It was her husband's diary for the two or so years he was in India. When she finished, she was in a state of utter shock. Folded inside was a piece of paper that conjured up her worst fears.

CHAPTER 17

J ustin couldn't settle to anything and found his mind drifting off
when he was supposed to be composing a speech he was to make in
the House of Lords, and it was always drifting in one direction, that
of Amanda Fletcher. He couldn't think of any valid excuse to go and see
her, although, of course, he didn't need an excuse to visit his mother, but
then Mrs Fletcher might not be in, and the visit would be wasted, or at
least the purpose of it would be.

However, his dilemma was resolved when a note, delivered by one of
his mother's footmen, came from Mrs Fletcher herself. It was brief, but the
marquis thought he discerned an underlying urgency. *"Dear Marquis"*, it
read, *"I am in need of your advice on a private matter concerning my role as
guardian. A carriage drive would not be a suitable meeting place"*.

The note was signed and sealed with the same small crest as before.
There was no overt sense of urgency in the message, but the felt that it
was there, all the same. The delivery was too late for him to comply that
day, but the following morning, he presented himself at Berkeley Square.
It was unfortunate that it was an *at-home* morning, and even more so to
find that Mrs Dearing, accompanied by Honoria Prideau, was prattling
away in the grand salon. He was obliged to join them and partake of tea,
cake, and small talk.

Honoria was all smiles and affability while conversing on the
probability of a good harvest on her father's estate, which, on reflection
later, the marquis thought was a strange subject for his mother's salon, but
then again, perhaps she was subtly fostering the advantages a match with

her would be. Eventually, he was able to make his excuses before another group arrived, and escape to the library, where he was sure Mrs Fletcher was waiting for him. As a footman opened the door, his assumption proved correct.

Amanda came forward immediately and barely bobbed a curtsey before saying, 'Oh, Lord Coverdale, I am so very glad to see you.'

'And I you, Mrs Fletcher, but you seem to be troubled.'

'I am indeed, Marquis. I have received information from the past, and I do not know what to do. I don't suppose you will, either, but at least I will be able to discuss possible courses of action.'

Amanda's distress was palpable, and Juatin decided that a calming influence was required.

'Perhaps the matter would be better explored if we were seated.'

Amanda sat, but before he did so, the marquis went over to the tray of decanters and poured her a small glass of port. 'Perhaps this will help,' he said, handing her the glass and sitting in his usual chair. 'Now, please, Mrs Fletcher, tell me about this new information.'

Amanda began by telling him about the box she received from Taunton, saying, 'It cannot have been opened since Agnew was in India; most of its contents were receipts and accounts and suchlike, but then there was this.'

She delved into her concealed pocket and drew out the diary. Throughout her account, Amanda's voice grew more and more agitated as she thrust the book towards him.

'Look, Sir; look what it says. It is too awful.'

The marquis was amazed at the woman's agitated state; he had thought little could unsettle her, but she was rapidly turning into a jelly before his eyes. He opened the book, perceived that it was a diary, and began to read.

'No, no, My Lord, further on, December 3rd.'

He turned several pages and began to read again.

Am beginning to worry about my friend. He seems to be becoming infatuated with an Indian lady. She is very young and very lovely in an oriental style. She is, in some sort, a princess, since her father is the son of the local maharajah. Percy has lot of dealings with him. I do not know if I should say anything; I find this often makes matters worse. Mrs Crawford has asked me to take tea with her tomorrow.

December 18. I was right to be concerned. Percy has come to me and told me about his feelings. I feel that I cannot counsel him, as he is older and more experienced in matters of this kind than I am, but I shall pray for guidance. The chapel was quite full today, and I think my sermon on righteousness was well received.

December 23. It will soon be Christmas, and I am very busy. The natives don't understand it, of course, but they like festive occasions. I have joined forces with my Roman Catholic counterpart for a carol service in the barrack square. I believe I saw Percy with the Indian lady there too, but not sure.

January 6, Epiphany. What I feared has occurred. Percy came to me today to say he wanted to marry the Indian lady. I counselled most venously against it, but he is adamant. I could refuse to perform the ceremony, but what would that do? He would probably go through some Hindu ritual instead. I argued that her father would object, but alas it seems he does not. It appears that he thinks an alliance with an English sahib will give him credit. I told Percy I would think about it and give him my answer in a few days' time. Supper with Colonel Brown; he really likes his curry hot.

Justin looked up, and smiled.

'You find something to amuse you, Marquis?' Amanda said, a touch crossly.

'No. I'm sorry, Mrs Fletcher. It's the juxtapositions of sentiment that diaries sometimes display.' He continued reading. 'The next bit is all about his daily tasks.' He turned over a few more pages, 'Ah. January 23.'

I have been persuaded against my better judgement to perform the marriage ceremony requested by Percy Abbot. It took place in the chapel at 6 o'clock this evening. Percy insisted that I use the full Church of England liturgy. There were only two witnesses, and no one else in the chapel. The bride spoke little English, but Percy, who is fluent in the native tongue, translated my words, and she replied in English. As we left, a native dignitary of some sort, dressed in colourful robes and accompanied by a liveried boy servant, came up to the couple and knelt down in front of them. The boy came forward bearing a cushion, upon which was a glistening yellow gemstone. The dignitary took it off the cushion and gave it to Percy. He then got up and, making the Indian sign of respect with his two hands together, as if in prayer, bowed and departed with the boy. Percy looked as if he didn't quite know what to do with it. The light was failing, but even as I approached, the jewel seemed to gather the last rays of the sun to itself.

The bride and groom departed in an ornate carriage drawn up outside the barracks, and I went home, but I am much troubled by the whole affair. Couldn't concentrate on my sermon for next Sunday.

The marquis turned some more pages, but there was only one more entry that he could see that referred to Percy

March 6. I have been having bouts of ill health. I do not think this climate suits my constitution, but today Percy and his wife came to sup with me. She has learnt a lot more English, so we were able to converse. Despite my misgivings, they seem very happy together, but it may not last.

Amanda looked anxiously at the Marquis as he closed the book.

'What should I do?' she asked. 'What do you think it all means? Was Sir Percy a bigamist? Are Piers and Rosalie illegitimate? What if they had a son? Who does the diamond belong to?' Her questions flooded out.

'Calm yourself, please, Mrs Fletcher. I understand how you must be feeling, but there is a lot here that needs closer examination. We cannot take everything that your husband wrote at face value, although he makes it clear exactly what occurred at the time.' He noticed the piece of paper still lying on the table. 'What is that?'

'It is a record of the marriage. Date, place participants.'

'Is it witnessed?'

'Yes and no; the names are written, but there are only crosses beside them, and it is dated.'

He took the paper from her. 'This may help any enquiries that have to be made.'

'What do you mean? How can you make enquiries?' Amanda clasped her hands together till the knuckles showed white.

'Mrs Fletcher,' Justin said gently. 'I suggest you take a deep breath and a long drink of my excellent port wine. My cellar is the envy of all my friends, and then we can discuss this admittedly distressful situation, logically.'

'I'm sorry. I'm afraid I am a bit overwrought, with no one to talk to. I am keen to hear what you have to say.' She took a sip of her drink.

'In the first place, I believe we should not speculate upon the rights and wrongs of the marriage of Sir Percy—Mr, as he was then—to this Indian princess, but consider the situation as regards the yellow diamond. My reason being that you've had several messages disputing its ownership, and whoever is sending these messages may well be right, or at least, believes he is right. From your late husband's description of the scene where Percy received it, it seems to me to have been handed over as some sort of dowry. Would you not agree, Mrs Fletcher?'

Amanda nodded. 'Yes, that could be so, and maybe that is why Rosalie's father meant it *for her* dowry.' She took another sip of the wine, and its rich warmth seemed to steady her nerves. 'When my husband Agnew was dying—he had contracted a congestion of the lungs following another bout of malaria, and the doctor said he could do no more …'

'I'm sorry.'

'No, no, please; he was delirious much of the time, talking about his childhood and a brother who died, but sometimes, he would ramble on about the light, the light of the sun. I thought he wanted the curtains drawn across, but I see now that he could be referring to the diamond, and just before he died, he sat up. I was holding him, and he said, "The sun, the sun, the light belongs to the sun" Oh, good God.' She closed her eyes in anguish.

The marquis leant forward and touched her on the arm. 'What is it, my dear Mrs Fletcher?'

'Don't you see, My Lord, he didn't mean the sun with a "U"; he meant the son, the son with an "O." Oh, poor Piers. What if it doesn't really belong to him after all, or the title, or Abbots Court? It's a disaster!' She cried.

Justin wished he was able to take Amanda into his arms to comfort her, but of course he could not; instead, he said calmly, 'I don't think we should cross bridges before we come to them, Mrs Fletcher.' Although he admitted to himself that what she had just said was a possibility. 'All that sort of thing should, if it comes to it, be put in the hands of lawyers, and I have very good ones, which I can place at your disposal, or the Abbots'.'

Amanda straightened up and replied, 'You are right, Marquis; I'm afraid I've let my emotions run away with me. What I need is your good advice and a sensible course of action.'

To himself, Justin said, *That's my girl*. Aloud, he told Amanda, 'Perhaps there are papers at Abbots Court that might clarify the position. Have you seen anything of the sort?'

'No, but that doesn't mean that there aren't any. However, I have no access to them. Piers owns Abbots Court outright; all archive material belongs to him.'

'Then, Mrs Fletcher, perhaps it is time to apprise him of the recent events.' Justin saw a look of dismay on Amanda's face. 'No, I don't mean about his father's so-called marriage, but about the existence of the diamond. Although he is still young, he is of age and the head of the family. His sister's welfare is as much his responsibility as it is yours, don't you think?'

'I hadn't thought of it like that, but I believe you are right. I will find a way to tell him what has been happening, and that might give me the opportunity to raise the matter of any papers.'

'I feel, Mrs Fletcher, there is nothing more that can usefully be done at the moment, but I can make some discreet enquiries in certain quarters.' He smiled. 'It will quite be like old times for me, that is, if you agree.'

'Of course I agree, but there is the other matter, that of Rosalie and Lord Benedict.'

'Is there good news on that front?' The marquis tried not to sound too eager.

'Yes, there is,' she replied. 'Unbeknownst to Rosalie, I've been in correspondence with the sergeant, and he writes that Lord Benedict has at last had the drapes that covered his windows removed, and that he and Rosalie have coffee together most mornings. I feel it best not to quiz her on the matter.'

'That is excellent news; perhaps there is real hope for his recovery, after all. I really miss him, you know.'

'I'm sure you do. Now, I must thank you most sincerely for being so patient with my concerns and those of the family. I can't say that I am not still worried, but I feel that perhaps there is a way forward, and that is all due to you.'

Contrary to protocol, Amanda held out her hand, looked up into the marquis's warm amber eyes, and smiled.

Justin took her hand in both of his. 'You are a wonderful woman, Mrs Fletcher.'

Amanda dropped her gaze, inwardly pleased by the unexpected praise, but she could think of nothing to say in reply.

Then the marquis added, 'One bit of advice before you go.' He picked up the diary, folded the paper with the marriage document, and placed it inside the book. 'Make sure this is kept under lock and key.' He handed it to her. 'I will be in touch if I have anything to report, Mrs Fletcher. I promise.'

Amanda, returning to formality, bobbed a curtsey before leaving the room, but the touch of his warm hands on hers still lingered.

CHAPTER 18

Rosalie's engagements over the next few days had prevented her from practising, but she always made sure that Lord Benedict had been made aware of the fact, via the sergeant. When she was finally free to play again, she was surprised to hear piano music issuing from the music room as she approached, and both surprised and pleased to find the captain seated at the instrument. He rose the moment he realised she had entered.

Giving a rueful smile, he said, 'I'm afraid I do not aspire to your virtuosity, Miss Rosalie. I am better at hearing music in my head than delivering it to the piano.'

'In that case, why don't I play the harp and you improvise an accompaniment? I think that would be good for both of us. It is always refreshing to try something new, don't you agree, Captain?'

Lord Benedict smiled. 'Yes, I do, but I think we had better partake of the coffee first, or it will be past all ability to refresh anything.'

The sergeant had set the table in front of the central French window, and Rosalie asked him if he could open it, if the weather was suitable, for her next practice session. Meanwhile, they quickly drank their coffee, and the two of them became so engrossed—enchanted, even—with their joint musical efforts that time was forgotten. A discreet tap on the door reminded her that an afternoon carriage drive was imminent, and she left the music room, but her spirits were soaring.

Rosalie was sure that it would not be long before Lord Benedict released himself from his self-imposed exile. But she knew that was not the whole story, by any means. He needed to overcome some deep-seated reason that had caused it in the first place, and about that, she knew nothing.

Amanda was walking up and down in her boudoir, which was quite a sizeable room, but only allowed a few strides each way for her long legs. Movement always helped her to think, and her thoughts were concerned with the best way to tell Piers what had been happening and just how much of it he ought to know.

After an initially poor start to his visit to London, Piers had become quite a man-about-town. His good looks and title had made him a favourite with the debutantes, and his charming manners with their chaperones. He was accepted as a good fellow to be with by his peers, and he had not fallen into either the dandy set or aped the Corinthians. Amanda was also well-pleased, both with the distinct improvement in his health and the fact that he appeared to be living within his (admittedly generous) allowance. Taken all round, he was becoming a young man to be trusted, and the marquis was right; it was time she did so. Finding him was another matter. She sent a note to Grooby, asking that Sir Piers wait upon her, at his earliest convenience.

Before dinner the next evening, he bounced into Amanda's boudoir. 'What's all this about, Amanda, sending me formal little notes to come and see you? You know you can talk to me any time.'

'Yes, well, but first I have to catch you,' she said, smiling, 'but never mind that. I have a lot of things we need to discuss.'

'I've not overspent, have I?'

'No, it's nothing like that. It's something perhaps I should have told you some time ago. So please just listen to what I have to say.'

'Yes, Amanda, fire away.'

'As you are aware, when your father died, my husband and Mr Smallbody became your trustees, then when Agnew died, I became your trustee.'

'Yes, yes, I know all that, Amanda; we went to Taunton …'

'Don't interrupt, Piers. What you don't know, and neither did I till I became a trustee, was that the trust included a very large, very valuable diamond.'

'Are you making a jest, Amanda?'

'No, I am not, and stop interrupting.'

'Sorry, go on.'

'I know little of its history, only that I presume it was brought back from India by your father.'

'Where is it now? Have you got it?'

'I'm coming to that. A month or so before Christmas last year, Mr Smallbody, fearing that his health was failing, which as you know was true, gave the diamond into my keeping, and I put it in the safe, in a plain box, at the Court.'

Piers looked disappointed. 'So you can't show it to me, then?'

'No, I can't, but neither is it at Abbots Court, and before you interrupt again, neither is it here.'

'Then where is it?'

'Lord Coverdale is looking after it.'

'Coverdale?' Piers exploded. 'What the … What in heaven's name has it got to do with him? He has nothing to do with our family.'

'You've changed your tune, Piers,' Amanda said with some surprise. 'In Taunton, you were all for making him a trustee. He has been more than kind in acting in our interests, but he suggested that it was time I told you about it, so that, as head of the family, you should take some responsibility, especially as the existence of the diamond might now be compromising Rosalie's safety.'

'Rosalie's safety? Of course I should know. I'm her brother. We should take her back to Somerset at once, Amanda.'

Amanda sighed. 'It's not as simple as that, Piers.' She went on to tell Piers about the notes and what had occurred at the masked ball. 'So you see, wherever she is, it seems that this person will find her.'

'But how can we protect her? What can we do?'

'His lordship has put a man to watch the house, and Rosalie has been told always to have a footman, as well as her maid, with her whenever she goes out, and we don't think she's in danger while she is in this house.'

'The marquis again!' exclaimed Piers, angrily. 'You told him all this before you told me? I think that's disgraceful, Amanda.'

'Do you, indeed?' she replied sharply. 'Well, just consider this, young man. I have your best interests to consider, too. When the first note came, you were just learning to walk again, let alone being able *ride ventre à terre* to the rescue of your sister. What good would telling you have done? And before you say another word against his lordship, just remember how he's helped you too, and I already said it was his idea that you should be told, and I admitted I was wrong not to do so sooner.'

'I'm sorry, Amanda, but now you've told me, can I see this diamond? Is it just as fabulous as you say it is?'

'I told you, Piers, the marquis has it.'

'You should have given it to me to look after; it belonged to my father, after all.'

'Use a bit of common sense, Piers. How could I put Lady Coverdale at risk, by keeping it in this house? I had to ask the marquis what I should do, and he very kindly offered to keep it safe. Not even I know exactly where it is, although I could probably find it if I had to.'

There was a pause before Piers said reluctantly, 'I suppose you are right, Amanda. So what happens now?'

'I don't know, because I recently received some old correspondence, letters, from when Agnew was in India, that throw doubt on the true ownership of the jewel.'

'Are you saying my father stole it?' Piers demanded, jumping up. 'That's a terrible thing to say. I won't listen to such lies.'

'For goodness sake, Piers, calm down. I'm not saying anything of the sort, only that it may not have been purchased by him, but received as a pledge of some kind, and there is someone out there who knows the family has it, and thinks it ought to be returned. At the moment, I know no more than that.'

Piers resumed his seat. 'I see. Perhaps that is why it was not mentioned in his will, and why I knew nothing about it.'

'Quite possibly. Now you are beginning to use your head and not behave like a petulant schoolboy.'

Amanda leant over and patted his knee. Piers gave her the dazzling smile that could charm the birds from the trees.

'For the moment, the most important thing is to ensure Rosalie's safety. You can resent his lordship quite wrongly, in my opinion, as much as you like, but he is devoted to the same cause and has the ability to do something about it, which neither you nor I have.'

Piers then stunned Amanda by saying, 'Well, what about the mad Lord in the attic? Is my sister safe with him?'

Amanda sagged in her seat. 'Who told you about that? It's all untrue, anyway.'

'Grooby, of course, and Rosalie asked me about someone called the sergeant, ages ago. I told her I thought I had seen him once, back view only.'

'Oh, servants.' Amanda sighed. 'I had better explain the situation, but only provided you talk to no one else, ask no questions, or listen to downstairs gossip.' Piers nodded in agreement. 'Briefly, Lord Benedict St Maure, Coverdale's younger brother, suffered some sort of illness of the brain and lives alone, in rooms on your side of the house, being looked after by the sergeant. Lord Benedict is very musical and enjoys listening to Rosalie playing, which she does most days. It has tempted him to leave his apartment for the first time in sixteen months. This leads Lord Coverdale to believe that his brother may, I *say may*, be on the road to recovery, and he has asked me not to interfere, and I most sincerely ask you not to, either.'

'It all seems a bit strange to me,' Piers said dubiously.

'So it may,' replied Amanda, 'but I can assure you that the situation is being carefully monitored, although Rosalie is unaware of that aspect of it, and you have no need to worry. But on no account say anything about this to your sister. I am adamant about that.'

'Oh, all right then, but I still think it's a bit odd.'

'It'll be even more odd if you are late for dinner. Go off and get changed.'

CHAPTER 19

J ustin sat in his study, wearing little but a dressing robe and a pair of drawers. The night was unbearably hot, and when he opened a window, the slight breeze bore nothing but unpleasant odours and little in the way of relief. Beside him was a glass of brandy, and an unread book lay on his lap. Nothing, or at least very little, seemed to be going right with his world.

His speech in the House of Lords was well received by the few members who had heard it. Parliament would soon rise for the long summer recess. And the prime minister's draconian measures to prevent unrest seemed to be having the opposite effect. To say nothing about the Corn Laws, which although intended to protect English farmers from foreign imports, had merely served to raise the price of bread to an extortionate degree and caused flour to be contaminated with substances like chalk (or worse). Unemployment increased, largely caused by the industries formerly producing goods for the war effort being idle or closed. The country was in a mess, as far as he was concerned, and more than likely set to get worse, and Parliament seemed unable to curb a head of state, in the person of the Prince Regent, whose lavish expenditures for high living and extravagant architecture was adding to the unrest.

He felt strongly, that a man in his position ought to be able to do something, but as his party was in opposition, he could not, except on a personal level. However, employing extra labour on his estates, and, together with Benedict, before he had his breakdown, setting up a home for maimed and sick ex-soldiers, who had nowhere else to go, was a mere drop in an ocean of misery.

He sighed and tossed down the remaining brandy. Getting up to pour himself another, he passed the bookshelf where the yellow diamond was hidden; he was tempted to take another look at it, and after filling his glass, succumbed. Carefully removing the book that concealed the precious volume, he took it down and carried it to his chair. He sat for a moment, fingering the raised spine. The moment he turned over the concealing pages, the jewel made its presence felt, glowing yellow with a deep heart of amber in the candlelight. He held it up, and its myriad facets immediately threw sparks of light into every corner of the room.

The Light of the Sun, indeed, he thought.

The diamond's amazing beauty belied the undesirable emotions it engendered in the human mind. Such value, such rarity, must surely be responsible for initiating most of the seven deadly sins, and a good many deviations from the Ten Commandments. He couldn't help feeling that if it really did not rightfully belong to the family, they would be better off without it. He held it in his hand. Who found it? Who dared to cut its scintillating facets? How many lives had been changed by it? How many hands had held it, as he was doing now?

He only knew it once had the best hiding place in the world when it rested on the warm skin of Amanda Fletcher's bosom; the memory of it aroused his desire for her. Without her pleasing and sometimes delightfully irritating existence, he would probably be engaged to marry Honoria Prideau, and his life set in a pattern of domestic mediocrity and unfulfilled passion.

He replaced the jewel and returned it to its dark prison, picked up his brandy glass, selected one candle from the branch, blew out the others, and went upstairs to bed. Tomorrow, he thought, would no doubt bring another set of problems, but then again, if they brought him together with Amanda, did he mind? No, he did not.

The next morning, he was surprised on receiving a card from Dr Amyas Pargeter and being informed by his manservant that the gentleman was awaiting his pleasure in the hall.

One baking hot day followed another, and London was becoming thin of company. Many members of polite society had travelled south to the fashionable resort of Brighton, especially those of the Prince Regent's coterie, among whose number the Coverdales did not count themselves, although the, due to his rank and position, Justin was obliged to attend at least one of Prinny's lavish parties, at his seaside palace (quite vulgar, in Justin's opinion). Instead, the Berkeley Square house would be closed, and the entire household would relocate to Coverdale Hall in Essex. But that event was still a few weeks away.

Despite the ban on early morning practice, Rosalie begged Amanda to be allowed to use the music room before the day heated up.

'Very well,' Amanda had said, 'but not before eight, and don't be late for breakfast.'

On entering the room, she was delighted to find that the French windows had been opened, and the coffee table and chairs had been moved away from them. Rosalie realised just how extraordinary thoughtful the sergeant was, and she did not even know his name.

The layout of the courtyard, accessed by steps, was similar to that of Alloa House in St James's, but smaller, paved with flagstones, and with a central tree surrounded by a rustic seat. She wondered how long it would be before she could sit there with Captain Benedict.

He came in while she was playing, followed by the sergeant, carrying a tray. From the corner of her eye, Rosalie could see the captain hesitate in front of the open window.

Please, she thought, don't turn back.

For what seemed like an eternity, he just stood there. As the sergeant placed the tray on the table, Rosalie kept on playing. At last, as though some great decision had been made, some milestone passed, Lord Benedict walked across the room and sat down at the table, and the sergeant withdrew. Rosalie finished the piece and joined the captain for coffee.

'I hope you didn't mind it being so early,' she began hesitantly. 'The heat, you know.'

'Why do you bother?' was his surprising question, ignoring her banal remark about the weather.

'Bother with what? I know I wasn't playing very well.'

'Don't be obtuse, Miss Rosalie. You know perfectly well what I mean. I know what you and the sergeant have been trying to do these past weeks. I'm not a complete fool, you know.'

Rosalie decided to ignore that remark, but noted the use of her Christian name. 'It's working, isn't it, My Lord?'

The captain narrowed his eyes, as if he realised he was being teased, and that it was a completely novel idea.

'You ask why I bother,' Rosalie went on, 'and I suppose you wonder why I connive with the sergeant to get you to come here. Well, if it benefits you, I am glad, but it benefits me too.' She poured them each a coffee.

'I don't understand; tell me more.'

'You are the first person ever, other than my music teachers, and not even all of them, who really appreciated what I am trying to do. I live with people who think that my love of music, and the playing of it, is just a useful social accomplishment. Oh yes, they know I do it well, better than most, even, but they have no idea at all what it really means to me. I think you do.'

She looked up just as Benedict looked down, and their eyes met for the first time, instantly communicating a mutual understanding.

He rose from the table and walked towards the open window. Rosalie held her breath. Would he take that one step into the outside world, albeit an enclosed one, that he had left more than a year ago? He stepped back and said, 'Play "Rosalie" for me.'

She returned to the pianoforte and began to play the sonatina Lord Benedict had composed specially for her. *Next time, perhaps*, she thought hopefully, *next time*.

CHAPTER 20

J ustin descended the stairs, to find Dr Pargeter examining the marble
statue situated on the hall table.

'One of the bits Lord Elgin overlooked,' Justin said, smiling and
holding out his hand. 'What can I do for you, Doctor? I don't suppose
this is a purely social visit.'

'You are quite correct, My Lord. I come on a matter of some delicacy,
and I know I can have your complete trust in not revealing anything I
have to say.'

'Naturally. Come into the study, where we can talk undisturbed, but
first some refreshment. What is your preference, Doctor?'

'A glass of ale would be very acceptable; the streets are very dusty with
this dry weather.'

They sat down with a glass of ale each, and a jug for replenishment;
the marquis began, 'In what way can I be of service to you, Doctor?'

'You may remember, sir, that when you visited me at St Bartholomew's,
you were keen to know about Mrs Fletcher's antecedents, and I was
probably, and rightly so, not very informative.'

'A somewhat unsuccessful fishing expedition, as I remember,' his
lordship replied with a wry smile.

'Quite so, but a circumstance has arisen that makes me believe you
should indeed know more about the lady's past history. But before I tell
you, I have to say that I have neither right nor permission to do so, only
that I sincerely believe it is in Mrs Fletcher's best interest you should know.

If you do not wish me to continue, I can enjoy your excellent ale, and we can talk of other things.'

'I understand your reservations, Doctor, but since I, too, have Mrs Fletcher's best interests at heart, please continue.'

Pargeter looked at the marquis intently from beneath his exceptional eyebrows, at the mention of the word 'heart,' and wondered, then began his story. 'I think I already told you that the crest you enquired about is that of an extinct viscountcy.'

'Yes, but you didn't reveal whose, if I recall.'

'It is of a family called Levenham. There were no male heirs, only a daughter. Her father was a debt-ridden spendthrift and virtually broke. The only opportunity to recoup was to put his daughter up for sale, to the highest bidder. At this point, Marquis, I must tell you that this is second-hand information, but from a very reliable source.'

'I understand. I imagine you are referring to some years in the past, is that not so?'

'Yes the girl was only sixteen, and the man her father wished her to marry was nearly sixty. As well as being very wealthy, he was a notorious womaniser and probably worse; one of his previous wives had died under suspicious circumstances, although nothing could be proved. I'll let you imagine how this young girl must have felt.'

'Trapped in an impossible situation, with little hope of escape, and possibly, even, in fear for her life, I suppose,' Justin surmised.

'That would be the fate of many in those circumstances, but this girl, Georgina was her name, was a girl of spirit and determined to prevent the marriage her father had devised. She had secretly been seeing a young man, an Oxford student, who had been tutoring in the local area.'

'I think I see where this is going now. When I saw you last, you mentioned a student of yours whose would-be academic brilliance was unfulfilled.'

'I congratulate you on your memory, Marquis, and it is as you say. The tutor, a scholarship boy, was making a little money before taking his final examinations. He fell deeply in love with Georgina, although I never believed that her feelings were engaged in the same way, but she must have been a persuasive girl, as she convinced him to elope with her to Gretna

Green, which they duly did, thereby forfeiting any chance my student had of an academic career, or, indeed, a degree.'

'I take it that the marriage was not a success,' Justin interjected. 'But before you go on, let me refill your glass, Doctor.' After refreshing both their drinks, Justin sat down, and asked, 'Were you aware of all this at the time?'

'No, I only knew that a very good student was no longer attending my tutorials, and later discovered that he had left Oxford entirely. It was several years before I made contact with William Kendal again. The couple seemed reasonably happy, and had a two-year-old daughter, Amanda.'

'How did he manage to make a living, if he never completed his degree?'

'He had become a schoolmaster at a so-called private academy. Higher education was not required for work of that sort, and the money was poor, but at least a schoolhouse was provided, so they got by. Kendal was able to save up enough money to buy a book from time to time, and it was in a booksellers in Bath that we met again. He recognised me. I doubt if I would have known him again, otherwise. After that, we corresponded; I had left Oxford by then and eventually received a letter saying Georgina had left him, but she had not taken the three-year-old Amanda.'

'And that's when you learnt what had happened?'

Well, most of it, anyway. I got to know his daughter, who as you know is now Mrs Amanda Fletcher. She had inherited her paternal grandmother's talent for drawing. I encouraged her and eventually arranged for her work to go to the Royal Botanic Gardens at Kew, but you know that bit, don't you, Marquis?'

'Yes, I visited Kew with Mrs Fletcher.'

'Kendal's mother lived at Weymouth, then a fashionable seaside resort for polite society; she had retired there from Bath, where she had made a good living as a miniaturist and silhouette cutter. When she became ill, Kendal sent Georgina to look after her, but unfortunately, his mother died. However, Georgina never returned. She met a French émigré, a Comte de Vailleux, and they ran off together.'

'Oh!'

'Oh, indeed. Now we come to the whole point of my story. When she was old enough to understand, Kendal told his daughter that her mother had died. I begged him to tell her the truth, but obviously he never did, and now the Comte and his wife, now legally married, have returned from America, where, apparently, he has made a fortune as an importer, particularly of French goods, and the couple are currently enjoying renewed acquaintances in town. My question to you, Marquis, is what should I do, or indeed, what, if anything, should you do?'

Justin sat in silence while, he tried to take in what Pargeter had just revealed.

Eventually, he said, 'Do you suppose her mother has information regarding Amanda's life?'

'I believe that that is possible; I suppose it must have been some eight years ago now, Georgina wrote to me, desperate for news of her daughter. I replied that William Kendal had died, and that Amanda was engaged to be married, but I did not tell her to whom.'

'So it amounts to two questions, Doctor. The first, should she be told? The second, who should be the person to tell her? Thirdly, I suppose one could do nothing and let events take their own course, but since you have come to me, I imagine you don't think that to be the right one.'

'I will not beat about the bush in this matter, Lord Coverdale. I think you should be the one to tell her, and for this reason: If I am the one, Amanda will surely blame me for keeping the information from her—'

'She will do that anyway, whoever tells her— 'The marquis interrupted.

'Yes, she will, but she cannot have a row with you, can she?' Pargeter smiled.

'That is devious.'

'That is my reputation.'

'I will think about it,' said the marquis, 'and let you know my decision.'

'Good, but do not take too long; the cat may jump out of the bag at any time.'

'I understand that. Perhaps you could do something for me, for Mrs Fletcher, too, as it happens.'

'I am at your service, Marquis. What is it you require?'

'I need to know all the legal requirements for a marriage to take place according to the liturgy of the Church of England.' He caught sight of the Doctor's face and added, 'And before you leap to conclusions, this has nothing to do with myself, and only indirectly with Mrs Fletcher; is that clear?'

'Perfectly.'

'I can explain briefly that I need to know, because it concerns the ownership of the aforesaid object, that was mentioned when we last met. Your enquiry must be conducted with discretion. Is that understood?'

'Perfectly,' the Doctor echoed his previous answer and then added, 'I don't suppose you would—?'

'Very well. I believe you have earned the privilege.'

Justinrose, understanding fully what Pargeter was asking. He went to his bookshelf, drew down the volume from its hiding place, and handed the doctor *The Light of the Sun*.

CHAPTER 21

The marchioness entered the small drawing room, where Amanda had also gone to work on some illustrations.

'I would be very pleased, Mrs Fletcher, if you would accompany me on a visit to my sister,' she said. 'She lives in Surrey, some twenty miles outside London. Providing the weather stays fine, we can go in the barouche.'

Amanda knew full well that this was not an invitation, but a command; however, she was happy to obey. Lady Coverdale had seen to it that the Abbots' stay in Berkeley Square lacked for nothing in the way of comfort and convenience, and anyway a trip to the country would make a nice change.

'I would be delighted to come, Lady Coverdale; have you a day in mind?'

'Tomorrow; we shall leave just after breakfast.' which Amanda knew could be translated to about half past ten, '… and should be there well in time for luncheon,' said her ladyship, adding, 'the barouche is a very comfortable carriage, as I am sure you will agree.'

Amanda now realised the real reason for the visit. Lady Coverdale's barouche was a fairly recent addition to her extensive range of coaches and carriages, and no doubt she wished to show it off to her younger sister. Who, although of lower rank, had married into considerable wealth, in the form of Sir Marcus Leigh, head of an old established private banking house, to whom, it was rumoured, the Prince Regent was heavily indebted.

The expedition set off on time and was due to return at about half past four. Piers, in the company of friends, was also in the country, in pursuit of the venue of a rumoured (but illegal) prize-fight. Amanda had made it abundantly clear to Rosalie that she was on no account to leave the house, unless accompanied by a footman and Jennie, her maid, or better still, Wilkins.

The evening entertainment was to include a trip on the Thames, ending at Vauxhall Pleasure Gardens. Rosalie was very excited by the prospect, as she had heard of it, but had not yet experienced the delights the gardens had to offer; her bosom friend Sophia had told her of the concerts, the mechanical wonders, and the fireworks that were part of every evening's entertainment there. Her real wish was that she could be taken there by Captain Benedict, whom, over the past days, she watched changing from a gaunt scarecrow into a handsome young man, but not yet fully confident or ready to face the world he had retreated from, into some dark, personal abyss.

She had selected a gown of silver tissue, embroidered with tiny rosebuds, short puff sleeves, and a lace-trimmed neckline. She would carry her favourite fan, with pierced ivory sticks, and the leaf hand-painted with roses, cherubs, and swags of silver ribbon. Long before she was due to get ready, she sent for Jennie to discuss her hair, but the housekeeper, Mrs Clarkson, arrived instead.

'I'm sorry, Miss Rosalie, but Jennie has been taken with the earache, and I have sent her to bed with a drop of laudanum and a hot poultice.'

'O, poor Jennie, I thought she was looking a little pulled this morning. I hope she feels better soon.'

'Shall I send for Miss Wilkins, Miss?'

Rosalie hastily answered in the negative. She always felt rather overpowered by Wilkins. 'Thank you, Mrs Clarkson, I shall be quite all right.'

After the housekeeper left, Rosalie sat down heavily on the dressing table stool, and immediately there was an ominous cracking sound. She got up, only to find that her beloved fan now had two broken sticks, and, what's more, none of her other fans matched her chosen outfit, but there was hope. The Burlington Arcade would still be open; there was time to purchase another.

Rosalie remembered Amanda's edict not to go out without her maid and a footman, but there was no way she was going to ask Wilkins, who would undoubtedly persuade her to choose a fan she didn't like, A footman, on his own, would just have to do. There was always one situated in the corridor, and he obeyed her request to find Clarkson.

Draped only in a light shawl over her day dress and a chip-straw hat, she waited in the hall. Clarkson appeared silently from the nether regions.

'You wished to see me, Miss?'

'Oh, yes, Clarkson. I wish to go to the Burlington Arcade. I have broken the fan I intended to use tonight, and I must have a footman to accompany me. Will you arrange for one, please?'

'Certainly, Miss, at once.'

Two footmen were already stationed in the hall, and one stepped forward immediately.

'I would be honoured to perform the task, Mr Clarkson,' the younger and taller of the two requested.'

Clarkson looked him up and down, checking that his livery was in order. 'Very well, Henry, but mind you take good care of Miss Abbot.'

Rosalie saw that the footman was one she had particularly noticed before. His white wig emphasised his swarthy skin, and there was also something about his features that seemed vaguely familiar. The walk to the arcade was quickly accomplished, the shopping rather less so. Rosalie was unable to choose between two equally suitable fans, and, in the end, decided to buy both. Exiting the arcade from the Piccadilly end, the two stepped into the bright sunshine.

As they set off, the footman said, 'I see you do not have your parasol with you, Miss. Do you not find the light of the sun too bright?'

'No, I am a country girl, Henry. I'm used to being out in all weathers.'

After they had gone a short distance, Rosalie realised the footman had used almost the exact words that had been spoken to her at the masked ball. She was about to turn and ask him what exactly he meant, when a closed carriage-and-pair drew up alongside. The door opened, and a man leant out, seized Rosalie round the waist, and clamped his other hand over her mouth.

Rosalie kicked out for all she was worth, and within seconds, Henry was struggling to prevent her abductor from dragging her into the coach.

He was tall and strong, and had the advantage of having both feet on the ground, while the aggressor was half-leaning out of the door.

The coachman shouted, 'Hurry up, the dock closes at four.'

A violent tug-of-war ensued, and Henry might have succeeded if the driver of the coach had not turned round, raised a pistol, and shot him through his upper arm, which fell, useless, and his grip loosened. The driver whipped up the horses, and Rosalie was flung back into the coach, as the horses galloped off, the door still swinging wildly, until the abductor managed to pull it shut.

The street was fairly empty at that time of day, but a small cluster of astonished bystanders had assembled, from which one man started to run after the receding vehicle, but soon gave up an impossible task, and returned to Henry, who was clutching his wounded arm, from which blood was now freely flowing.

While taking out a handkerchief and binding up Henry's arm, he said, 'I am in Lord Coverdale's employ, to ensure Miss's safety, but I was too far away to help.' He tied the makeshift bandage in a tight knot. 'That's the best I can do.' He lifted Henry's limp arm and thrust it inside his livery coat. 'I must go at once to Lord Coverdale, in Mount Street, and inform him of what has happened. Are you able to go back to Berkeley Square and tell them? Speed is all important now.' He picked up Henry's wig, which had fallen off in the struggle, and handed it to him. 'Go as quickly as you can, man.' He ran off in the direction of Park Lane.

Henry, refusing all offers of help, replaced his wig and set off, but before long, his strength began to fail, and it was only with an extreme effort and determination that he was able to reach Berkeley Square before collapsing in the hallway, gasping out, 'Fetch Mr Clarkson,' to the hall porter.

The butler arrived in less than a minute.

Henry managed to utter, 'Miss Rosalie ... abducted ... two men ... coach ... tried to save ... shot me ...'

'Where ... where have they taken here?'

'Don't know ... docks, I think. Tell his lordship ... coach ... one red wheel,' gasped Henry, and then he fainted dead away.

Clarkson immediately ordered two footmen to carry Henry to his own quarters across the courtyard.

'Get Mrs Clarkson to attend to him and send at once for a surgeon, on my authority. Where is the sergeant?'

'With Lord Benedict, Mr Clarkson,' said one of the footmen, as they lifted the inert figure of their fellow servant.

But they were not together; Clarkson could hear the sound of the piano, issuing from the music room. It could only be Lord Benedict. He entered swiftly and received an admonishing glare from the pianist.

'I'm sorry, My Lord, but there has been an unfortunate incident that I need to apprise you of immediately.'

'Well, man, what is it?'

'Miss Rosalie has been abducted.'

Benedict leapt to his feet. 'What? What do you mean, abducted?'

'From what I understand, My Lord, she was taken in the street by two men and carried away in a carriage.'

'Oh, my God. Where is Mrs Fletcher, or Lady Coverdale? They must be told.'

'Her Ladyship and Mrs Fletcher are out of town, M'lord; they have gone to visit her ladyship's sister and are not expected back until after four o'clock.'

'I must go at once; send someone to the stables to saddle two horses. Tell the sergeant to join me there, and tell him to arm himself. Then come to my quarters and tell me all that you know. Go, man, go, at the double.'

Lord Benedict quickly pulled on his boots and was shrugging himself into a riding coat when the butler arrived.

'Now, Clarkson, tell me all you know. Why wasn't Miss Rosalie being accompanied? Who allowed her to go out alone?'

'She was accompanied, My Lord. A footman was with her; unfortunately, one of the men in the coach shot him.'

'Shot the footman? Is he dead?'

'Fortunately, not, My Lord, but he is in a bad way; he lost a lot of blood. But he managed to get here, before collapsing.'

While he was speaking, Benedict was emptying drawer after drawer of his chest-of-drawers, flinging the contents on the floor, muttering, 'Where the hell has the sergeant put them? 'Ah,' as he pulled out a wooden box containing a matched pair of duelling pistols. 'Was the footman able to tell you anything before he collapsed?'

'Yes, M'lord. He thinks the coach, which he said had one red wheel, was headed for the docks, and also that Lord Coverdale is being informed. I expect he will be here shortly.'

'I can't wait for him; he may not have been at home. The sergeant and I will go. When his lordship arrives, tell him everything you have told me, Clarkson.' He shouted back up the stairs, 'Is the footman getting proper attention?'

He barely heard the reply, as he leaped down the last few steps, his knees almost buckling; he ran down the passage to a door and into the outside world, saying to the waiting sergeant, as he was given a much-needed leg up, 'I may have deserted my men on the field of battle, but I'll never desert Miss Rosalie.'

CHAPTER 22

Lord Coverdale was at home, restlessly wondering, as he had been for the past few days, what he should do about Dr Pargeter's news concerning Mrs Fletcher's mother, when his front door received a battering fit to wake the dead. Roberts, who answered it, was practically knocked over by a man who rushed past him.

,Coverdale…,' gasped the man. 'Must see the … his lordship.'

'Whom shall I say wishes to see him?'

'Say … say, the man from Bow Street; quickly, man.'

The altercation in his hallway brought Justin out of his study to find out what was going on. Recognising the man who had been set to watch over Berkeley Square and Rosalie, he said, 'That's all right, Roberts. Come in, Simmonds; what has happened?'

After the runner related all he knew, including the probable destination of the coach, in quick succession, Justin ordered his curricle and fastest horses; scribbled and sealed a note to the Intendant at Bow Street, and despatched Simmonds there, to summon assistance, directing them to the new East India dock.

Thus, it was barely twenty minutes later that the marquis drew up to Berkeley Square, to be met by an anxious Clarkson with the latest news, and the fact that his mother and Mrs Fletcher were out. Justin was astonished to hear that Benedict and the sergeant had already set off in pursuit. He would have liked to question the footman who had been shot, but Clarkson assured him that the young man was with the surgeon and in no state to be interrogated.

'Besides,' he added, 'I do not think he can tell us anything further. He was only just able to speak before he collapsed.'

'Well, then, when my mother and Mrs Fletcher return, on no account is her ladyship to be informed of these events, but you must make sure that Mrs Fletcher is made fully aware, and of what is in hand to rescue Miss Rosalie. Do I make myself clear on that point?'

'Yes. M'Lord. Quite clear.'

'Good, because if I find my orders have been disobeyed, there will be dismissals. Is that clear, also?'

'Yes, M'lord'

At that moment, the hall porter opened the door, and the marchioness and Mrs Fletcher entered.

Immediately after greeting his mother, the marquis said, 'Ah, Mrs Fletcher, how fortuitous. I have just arrived to beg you to take a turn round the park with me and was desolated to find you not at home.'

'I'm sorry, My Lord, but as you see, we have just returned from a long drive, and I am in need of –'

The Marquis turned to his mother and said, 'I'm sure you do not require Mrs Fletcher for anything, do you, Mama?'

'Not at all, my dear. I shall go to my bedchamber and rest till dinnertime. Clarkson, have my maid bring tea to my room.' She pointed to a footman and said, 'James, assist me upstairs. I am fatigued by the journey.'

Justin watched the stately ascent begin and then turned to Amanda. 'We will go for that drive now.' He put an unexpectedly firm hand on her arm. 'Now, Mrs Fletcher.'

Recognising his urgent tone, Amanda obeyed and was hurried down the steps to the waiting curricle.

'We will be quicker on horseback than the coach, Captain, as we can go down narrower alleys, so we 'ave a good chance of catching 'em up,' the sergeant said to Lord Benedict. 'An' I knows the ways through London better'n you, sir, if you'll pardon me.'

'Time is of the essence, Sergeant. I am in your hands.'

In fact, Benedict was having a bit of trouble managing his horse. His legs did not want to obey him, and his balance was not what it should be, as a result of being out of the saddle for over a year. They had travelled several miles and were somewhere in the East End, when they noticed some kind of commotion at the far end of the street.

The sergeant pulled up his horse, dismounted, and handed his reins to Benedict.

'Stay there, Sir. I'll 'ave a look-see.' He peered round the corner and could see, at the other end of the street, a partly overturned carriage and the remains of a red wheel lying in the middle of the street.

'Can you see any people?'

'Yes, Captain. Yes, there's someone standing on the flagway. It must be them.'

'No one's come out to help, have they?'

'It ain't the sort of place folks come out to 'elp, sir; more like to run indoors and pull the door shut be'ind 'em.'

'Is your pistol loaded, Sergeant?'

'Yes, sir.'

'There hasn't been time to load mine, but they won't know that, will they?'

The sergeant looked doubtful. 'I 'opes not, sir.'

'Right, now, since we don't know the exact situation, except that there were two men, at least one of them armed, we'll just approach casually, as if we're out for an afternoon's ride.' Benedict looked around him at the filthy street and run-down houses. 'Not that that seems very likely in this district. If pressed, we'll say we got lost. Mount up, Sergeant; let's go.'

They urged their mounts to a gentle trot and approached the overturned carriage. As they drew alongside, they could see that although the man on the flagway had his back towards them, he was actually holding Rosalie, who appeared to be gagged, with her hands tied behind her back.

Benedict realised at once that this was to their advantage. It meant that she could neither cry out in recognition, nor attempt to rush towards them; any such movement might result in disastrous retaliation.

'I say, bit of a bother, what?' Benedict dismounted, clinging onto the stirrup leather for momentary support, hoping it didn't show. 'Can we be of any assistance?'

'Nah,' said the man holding Rosalie, who had watched the arrival of her saviours, relief and anxiety in her expression. 'Sent a boy for 'elp.'

'Anyone hurt?' enquired Benedict.

'Nah,' replied the man, who seemed to have a limited vocabulary.

'Why is that woman tied up like that?' asked Benedict, buying time to assess the situation.

'Runaway; beat her black an' blue, when I gets 'er 'ome, little varmint.' He gave Rosalie a shake.

Benedict could see she wasn't being held tightly, but knew that could change in an instant, if he made the wrong move.

Meanwhile, the sergeant was engaged with the other man in seeing to the two coach horses. One was still harnessed to the shaft and shaking like a leaf, and the other was on the ground, entangled in the traces.

'Can't leave 'em like that,' said the sergeant.

'Wot's it to you, mister? We'll just take one o' yourn,' said the man, making to where Benedict and the sergeant had tethered their horses to a lamp post.

'Oh, no you won't.' The sergeant fetched the man a hefty swipe to the jaw, but the man dodged, receiving only a glancing blow, and a fist fight ensued.

The man confronting Benedict was momentarily distracted, and believing this was his chance, Benedict lunged forward to make a grab for Rosalie, but his year's incarceration, and self-exile had taken its toll, and he was neither quick enough, nor strong enough to effect the manoeuvre successfully. Taking a step back, the man increased his grip round Rosalie's waist, at the same time pulling a pistol from his belt and pointing it at Lord Benedict.

'You stays right where you are, mister, or you won't be goin' nowhere.' He waved the pistol menacingly.

Benedict, realising that brute force was not within his power, tried reason. 'Who is that lady you're holding onto so tightly?'

'None o' yer business,' he growled, adding, 'my wife, thought she could leave me, din't she? You ain't getting her, neiver.'

'Nor will you, if you shoot me, will you?'

'Dunno wotcher mean. She's mine, that's wot.'

'Well,' said Benedict in the most reasonable voice he could muster, 'if you shoot and wound me, you will go to prison for a very long time. On the other hand, if you kill me, you will hang. Either way, you still won't have her. So best to put that gun down, don't you think?'

The next moment, several things seemed to happen at once. The sound of a heavy fist meeting a jawbone, and that of a body hitting the ground, was followed immediately by a loud howl from the man with the gun, who doubled up in pain, releasing his grip on Rosalie.

Benedict seized his opportunity and went for the arm holding the pistol, forcing it up; the gun went off, with a loud report, followed by the sound of breaking glass. Benedict extracted his own pistol from his boot and pointed it at Rosalie's captor, but the man thrust her aside and ran off down the road, still awkwardly bent forward.

Benedict caught Rosalie as she staggered sideways, quickly undoing the gag and releasing her imprisoned arms; they clutched each other tightly, as she sobbed with relief. Just at that moment, the marquis and Mrs Fletcher arrived at speed, the sudden stop causing the horses' shoes to strike sparks from the cobbled street.

He turned to Amanda and said, in a calming tone. 'It seems, Mrs Fletcher, that we have missed all the action.'

CHAPTER 23

Without waiting for assistance, Amanda leaped down from the curricle and ran towards Rosalie, who was now attempting to smile up at her rescuer and thank him with a wobbly voice.

'Rosalie, Rosalie, are you all right?' she cried. 'Are you hurt? What did they do to you?'

Her ward, showing no signs of wanting to exchange the comfort of Benedict's arms for those of her guardian, said, 'Oh, Amanda, he was so brave; the man had a gun. I thought he was going to shoot. I'm not hurt, but poor Henry, the footman, they shot him, you know. How is he?'

Amanda, seeing that Rosalie had not suffered much physical harm from her ordeal, was sure some sort of reaction would probably set in later and kept her voice calm. 'I see you have lost a shoe. Do you think it is in that coach?' She pointed to the wrecked vehicle lying half-overturned along the street.

'Yes, Amanda, I expect so, and my straw hat, and my shawl … oh, and a parcel. I had just been shopping, you know?'

Mrs Fletcher addressed Lord Benedict. 'I am afraid these are unusual circumstances for introductions, My Lord, but I am Amanda Fletcher, Miss Rosalie's guardian, and I thank you most sincerely for effecting her rescue.'

'I am indeed pleased to meet you, Mrs Fletcher, under any circumstances, and I have every reason to believe that we have rescued each other. Perhaps, if you could retrieve Miss Rosalie's belongings, I will endeavour to carry her over to my brother's curricle, and you can sit with her there.'

Fortunately, Rosalie was very light, but Amanda could see that it cost Lord Benedict a superhuman effort to reach the vehicle.

After the marquis had descended from his curricle in a rather more leisurely manner than his passenger, and seeing that Rosalie was being well attended to, he ordered his tiger to rug up the horses.

He strolled over to the sergeant, who was guarding the inert body of the second man, and asked, 'Is he dead?'

'No, Sir, just knocked out a bit.'

'Quite a bit, I would say, Sergeant, wouldn't you?' He gave the prone man a poke with the toe of his boot, eliciting a groan. 'Get him tied up before he tries anything again. Then we'd better see to those poor old nags over there.'

'I was about to do that, My Lord, when this ruffian come at me, wif 'is fists. It weren't a long fight, Sir.'

'No, Sergeant, I imagine it was not.' They managed to get the second horse to his feet, and he seemed more frightened than hurt. 'Stay with them, Sergeant, for now; I'm going to see to the comfort of the other parties involved.'

Benedict was standing next to the curricle in his shirtsleeves, having given his jacket to put round Rosalie's shoulders, as she had started to shiver despite the warmth of the early evening. Justin put his arm round his brother. The two men were about the same height and of similar colouring, but Benedict seemed to be but a thin, pale copy of his older brother. He also looked as if he was about to collapse with fatigue.

'Good to see you back, Ben,' Justin said, smiling. He then asked Amanda, 'Will Rosalie be all right going home in the curricle?'

But before she could reply, Rosalie answered, 'Of course I will. Who is going to drive?'

'Benedict, do you think you are up to it? My bays are easy, even for a ham-fisted pilot like you, and anyway, the steam has already been taken out of them.'

'I am not ham-fisted; I'm very hurt,' Benedict said in mock indignation. 'Yes, of course I can drive these two lovely ladies back to Berkeley Square. What are you going to do?'

'I am expecting some professional assistance from Bow Street to arrive any minute, and I'd better settle with that man.' He pointed to a red-faced man, whose window had been broken. 'Before he has an apoplexy on his front doorstep. Just leave it to the sergeant and me to clear things up.'

'What was this all about, Justin? Do you know why Miss Rosalie was abducted?'

'Not now, Ben. I'll talk to you about it later. Now get going.'

Benedict climbed into the curricle, with Rosalie happily squeezed between him and Amanda. He told the tiger to unrug the horses, and they set off at a steady pace. At first, it was in silence, as Lord Benedict accustomed himself to driving again. Amanda wasn't sure if she should ask Rosalie about her horrible experience, or if it was best to let her say something in her own time, but it was Lord Benedict who spoke first.

'I am truly honoured and grateful to be driving you two very brave ladies.'

Amanda was a bit surprised at this remark, as she could not think of anything she had done that could possibly be construed as brave, and said so.

'You are quite wrong there, Mrs Fletcher. You allowed Miss Rosalie to visit the music room and play so beautifully for me, although you must have known she was being listened to by the "Mad Lord in the Attic."'

'Don't ever say that, Captain,' Rosalie interrupted angrily. 'You are not mad, you are ...' She wanted to say wonderful, but realised that it would not be appropriate, so ended, '... the really brave one. That man pointed a loaded pistol at you.'

'But I had the advantage, at least I did, until I failed to disarm him the first time. It was only your intervention, even although you were bound and gagged, that enabled me to grab him.'

'What did you do, Rosalie?' Amanda was astonished. 'I had no idea they had done that to you. How could you possibly have helped?'

'I pinched him, very hard, with both hands, Amanda, and you know that harpists' fingers are very strong.'

Lord Benedict laughed. 'No wonder he let out such a howl. A pinch in that region is enough to disarm any man.'

'What region?' Amanda asked and then said, 'Oh ... oh, Rosalie, you didn't.'

'Well, my hands were tied behind my back; I just grabbed the nearest bit. But Captain, why didn't you shoot the man after he let me go?'

'My dear Miss Rosalie, there are two very good reasons why. In the first place, it is not good form to shoot a man in the back when he is running away, and secondly, my pistol wasn't loaded.'

The occupants of the curricle fell into silence after this revelation, and as the journey continued, Rosalie noticed that Lord Benedict was coming to the end of his tether; she could feel his body beginning to sag, and his legs to tremble. He had nothing more to give. Surreptitiously, and under the cover of his jacket, which she was still wearing round her shoulders, she slipped her arm round his back and embraced him. She could hardly believe how thin he was.

It's a good thing the horses know where they live, thought Rosalie.

She whispered to Amanda, 'When we get there, can you get down first, and call the porter? I don't think Lord Benedict will be able to get down, or even stand, on his own; he is close to collapse.'

Amanda glanced across at their driver, and one brief look was enough to agree with her ward. When they finally arrived, Amanda quickly went inside and explained that the gentleman had been taken ill and required assistance. Between them, the porter and a footman smoothly organised Lord Benedict's safe transfer to the library. Amanda attempted to administer some brandy. But he turned his head away. It was his silence that worried Rosalie the most.

She took Amanda aside. 'I don't think he should be left alone; it's like Piers.'

'What do you mean, "like Piers"?'

'When his injuries were getting better, he went all silent and wouldn't eat, like the captain. Lizzie and I took more than a week to get him over it. Lord Benedict has been much worse; he might just slip back again into whatever dark world he has been inhabiting. I need to stay with him.'

This was the second time Amanda had been informed of Piers' depression and Rosalie's role in his recovery, but Lord Benedict was a different case altogether.

'I'm sorry, Rosalie,' she replied. 'I can't let you stay with him. If anyone found out, you would be ruined.'

'He would never do anything to hurt me or my reputation.'

'I know, but that is not the point; others wouldn't, and besides, you need to rest too, after such an ordeal.'

'There'll be a footman in the hall; ask him to send for Clarkson, Amanda.'

Throughout this, Lord Benedict sat as if in a trance, seemingly once again abandoning the outside world he had only just re-entered.

Rosalie pointed to him and said, 'You see how he is, Amanda. It would be a tragedy if he lost himself again. He needs me. You must see that, but I have an idea.'

Clarkson entered. 'You require me to do something, Madam?'

'Miss Rosalie, does, Clarkson.'

'First, can you get Lord Benedict to his rooms? Is there a settee or a couch in his living room?'

'I believe so, Miss.'

'Could you put him on it and make him comfortable, do you think?'

'I will endeavour to do so, Miss.'

'Good, then can it be arranged for my harp to be brought up there?'

'If that is your wish, I have no doubt I can arrange it.'

'As soon as possible, please Clarkson, and when you have done so, let me and Mrs Fletcher know. We shall be in our apartments.'

'Very good, Miss. Will that be all?'

'Yes, thank you, Clarkson.'

The butler bowed and withdrew.

'What are you thinking, Rosalie?'

'I am not going to abandon the Captain Benedict, whatever you say, and that is the best I could come up with. He likes the harp above all, and I hope it will remind him that it was the music that brought him out of his exile. But his body is not strong; I felt every rib when I tried to support him near the end of the drive.'

'You did what?'

Rosalie ignored the interruption. 'He would probably have fallen off, if I had not, and I know his mind must still be fragile.'

'But you must be so tired yourself, Rosalie, and you've been through such a lot, had such a terrible shock. You need rest as well.'

'I can rest any time,' she retorted sharply, 'besides, I find playing my harp restful, too, and that reminds me, you had better send a note saying I've caught a chill or something, and make our excuses for tonight's party.'

Two hours later, Justin and the sergeant entered Lord Benedict's apartment to find him lying on the couch, with Rosalie on the floor, beside him, her head on his chest, and holding his hand, both of them sound asleep. The marquis picked her up and carried her back to her own rooms.

Amanda had been waiting for Rosalie to appear and was quite surprised (and more than a little agitated) to find her in the arms of the his lordship.

'She doesn't look like she's been playing the harp recently, does she?' Amanda asked.

Justin smiled. 'Where shall I put her?'

Amanda opened the bedchamber door. 'Just lay her on the bed; Wilkins and I will attend to her later, when she wakes.'

'I don't think you need worry; she *was* playing the harp earlier, Clarkson has been keeping an eye on the situation, as he knew you might worry.' Justin had already decided not to say exactly, in what position he had found Rosalie and his brother. 'The sergeant is with Benedict, now.'

'I'll be staying the night here, possibly more, so if you are up to it, after today's events, I will see you at dinner. If the subject comes up, and I am sure my mother will have heard something, the story I am putting about is that Henry got his wound while trying to prevent an unknown woman from being abducted on the street. Rosalie was only a spectator. Do you agree?'

'Certainly, an excellent plan, Marquis.'

'Good, because I have already informed Clarkson and the sergeant.'

'Clarkson is a marvel, and I think the sergeant is too.'

'Yes, I agree, and so are you, Mrs Fletcher.'

Marvel wasn't exactly the word she wanted to be called by Justin; perhaps it was better than nothing, but what did it matter, anyway?

CHAPTER 24

D inner was a quiet affair, with more footmen than diners, and when the marchioness expressed surprise at Rosalie's absence, she was told she was not feeling well and that the planned river trip and visit to Vauxhall Gardens had been postponed. Once again, Clarkson had performed his duty, and it was clear that no hint of the true events of the afternoon had reached her ears. The marquis had been particularly concerned that his mother did not discover that Benedict had at last left the confinement of his room. Both sons were fond of their mother, who had a generous disposition and, unlike many others in her high-ranking position, was always mindful of the welfare of her servants and others less fortunate. But her understanding of emotional needs was somewhat limited.

Justin was determined that Benedict should be allowed to re-join the family in his own time, untroubled by any coercion from an overenthusiastic mama. Fortunately, Lady Coverdale, still feeling the effects of the long carriage drive and the exuberance of her sister's children, decided to retire early, leaving Amanda in charge of the after-dinner tea tray, in the small salon. Being together, enabled them both to raise the questions each had been bursting to ask throughout the tedious dinner.

Immediately, Amanda began, 'What happened after we left? Did you catch the man who abducted Rosalie? Why was she abducted? Was it anything to do with the you-know-what?'

'Hold your horses, there, Mrs Fletcher. One question at a time, please. No, I'm afraid the man got away, but they have every hope of catching him in due course. Your final question is an interesting one, but I don't know the answer. On the face of it, it would seem that it was, but the sergeant and I went with the Bow Street men to the East India Dock. After I told the dock-master about the abduction, he was persuaded to search a ship, about to sail on the tide, and there, on a lower deck, discovered half a dozen other unfortunate women who had also been taken and forced on board.'

'But surely those women were not of Rosalie's social class?'

'No, they certainly were not, but they all had one thing in common with her: They all had blonde hair. Which makes me think her seizure had nothing to do with the you-know-what, as you call it, but more to do with white slave-trading. Have you had an opportunity to talk to Rosalie about any of it?'

'Not in any detail, but she was adamant that, apart from the gag and her tied hands, they didn't hurt or even touch her, until the coach overturned. She is very concerned about the footman, Henry. Have you any news?'

'Not good, I'm afraid. His arm is very badly damaged, and he has lost a lot of blood. We owe him the very best of care; without his courage and determination to get back to Berkeley Square, despite his injuries, we would not have known about the abduction till quite a bit later, when it just might have been too late.'

'Who is looking after him?'

'A surgeon was called, and Dr Griffiths informed Mrs Clarkson that the ball went right through Henry's arm, unfortunately carrying a considerable portion of his arm with it. He is being looked after in their quarters, which are separate from the other staff, but I know she is worried about him.'

'Would you consider calling Dr Pargeter? He is an expert on bones, and he has some *avant garde* methods, which are not always accepted by conventional medical practice. I don't believe Dr Griffiths would object to a second opinion from such an eminent colleague, do you?'

'An excellent suggestion, Mrs Fletcher,' the marquis agreed immediately. 'I shall send for him to come and bring medical equipment with him, as soon as possible tomorrow.'

It was just the opportunity that Justin wanted, an excuse to have another talk, in private, with Pargeter about the problem of Amanda's mother.

'You know, Marquis, it was Rosalie who realised that your brother was so exhausted by the drive home, and what had gone before, that she didn't think he'd be able to get down from the curricle without assistance. I have to say, it never occurred to me.'

'Are you concerned about those two?'

'She's very young.'

'In years, perhaps, but I believe she has wisdom beyond her youth.'

'But they hardly know each other, and Lord Benedict has been, well, you know, in a bad way.'

'I think they do know each other, Mrs Fletcher; in the future, they may even fall in love, but just now, it's something different. I don't believe it was only music that brought Benedict back to us. I think it was *specifically Rosalie's* music. They connected on some very deep level that we, or at least I, don't understand, but which started the process of healing Benedict's broken mind.'

'As her guardian, what should I do about it? One thing I do know is, that without your brother's courage and incredible willpower, stretched to the absolute limit, things might have had a very different and tragic outcome. The debt of gratitude I owe him for that is beyond imagination.'

'If you really want my advice, and I'm thinking of both of them, my answer would be, do nothing. Just observe and wait.'

Amanda heaved a sigh. 'Sometimes, Marquis, we have very difficult decisions to make.'

His Lordship looked at her closely. 'Yes, Mrs Fletcher, we do indeed. You must be exhausted too. I will take my leave and let you retire.' He rose from his chair, but Amanda stayed him. 'There is just one thing perhaps I ought to mention. Rosalie said a rather strange thing to me.'

'Yes?'

'She asked me, "What is this thing about me and the sun?" So I asked what she meant, and she replied that Henry had seemed very concerned that she had gone out without a parasol, because the light of the sun was very bright. What do you make of that, Marquis? Of course, they had just emerged from the Burlington Arcade, which is quite dark.'

'Oh, dear, more and more questions without answers. Frankly, Mrs Fletcher, I don't know, and I think we are both too tired to concern ourselves with it now. Let us think about it in the morning. I bid you goodnight, and hope you sleep well. We will talk again tomorrow.'

CHAPTER 25

D r Pargeter arrived at Berkeley Square promptly at nine o'clock. Together, they went immediately to the Clarkson apartments, during which time Justin explained the nature of the footman's injuries. Dr Griffiths was already in attendance.

Henry lay motionless on the bed, his light, coffee-coloured skin, now a distressing shade of greyish-green. Dr Griffiths was by the bed, holding a bleeding bowl and a blood-letting knife. Pargeter at once stepped forward and introduced himself.

'I often find, Doctor, that extreme loss of blood, such as I believe this patient has suffered, is not generally improved by the removal of more.'

Griffiths, from his expression, clearly did not agree but acknowledged the presence of a distinguished colleague; he put down his instruments and said, 'I am glad of your advice Dr Pargeter, but I was thinking of the fever, Sir.'

'Yes, Doctor, quite right, but now we must look at this wound.'

Together, they carefully removed the bandages on Henry's left arm, and what was revealed shook Justin to the core. Ragged flesh, dried blackened blood, visible bone. He turned away, sickened by the sight, disbelieving the damage a single pistol shot could do.

'This needs complete cleaning out or he will certainly lose the arm; most probably will anyway, and maybe his life, but we must do our best, Doctor.' He turned to Mrs Clarkson, hovering in the doorway. 'Boiled water, white vinegar, and plenty of clean linen, if you please, madam.'

When it arrived, the two surgeons set to work, Dr Griffiths holding the wound open with forceps, while Pargeter probed for fragments of cloth that had been carried into it; this was often the main cause of gangrene, especially on muddy battlefields.

'It is fortunate that the bone has not been completely shattered, but a portion of it has splintered, and I must remove all the fragments.'

Pargeter was meticulous, examining the wound with a powerful magnifying glass before declaring himself satisfied.

'I shall not attempt to close the wound at this time. If infection arises, as I'm afraid it will, the wound will have to be cleaned and dressed every day. You will see to that, Dr Griffiths. You did a good job, but please, no blood-letting. For the dressing, use basilicum powder, several layers of fine linen, and a firm, but not tight, bandage. Immobilise the whole arm with a sling fixed thus.' He placed his own arm up, so his left hand was touching the centre of his chest. He spoke with the authority of someone whose orders were always obeyed without question. He then addressed Mrs Clarkson, 'Now to the patient's regimen …'

Throughout all this painful attention, Henry barely moved; he groaned several times but never opened his eyes. Dr Pargeter looked back at his patient, as the marquis stood by the door, ready to leave, and shook his head.

'I don't know, Coverdale, it's going to be touch-and-go for the next few days; yes, indeed, touch-and-go. Griffiths seems a good man, if he follows my orders, that is. I shall get my apothecary to make up some draughts to ease some of the poor man's pain, which will be very bad, I'm afraid. At the moment, he is feeling very little, but the better he gets, the worse the pain will get. I don't suppose you will tell me how this happened, Marquis?'

'Some sort of street robbery, I believe. The footman went to the aid of the victim, and that is what he got for his trouble. Bow Street are looking into it. I must thank you for your prompt attendance, Pargeter. I believe your ministrations are the poor man's only hope.'

They reached the hall, and Pargeter said, 'If you have a moment, I'd like to have a word about that other matter. I've been thinking and came to the conclusion that you are definitely the right person to tell Mrs Fletcher, you know, about her mother.'

'Yes,' Justin replied, 'as to that, there is now no immediate concern, because I have learned that the couple in question have taken a house in Brighton, so the problem is not likely to arise in the near future, but I will keep you informed.'

'Thank you, My Lord; at any rate, I shall return in a few days' time to check on the patient, but call me if there is a crisis. However, there is also the matter you raised with me last time we met, Coverdale.'

'Remind me. I've had a lot to think about recently.'

'A question of legal requirements for marriage.'

'Yes, of course, and …?'

'I applied to the Palace, discreetly, of course.'

'Buckingham?'

The Doctor smiled, 'No, Lambeth, and without going into detail, since the 1753 Marriage Act, a marriage is only legal if it is conducted by an ordained Church of England priest and takes place in a church or chapel registered by the Church of England. I hope that satisfies your … er … curiosity, Marquis.'

'Perfectly. I thank you,' Justin replied with a smile, as Dr Pargeter collected his hat and cloak from a waiting footman and took his leave.

Later in the morning, Justin sent a message requesting Clarkson's presence in the library. While he waited, he poured himself some ale and another for his butler, who arrived minutes later.

'You wished to see me, My Lord?'

'Yes, Clarkson, please be seated.'

'I prefer to stand, My Lord.'

'Oh dear! Oh dear! Oh dear! Clarkson. If I cannot sit and talk to the man who has known me since I was in leading strings, who can I talk to? Please, have a seat, and take a glass of ale with me. You only serve the best, I know.'

'Yes, indeed, My Lord.'

'Now, I need to talk to you about Henry. Everything you know, Clarkson. For a start, how long has he been in my mother's employ?'

'Since March, My Lord.'

'Before or after the Abbots arrived?'

'Let me think, My Lord. Yes, it would be about ten days before.'

'You're certain of that, Clarkson?'

'Yes, because Thomas left, his mother was ill, on March the first, I remember that because it was St David's Day.' He cleared his throat. 'Mrs Clarkson is Welsh, My Lord. She doesn't let me forget it.'

'So how did you fill the vacancy?'

'Through the usual agency, but it not being a quarter day, they didn't have much on their books. I interviewed three, including Henry, I believe. I have it all in my books, My Lord. I can get them …'

'No, that won't be necessary.' The marquis took a sip of his ale. 'Why did you choose Henry?'

'He seemed to have everything I required in a footman: a good figure, well spoken, better than most, as it happens. He was respectful without being obsequious, and when I questioned him about the duties he would be expected to perform, he appeared knowledgeable about table service and the care of silverware; he was by far the best candidate, so I hired him on the spot. Did I do wrong, My Lord?'

'Not at all, Clarkson; without him, I don't know where Miss Rosalie might be now. I hate to think. Does he get on with the other staff?'

'I believe so; I have had no complaints. I suppose one might call him reserved in his manner, but never unpleasant.'

'References?'

'That is why I employ an agency, My Lord; they have better ways of checking them than I have.'

'Is there anything about him that suggests he is different from the usual run of footman?'

Clarkson thought for a minute and then said, 'There is one thing: He doesn't eat meat. Poultry and fish, but no red meat.'

'Anything else? You're not drinking your ale,' his lordship remarked.

'No, Sir, I do not think it would set a good example to the rest of the staff if I returned to my duties smelling of liquor, however good. But yes, My Lord, there is something a little strange. You would have to understand the way the household is organised to find it so.'

'You'd better tell me, then.'

'Every member of staff gets one whole day off, once a month, alternate Sundays, after church, and a half-day once a week.'

'That seems very generous.'

'Yes, it is, compared to some households, but I find that the better the staff are treated, the better they work, and the more loyal they are. Loyalty is very important in an establishment like this. There is always something for them to look forward to, you see, My Lord.'

'Yes, I understand that, but what has it to do with Henry?'

'Well, he asks me if he can have his half-day on the day before his monthly day off, and during that time, he doesn't sleep in the footmen's quarters.'

'Interesting; what is your opinion?'

'I assume he must have somewhere else to go for those two days, although he is never late for work.'

'I'll bear in mind all that you have said, Clarkson, but there is another matter of great importance. The marchioness must never know the truth of what happened yesterday; to that end, I will tell you the truth. Briefly, Miss Rosalie was abducted, for reasons I have yet to ascertain, and Lord Benedict managed to rescue her, although God knows how, and by the time I arrived on the scene with Mrs Fletcher, the abductors had fled, or been captured. I sent Miss Rosalie and Mrs Fletcher back in my curricle, with Lord Benedict driving, a feat almost beyond his strength. The story now devolves upon you, Clarkson.'

'Yes, My Lord. On their return, Mrs Fletcher, realising that Lord Benedict was in a sad way, called me to help. I was in the hall at the time, My Lord, and the hall porter and I managed to get his lordship into the library, and from thence to his room. I am afraid that the porter, to whom Lord Benedict is unknown, him being fairly new, was under the impression that His Lordship was drunk. I did not disabuse him, but enjoined him to silence, on pain of death.' Clarkson smiled.

'Good, just so long as you say nothing about Miss Rosalie's involvement. As far as you, or anyone else, is concerned, she was just a spectator, you understand?'

'Yes, My Lord, of course.'

'One other thing: please tell Mrs Clarkson to devote all her time to the well-being of Henry. Delegate her housekeeping duties to an upper housemaid if necessary; she may do this on my authority, should her ladyship query it. Now, you'd better return to your duties, Clarkson, alcohol-free, and I thank you most sincerely. I don't know how this household could manage without you.' The marquis smiled and looked at his watch. 'Now it is time for me to visit Lord Benedict, something I have been hoping to do for a very long time.'

The butler cleared his throat. 'My Lord, would you consider it forward if I asked you to convey my good wishes to his lordship?'

Justin slowly shook his head. Looking at his butler, 'You, you couldn't be forward if your life depended on it. Certainly, I'll pass on your good wishes.'

'Thank you, My Lord. It has long been my pleasure to serve this family.'

CHAPTER 26

Lord Benedict St Maure woke up and attempted to move; immediately, every muscle and joint in his body screamed for mercy. He lay still, trying to sort out his confused mind, instead. It seemed like one of the dissected wooden geographical puzzles he had had as a child, lots of different pieces with parts of a map glued onto each one, but he had to put them together, before it all made sense. An image of Rosalie. Being held prisoner? Was she safe now? Going outside, riding? Driving? His mind clouded; he moved. His body objected. What time was it? There was daylight coming through the window. There was a strange sensation in his stomach. It was hunger. He couldn't remember when he last actually wanted to eat. The sergeant came in with a tray; it had a coffee pot and covered dishes on it. Benedict struggled to sit. It was too much; he flopped back down.

The sergeant put the tray down, and went to help. 'Just relax and let me do it, Sir.' He eased Benedict forward and packed pillows at his back.

'I'm sorry, Sergeant, I'm just so damned weak. I don't know why.'

'Well, *I* do, Sir. No one, an' I mean no one, could do what you done yesterday, after staying in one room for over a year, an' not feel the consequences, sir. It'll take a day or two before you feel yourself again.' The sergeant knew he was being optimistic. It could take much longer, but he was cheered by his captain's next remark.

'Bring that tray over here. I feel as though I could eat a horse.'

The sergeant settled the tray, which had folding legs, on Benedict's lap, and removed the covers, revealing scrambled eggs, mixed with small pieces of bacon. He poured the coffee and buttered a slice of toast.

Benedict fell upon it eagerly, but he had barely eaten half when he said, 'I don't think I can eat any more, Sergeant, and yet I felt so hungry.'

But the sergeant, who loved his commanding officer like a son, although he was not more than ten years older, was delighted. It was the first proper meal the captain had eaten for months.

'You done very well, Sir,' he said, giving his lopsided grin.

Without moving Benedict from the couch, the sergeant managed to wash his captain, shave him, and ease him into a maroon-velvet dressing gown with silk lapels. Benedict looked to where he remembered, or thought he remembered, that Rosalie had played her harp, but it was gone.

'Did I dream it, or was Miss Rosalie in here, with her harp?' he asked the sergeant.

'Yes, Captain, she was. When 'is Lordship an' me come in, you was both asleep.' He saw the look of dismay on Benedict's face. 'Oh, no, sir, she was on the floor, like, an' you was on the couch.' He thought it better not to say anything about them holding hands.

'The harp's not here now.'

'No, sir, it was took away when you was asleep.'

Benedict noticed that the sergeant looked as if he wanted to say something; there was much clearing of the throat and perfectly arranged objects on the mantelpiece were being rearranged.

'I think you have something on your mind, Sergeant; what is it? Spit it out.'

'Yes, Sir, I 'ave, sir.' He cleared his throat again. 'It's this. Yesterday, when we was goin' out to get the 'orses, you said, somefing like this: "I may 'ave deserted my men at Waterloo, but I'm damn sure I'll never desert Miss Rosalie." Do you remember, Sir?'

A pained expression crossed Benedict's face. 'Did I really say that?'

'Yes, Sir, you did, an' pardon me if I'm speakin' out of turn, but I wants to know what you meant by it, Captain, Sir.'

'I should've thought that was pretty obvious, Sergeant,' Benedict replied gruffly.

'Not to me it ain't, sir.'

'Then I shall make it plain, Sergeant. At the height of battle, I found myself nearly a mile back from where my battery was. Sitting on the ground, not a mark on me, except for a fearsome headache and ringing in my ears. A horse, not mine, with a flesh wound on its flank that had already dried, was cropping grass at the edge of a sort of wood or coppice. I could hear that the battle was still raging, and there was a large crater, about twenty or thirty yards to my left. I had no idea exactly where I was, or any recollection of how I got there, still haven't, for that matter.

'I caught the horse,' he continued. 'It wasn't badly wounded, and I rode back towards the guns, but when I eventually found my battery, every man was dead except you, and you had this terrible wound in your head and were unconscious. So I did the only thing I could think of, and took you back to the dressing station. That's the whole dreadful story. I must have deserted my post and all my poor brave gunners. Why else was I so far away? I was a coward.' Benedict buried his face in his hands in despair.

The sergeant listened, amazement growing in every vestige of what was left of his face. 'No, Captain, Sir, that ain't what 'appened at all. You never deserted nothin'. You couldn't, sir; it's not in you to do a thing like that. Nobody's less cowardly 'an you, sir, on my life.'

'But I saw it, Sergeant. Bodies everywhere, guns off their limbers, wheels broken, not a man alive except you, lying in the mud. I still see it, in nightmares, and sometimes in the day, I'm suddenly there again in the midst of it, and I know I couldn't have been there with them.'

'Well, sir, some of that *is* true, I can't say otherwise, but not all of it, nor at least, the reason for it.'

'How do you mean? Please, Sergeant, explain, I beg you.'

'We was almost out of ammunition, an' only one gun left firing, when a staff officer rides up an' speaks to you, Sir, an' when 'e left, you tells us that we was to be redeployed at another battery, some five hundred yards along the line; they had ammo, but not enough gunners. We'd lost a lot of men too, but there was about eight of us left to send. You was to go first, 'aving an 'orse, like, an' me, being the sergeant, was the last to leave, but one of them Frenchies, on 'orseback, them with the brass plates on their chests, got me. I'm sorry, sir, I don't remember nothin' after that, till I woke up in a house in Waterloo, with 'alf my face missin'.'

Benedict was silent for quite a long time, then he said, 'And that is the absolute truth, Sergeant? You're not just telling me this to make me feel better?'

'As God is my witness, Captain, Lord Benedict, Sir, that is the absolute truth. I'll swear to it on the Holy Bible, Sir.'

'And you didn't know, until now, that I believed I was a deserter?'

'You wasn't, but no, Sir, not until I 'ears what you said before we set off to rescue Miss Rosalie. An' I couldn't rightly understand then, why you said it, Ssir. That's why I wanted to ask you about it.'

'I'm very grateful that you did, Sergeant. I can't tell you what a weight off my mind it is, although it still doesn't explain why I found myself on the ground, not knowing how I got there, like I said, does it?'

'I don't suppose we'll ever know for certain, as you was all alone at the time, but my guess would be that the 'ole you said was near you was made by a shell exploding, or one of Mr Whinyates' rockets, gone the wrong way, as they sometimes did, an' it knocked you off your 'orse, an' the blast did something to your 'ead, sir. An' you forgot what you was meant to be going, an' don't remember nothing about the order to move your gunners, even now.'

Benedict gave a sigh. 'I expect that's as good an explanation as any, Sergeant.'

'If I were you, Sir, I wouldn't bother my head about that, only be sure you was no deserter.'

'Perhaps you're right.' He leant back against the cushions. 'What time is it?'

'Eleven o'clock, Sir.'

'Ask Lord Coverdale to come and see me in about an hour.' Benedict closed his eyes.

'Very well, Sir, now you have a little rest.'

Justin entered the room quietly and saw his brother stretched out on the couch. It was not without some trepidation. His fear was that Benedict could have slipped back into whatever dark place he had been inhabiting for the last year, despite the sergeant's assurance that it was not so.

Benedict opened his eyes and smiled.

Justin sighed with relief. 'I don't suppose it's much use asking how you are feeling. The sergeant said you could hardly move.'

'The sergeant exaggerates; look.' He raised his arms and groaned.

'Really?'

'It's those damned horses of yours; pull like the devil.'

Ignoring this supremely unfair remark, Justin came forward, knelt by the couch, and took his brother's hands in both of his. 'Oh, Ben, you can't imagine how much I've longed for this moment. I would hug you if I didn't know how much it would hurt.'

'Consider me hugged, brother.'

Justin stood up, then seated himself in the armchair. 'Do you want to talk?'

'What about?'

'Anything. What's going on in the world, what's going on in this house, what's going on with you?'

'Yes, lots of those things, but first, is my guardian angel, Miss Rosalie, all right? And what about the footman who was shot; is he in any danger?'

'I received a message from Mrs Fletcher; Rosalie's tired but in good spirits. I saw the footman earlier; his name is Henry, and I'm afraid he's not too good. The ball has damaged his arm very badly, and the doctors are very concerned.'

'I definitely want to know more about Mrs Fletcher and the Abbots, but first, I think I owe you an explanation of some sort, not that I can give a very clear one, because my mind has been troubled for so long,' Benedict replied.

'I'm always ready to listen, Ben, you know that.'

'You always were, Justin, ever since I was a boy.

'Go ahead, little brother.'

'Until today, this very morning, in fact, I always thought I'd deserted my battery at Waterloo.'

This statement so shocked Justin that he burst out, 'You couldn't. Ben, it's not in you.'

Benedict gave him a look. 'If you're going to interrupt after every sentence, I won't say another word.'

'Sorry.'

'This morning, the sergeant put me right about a number of things, especially the reason I was not with the battery when he was wounded. I won't go into that now, but the consequence was, something, probably an exploding shell, caused me to lose all memory of the events leading up to it. In fact, I still have no recollection of it.'

'But surely you could've asked someone; the sergeant, he could've told you.'

Benedict smiled wryly. 'He just has.'

'I mean before, at the time.'

'Have you seen the sergeant?'

'Yes, of course, often. He was my only contact with you.'

'Well, then, how long do you think it was before he was able to speak at all, never mind give long explanations about anything?'

'I'm sorry, I wasn't thinking—'

'And besides, it wasn't until several months after the war that I found him again, and he came to work for me, and subsequently look after me so tirelessly. Perhaps I should have talked to him, or to you, but I couldn't. I just couldn't. It was all too appallingly shameful.'

'Ben, you could always talk to me; you know that.'

'But this was different, Justin. You were not a military man; you couldn't begin to imagine how I felt. Gunners are different from the infantry. A battery is a small group; the officers know every one of the men by name and usually quite a lot about their families too. They get close …' Benedict lost himself for a moment. 'Bombardier Williams, gunner Harris, boy soldier Jenks, and the others … all dead, and I thought I had deserted them. The guilt was unspeakable, and every day, it just seemed to get worse. I couldn't go back to Woolwich, couldn't look my fellow officers in the face, and then … I don't know. I can only suppose it got all too much, and one day, I just fell into a pit of despair I couldn't climb out of until … until Rosalie.' Both men were silent, and then Benedict said, 'That's it, really. I believe I've left that dark place for good now, but I'll never forget the scenes of carnage, or the loss and the waste that war creates.'

Justin's experience of being with Henry while Dr Pargeter had attended to just one wound had made him sick to his stomach. He couldn't imagine the horrors that his brother had seen on the battlefield. 'It creates heroes, too.'

'Don't look at me, Justin.'

'No, I was thinking more of the sergeant. His devotion to you goes beyond the heroic, don't you think?' And so does Mrs Fletcher's; it was a difficult choice for her to allow Rosalie to play for you every day, alone, you know, and Rosalie herself, of course. She was extremely brave, especially when she was being held prisoner.'

'Yes, she was.' Benedict smiled. 'Harpists have very strong fingers, you know. Now, Justin, tell me about Mrs Fletcher.'

'You've seen what she looks like.'

Benedict observed a certain look in his brother's eyes. 'Yes, very beautiful...'

Justin ignored this. 'She is the widow of a clergyman, and the guardian of Rosalie and Sir Piers Abbot. I believe her to be a very clever woman.'

'I think you believe her to be a lot more than that.' Benedict saw Justin's expression and added, 'I'll say no more on that head, but you are right; without Rosalie and her music, who knows? The pit might have closed over me forever. She is all right, isn't she?' Benedict asked again. 'She played her harp for me last night, you know.'

'Yes, I know; she insisted, despite Mrs Fletcher's misgivings and her own fatigue. Yes, she is fine. She was just worried because you became so unresponsive and was afraid you might relapse, so she demanded that her harp be brought up here. I think she cares very deeply about you, Ben. How do you feel about her?'

'We connect through the music in our souls, I think. I have never known anyone else who understands how I feel about music like Rosalie does. Nor, I believe, has she.' Benedict then asked, 'Why was she abducted?'

'Probably something to do with white women being taken to the East as slaves. After you had gone, I went to the docks with the Bow Street men, and we found others hidden away in a ship.' Justin knew this was not the only possible explanation, but it was the only one he was prepared to give. This was not the time to burden his brother with other worries.

Any further discussion was interrupted by the sergeant coming in with a tray, this time with a light luncheon, which, he said had been specially prepared for Lord Benedict by the chef.

'I had better go and have mine, Ben, or Mother will be cross if I'm late. By the way, do you want to see her?'

'Not yet, Justin. She might not be able to resist hugging me.' They both laughed. The sergeant nearly dropped the tray. His captain's laugh was something he had not heard for a very long time.

CHAPTER 27

J ustindecided it was time he visited Brighton, and showed his face
at one of the Prince Regent's interminable parties, but this time,
he definitely had other business to attend to as well. The drive, in
a post-chaise, gave him plenty of time to think. He could contemplate
the political and economic state of the country, he could consider the
improving condition of his brother, or he could review the dramatic events
of the past week, but in fact, all his thoughts kept slipping back to his
feelings for Amanda Fletcher. She was beautiful; she was intelligent; she
could make him laugh, and, he thought, she could probably make him cry,
but above all, he wanted her, all of her: her beauty, her mind, her body, her
spirit, her courage, and he couldn't have any of it. It was driving him to
distraction. He hadn't given Honoria Prideau a single thought.

An invitation to one of the Prince Regent's overheated, overlong
gatherings, at his architectural monstrosity, was not long in coming, once
it was known that Coverdale was in Brighton. He duly presented himself at
the Pavilion, exchanged pleasantries with the Regent, and sought out more
congenial company. It wasn't long before he spotted Colonel Fortesque
and drifted towards him, managing to subtly detach him from his party.

'Playing soldiers-by-the-sea, Fortesque?'

'Yes,' the Colonel smiled, 'our master likes to see us marching up and
down, and actually, it makes a nice change from Horse Guards, at this time
of year. Knowing you, Coverdale, I don't suppose you struggled through
this crowd just to say good evening. What do you want?'

'That's the trouble with friends; they always jump to the right conclusions. I want to know if you have come across a bit of French nobility, a Count and Countess de Vailleux, to be precise?'

The colonel looked at the marquis quizzically. 'I haven't been introduced, but I can point them out to you; they have become quite favourites here in Brighton. Noble French émigrés, father went to the guillotine; you know the sort of thing I mean.'

'Yes, indeed, but I want an introduction.'

'I don't suppose you'll tell me why, if I ask.' The colonel laughed.

'You suppose correctly, Fortesque.'

'I will do my best on your behalf. Does it have to be here and now?'

'If possible.'

They parted, but it wasn't long before Fortesque returned with another couple and introduced them. 'The Honourable Horace Dampier and Mrs Dampier. They were just telling me how much they had enjoyed a visit to Coverdale Hall on one of its Open Days, so of course I offered to introduce them to its owner.' The colonel went on to say, 'Mr and Mrs Dampier have lodgings in the same house as the de Vailleuxs.'

Justin's initial surprise at the introductions was immediately understood, and after some flattering conversation about his house, he expressed a wish to meet the French couple he had heard so much about, but had not had the pleasure of being introduced to, in London. The Dampiers offered at once to do the honours, delighted to claim such an important peer of the realm as a new acquaintance.

The French couple were somewhat of a surprise to Justin. He had expected a dashing aristocrat in the high romantic mould, but instead, de Vailleux was barely above medium height, dressed in sober black, and wore his grey hair long enough to be tied back in an old-fashioned queue. His looks were undistinguished, except for bright, intelligent brown eyes, which not even gold-rimmed spectacles could hide. His countess was as tall as, if not taller than, her husband. Justin knew her to be in her late forties; her abundant hair, which now was snowy white, he guessed had once been auburn, like Amanda's. Her gown was of the finest quality, but not in the height of fashion. She was clearly nervous, making much play with her fan.

Once the introductions were completed, the marquis turned and addressed her directly. 'I hope you and your husband are enjoying your stay in Brighton. It must be quite different from America, where I understand you have been living for some years.'

'Oh, yes, Lord Coverdale, very different. It has been more than twenty years since I was last in this country.'

'You must have found much to have changed since then, Countess.'

'That is true, Your Lordship.'

'For one thing, this place wasn't here, or at least not as you see it now,' Justin continued, waving his hand to indicate the building. 'In fact, Brighton may still have been not much more than a little fishing village, called Brighthelmstone. The fashionable seaside town was Weymouth. His Majesty always favoured it; you know.'

The countess fluttered her fan. 'Really, is that so? She said weakly.

The marquis was determined to speak to Amanda's mother alone, but the Prince Regent's reception was not the place for such a conversation. He racked his brains for something personal enough to make her come and see him, then had an inspiration. 'I mentioned Weymouth, Countess, because I have seen a miniature by a well-known limner, a Mrs Kendal, who worked mainly in Bath and later retired to Weymouth. There is something about you, Countess, that reminds me of that portrait.' This was an outright lie. Justin had never seen the miniature, only knew of it because Dr Pargeter had told him of its existence. But it did the trick.

The countess began fanning herself rapidly, and her husband, who had been watching the conversation between the marquis and his wife, came forward.

'My dear, I fear you are being overcome by the heat.' He addressed the marquis. 'I'm sure Your Lordship will excuse us; my wife needs some air.'

'By all means, Count, there is a smaller room through there, with some chairs and hopefully an open window.' He smiled and added, 'But before you go, let me give you my card.' Matching the word to the action, he slid a card from an engraved gold case and handed it to the Count. 'Please do not hesitate to call. I would be delighted to hear more about your life in America. I shall be in Brighton for the rest of the week.'

Justin's little subterfuge worked, and two days later, just as he was finishing breakfast, his manservant brought him a card. 'My Lord, the Count and Countess de Vailleux are downstairs and are awaiting his lordship's pleasure.'

'Show them to the front parlour, and bring fresh coffee.' As he entered, he saw his two visitors standing close together and looking very nervous, as they bowed and curtsied.

'Please, Countess, Count, please be seated.'

'Your servant, Lord Coverdale. I believe we know the reason why you've asked us to call.' The Count's English was excellent, tinged with a pleasing French accent.

'I'm sure you do, and I had no wish to embarrass you by mentioning it at the Prince Regent's reception. Would you care for a coffee, Countess, or something stronger, Count?'

'No, I thank you, My Lord. May we come to the point?'

'By all means,' replied Justin, mentally noting how like her mother Amanda was. 'To save beating about the bush, I will tell you that I know, Countess, that you are Mrs Fletcher's mother, and I am also aware that she does not know it, also that she believes you to have died when she was about three years old. Is that not so?'

'Yes, all quite true, My Lord,' said the countess immediately, 'and very unfortunate. It is not how I would have wished it to be, but it is what my late husband, William Kendal, told her, and I respect his right to have done so. Now I very much want to meet her again, and we know she is currently staying with your mother, the Marchioness of Coverdale, and that her married name is Fletcher.'

'Yes, along with her two wards, a brother and sister, and before we go on, I would like to say that none of this is any of my business. I desired you to come here, so I could assure you that I would never say anything to Mrs Fletcher without your permission. It is your secret, not mine.'

After he said this, Justin could sense an almost palpable relaxation in the atmosphere and chose the moment to re-offer coffee, which was accepted.

The Count spoke out for the first time. 'How did you find out about us and Amanda?'

'A Dr Pargeter recognised your wife and told me. I think he is the right person to tell Amanda that her mother is, in fact, still alive.'

'Ah, yes, Dr Pargeter; he was a friend of William's, and we kept in touch for a little while after I left. He wrote that Amanda had been told that I had died.'

'He believes that to have been a mistake,' the marquis added, and went on, 'Do you want him to be the one to break the news to her?'

The countess made a little gesture with her hand, and there was a pleading note in her voice. 'Could you not do it, Marquis? I know you will be discreet and, I hope, kind. You would not have chosen to meet us in this way, if it were not so.' She reached for her husband's hand. 'Etienne and I would both prefer it, wouldn't we, *ma cher*?'

Husband and wife smiled into each other's eyes with such intensity that Justin could see they still loved each other, even after twenty-four years.

'If that is what you really want, I shall need more information. Imagine how your daughter is going to feel when I tell her, and the questions she will ask. I will have to have answers.'

'Yes, of course, we will tell you everything you want to know, but how much do you know already, My Lord?' the Count asked.

'I know from Dr Pargeter that the countess, as a young girl, eloped to Gretna Green, to escape what would have been an appalling marriage to a known degenerate, in return for money. I know that you, Countess, are the daughter of a viscount. I know that William Kendal became a schoolmaster, and that you left him, and your daughter, to flee with the Count.'

'Said like that, it does sound terrible,' said the countess, 'but it is true, all of it. I cannot make excuses, but I can try to make you understand.' She paused.

'Please go on; I'm listening.'

'I didn't love William Kendal. I'm not ashamed to say so, but he was my only way out. I was pretty and high-spirited in those days, and I unashamedly seduced him. We were not very compatible. He was an intellectual, a scholar. I am more instinctive, more imaginative perhaps, but he was a kind man, and we would have stayed together, but for one thing. I fell in love, *c'est tout*. Really, truly, in love.' She gripped her husband's hand and looked at the marquis.

'Yes.' He smiled. 'I think I can believe that. So where did you two meet?'

De Vailleux took up the story. 'I was a French émigré, an escapee from the revolution. Our chateau, it was burned, but my father managed to find

159

a way to get me to England. It took many days; I didn't know exactly how many, as it was either dark, or I was blindfolded. Eventually, I was given papers, saying I was a Belgian apprentice shoemaker.' The Count smiled. 'It was a good thing nobody asked me to make a pair of shoes. Eventually, I was put on a boat and arrived in Weymouth. Later, I learned that my father had been sent to the guillotine, and my mother died soon after.'

'I'm sorry to hear that; they were terrible times. But I am curious. Why Weymouth?'

'At the time, I didn't know, but I have since learned that if the French didn't know where the escaped émigrés were, if they were not seen in London, they kept looking for them; it kept them busy.'

'Do you know who arranged your escape, Count?'

'No, not even to this day, but there was always a name in connection with escapes, but it too, was probably just a ruse: *"Le Chat Noir."'*

Justin controlled an expression of surprise. 'Do go on, monsieur.'

'William Kendal's mother took me in. I did odd jobs for her and for neighbours. I was eventually meant to go to London to join other émigrés, but I had not enough money for the journey. Then Georgina came to stay with her mother-in-law, who had fallen ill, and we fell in love, *c'est tout.'* The Count reiterated his wife's statement.

Justin couldn't help turning to the countess. 'But you left your child?'

The countess's eyes glistened. 'Yes, it was the hardest thing I ever did, but what else could I do? Under English law, any child of a marriage belongs to the husband; a wife who deserts has no rights, and we had no money. We boarded a ship for Liverpool, working our passage, and the same to the Americas.'

'How did you make a living there, de Vailleux?'

'At first, I found various odd jobs, and then I discovered that Americans like the French, and French goods, so I was able to borrow some money and start an import business.'

'And you were very successful, I understand,' said the marquis.

'Yes, but following Napoleon's exile, we wanted to come back to Europe, especially England, so I sold the major interest in my business to my partner, *et voici, ici nous sommes,'* he smiled, 'and that is really the whole story, Milor.'

Justin addressed the countess. 'So, Ma'am, what do you want to do now?'

'I long to see and talk to my daughter, but I am afraid to cause an upset in her life and the lives of those she cares for. Nor do I want to drag up old scandals. People, especially in the so-called polite society, can be so cruel, you know.'

The marquis nodded. 'But I must ask you this. I know it is a personal question, but I believe a very important one.'

'Please,' answered the count. 'You may ask anything at all.'

Deciding there was no way to wrap it up in fancy language, Justin came straight to the point: 'Are you and the countess legally married?'

'Yes,' said de Vailleux.

'We are now,' his wife added, smiling at her husband.

The Count leaned over and held his wife's hand again. 'It is true that although we lived as, and pretended to be, husband and wife, after Kendal died, we had a legal but private ceremony in Philadelphia.'

The news was a great relief to the Justin; since, if they were not married, and it got out, it would cause a very damaging scandal. With a sudden realisation that hit him with almost physical force, he knew that he wanted to protect Amanda from anything and everything that could possibly harm her. He loved her.

It took a moment to pull himself together and ask, 'How did you find out about Kendal?'

'My wife was desperate to know how Amanda was,' replied the Count, 'so she wrote to Dr Pargeter, who told us that Kendal had died and Amanda was married, but he did not tell us to whom.'

The couple sitting there in front of Justin personified the meaning of true love. Throughout many difficult years, they had suffered the kind of hardship he couldn't even imagine, and yet they were still in love, enough to hold hands in front of a stranger. It was what he longed for but could never have.

The long pause, and perhaps the look on his face, made the count ask, 'Are you satisfied with what I have told you, Milor?'

Realising that his mind had been momentarily elsewhere, he immediately replied, 'Yes, that is very good. Do you have children?'

The Countess answered, 'Yes, My Lord; we have a son. He is studying to enter college, so he has stayed in America, for the time being.'

Now that several things had been made clear to him, Justin decided on a course of action. 'Count and Countess, I believe it would be best if you met Mrs Fletcher away from the prying eyes of society. Therefore, I suggest that you come to Coverdale Hall. My entire family will be moving there shortly, and I shall be joining them not long after. I shall be staying in the Dower House and will invite you to join me there. If you approve of that arrangement, I believe that will give us all time to prepare for what may be a very upsetting revelation for Mrs Fletcher, but I hope, in the long run, a happy one, for her.'

The de Veilleux's turned to look at each other with smiles of relief. 'You are most kind, My Lord; it is an excellent plan. We cannot thank you enough for your understanding.'

When they had gone, Justin sat down and buried his face in his hands. He had every hope for a successful outcome for Amanda and her mother, but no such hope for himself. How much longer could he put off tying himself for life, to Honoria Prideau

CHAPTER 28

Amanda felt that the household's move to the country was rather like a swan paddling in the river. On the surface, everything seemed serene. Meals appeared on time, bedding was changed, furniture was polished, floors swept, but underneath, there was a definite feeling of increased activity. Strange thumps and bumps were heard as boxes and trunks were heaved down from attics or brought up from basements. She presumed that Coverdale Hall was fully equipped for every eventuality, but she had learned enough about the marchioness to know that her demands, though softly given, were paramount.

Two events, one delightful, the other not so, occurred in the next few days. Lord Benedict came down to dinner. It was an evening in which no guests were present, which is probably why he chose to do so, thought Amanda.

He entered the small salon, just prior to dinner being announced. 'Good evening, Mother. I hope I find you well.'

'Ah, Benedict, my dear, come and give your mother a kiss. It is such a long time since you have graced us with your presence. Are you feeling better?'

Dutifully, he approached her chair and kissed the proffered cheek. The marchioness looked him up and down. 'You're looking rather thin, Benedict. Have you not been eating properly?'

Looking at the small gathering, Amanda saw Rosalie's eyes shining and Piers looking surprised, but also caught a fleeting expression in the

Marchioness's pale blueeyes that spoke of emotion, despite her casual words.

'Benedict, I do not think you have met my guests. Mrs Fletcher, who is the guardian of Sir Piers Abbot, and his sister, who is my very dear goddaughter, Rosalie.'

Keeping a straight face, Benedict bowed. 'Your servant, Sir Piers, delighted to make your acquaintance, Mrs Fletcher. Miss Rosalie, I am told you play the harp. Is that not so, Miss Rosalie?'

'A little, Your Lordship.' Rosalie could barely keep up the pretence.

'Then you must let me hear you play. I am very fond of music, you know.'

Rosalie replied, 'Yes, Sir,' but kept her head down for most of the meal. Benedict excused himself from after-dinner tea.

The following day, Justin arrived back from his trip to Brighton and was told that Mrs Fletcher was to be found in the Clarkson's quarters. He was surprised to find her at Henry's bedside, bathing his forehead with cool water, slightly perfumed with lavender.

'This is not what I expect a guest in this house to be doing, Mrs Fletcher.'

'No, Your Lordship, you expect poor Mrs Clarkson to be on duty twenty-four hours a day, nursing a very sick and feverish patient, as well as being in command of the move of almost the entire household, and half the furniture, to the country,' she retorted tartly.

Anything Justin might have replied was forestalled by a groan, followed by a string of disjointed words in a foreign language.

'Is he very bad? Will he recover?'

'Dr Pargeter thinks the fever is at a turning point, and he has hopes that it will not turn for the worse, although he is pleased with the progress of Henry's wound, but you had better speak to him yourself; he is at the moment assessing Piers, to see if he is fit to ride once we are at Coverdale Hall.'

'I'm sorry, I was less than thoughtful just now. Do you know what language that is, Mrs Fletcher?'

'I have no idea, Sir,' she replied, renewing the cloth from a bowl nearby. 'He has just had his wound redressed and is in considerable pain. It is no surprise that he cries out in any language, is it?'

Justin was momentarily diverted by the sight of the delightful curve of Amanda's neck, as she bent over her patient. He cleared his throat.

'I am really very grateful for your concern, and now I have another request: I know your botanical drawings are excellent. How are you with faces?'

'Not as well as my paternal grandmother, but I can capture a likeness.'

'Good; would you draw a small portrait of Henry and give it to Clarkson? He will probably ask for it later today. Nothing more than a pencil sketch, but something that would serve to identify him.'

'I will certainly try, sir. When do you want it?'

The marquis pulled out his watch. 'Could you manage to do it by noon, Mrs Fletcher? I have an errand for Clarkson this afternoon.'

'That will not be a problem. Have you seen your mother this morning, Marquis?'

'Not yet, I came straight here.'

'Well, when you do, I think you're going to be in for a pleasant surprise. I will say no more on that head, but if you also want to see Dr Pargeter, you will find him in Piers' apartment.'

'Is there anything I can do for you?'

'If you could send someone to bring me pencil and paper, I will commence the sketch immediately. I cannot leave here until Mrs Clarkson returns.'

'No, of course not. You are doing noble work, Mrs Fletcher.'

'No, I am not. I owe this man more than words can say. Without his courage, not only in trying to save Rosalie, but for making a superhuman effort to get back here to tell us what had happened, I dread to think of the outcome, if he had not.'

'You are right, of course, but now I will take my leave.' Justin bowed, giving one last look at the woman he now knew he loved with all his heart, before quietly closing the door.

He found Dr Pargeter about to leave Piers' room, with that gentleman in a high state of excitement.

'Oh, Coverdale,' he exclaimed, with a huge grin, 'you'll never guess what ...'

'Good news, I imagine.'

'Dr Pargeter says I may ride again, once we get to Coverdale Hall.'

'But for no more than fifteen minutes a day, to begin with, young man, and then only gradually increased,' Dr Pargeter put in sternly, but with a smile on his face.

'Will you excuse me, sir? I must tell Amanda and Rosalie the good news.'

'Yes, run along. Mrs Fletcher is with Henry, Piers, so if you go there, keep your voice down and your high spirits at bay; he is still very ill.'

'He is, indeed, Marquis,' added Dr Pargeter, 'but I have reason to hope, tomorrow will be a crucial day.'

'What of his arm? Will it recover completely?'

'I fear not. I am optimistic of some useful movement, but it is early days.'

'And young Piers, you are pleased with his progress, too, Doctor?'

'Yes, sir, his strength has improved much faster than I expected, no doubt due to the exercise that fencing and dancing have created. I believe I have you to thank for that.'

'It was nothing, but what of the long term?'

'He will always have a problem, but how much that affects him in the future is difficult to say, but as with your footman, time will tell.'

'On another subject, I have to tell you that I have just come back from Brighton, where I made myself known to Mrs Fletcher's mother and her husband.'

'Did you say anything to them?'

'They came to me with the whole story, very dramatic, I must say. The countess is very keen to be reunited with her daughter. I have invited them to the Dower House at Coverdale Hall, where I shall be staying in about three weeks' time. I should very much like you to be there too, Doctor; would you be agreeable?'

'That's very kind; a visit to the country is always agreeable.'

'When will Henry be able to travel?'

'If he survives, that is. I cannot say at the moment, but I will visit again at the end of this week and let you know.'

'Thank you for all your attention, Pargeter.' The marquis held out his hand. 'Now I must go and pay my respects to my mother.'

Perhaps the greatest surprise of the day greeted his eyes, as he entered the small salon. The marchioness was seated in her usual chair, but ensconced in another close by was Benedict, and on a small stool between them, Rosalie was reading aloud. Justin made a quick bow to his mother, but went straight over to his brother, who made an effort to rise, but Justin pressed him on the shoulder.

'Well, brother, how are you enjoying *Sense and Sensibility*? According to our mother, the reader is greatly to be admired, too.' He smiled down at Rosalie.

'The book is better than I expected, Justin, but in my opinion, the reader excels both Miss Austen's heroines.

'I'm very glad you think that is so, Ben.' Justin understood the subtle meaning of his brother's woods.

In a thoughtless moment, Rosalie blurted out: 'Do you know how Hen., I mean the footman who was wounded, goes on? 'I have been to see … I mean, Amanda has told me … Mrs Clarkson has said …' Rosalie, having helped Amanda in the sickroom, suddenly realised that her godmother was not fully aware of all that had happened and stuttered to a halt.

Realising Rosalie's confusion, Justin replied. 'He is being well looked after,' and quickly changed the subject. 'I shall need the services of Clarkson this afternoon, Mama.'

'But I want to discuss which silver service to take to the hall and whether my small bureau should go with the wagoner or with the coach; you will have to wait.'

'No, Mother, *that* will have to wait. May I remind you that the Clerksons and Antoine, my chef, are in my employ.' Justin spoke gently but firmly. 'Good to see you, Ben. Carry on reading, Miss Rosalie, before your listeners lose the plot.' He could be heard saying, 'Please ask Mr Clarkson to join me in the library,' to a passing footman, as he left.

As soon as Clarkson entered, the marquis came straight to the point: 'Does Henry have any personal belongings here, other than a change of clothes?'

'I couldn't say, M'lord. but every servant has a cupboard by his bed, in which to keep such things.'

'Can you access Henry's cupboard?'

167

'Yes, M'lord., but it is not something I am accustomed to doing.'

'No, of course not, but in this case, I wish you to do it. Believe me, it is in Henry's best interest. Go now, and bring me everything you find there, please, Clarkson. I will await your return.'

Fifteen minutes passed before Clarkson returned, carrying some clothes and a wooden box. He put it on the table in front of his lordship

'I have placed in this box all that was in his cupboard, M'lord.' He put a suit of clothes, two shirts, and a pair of shoes on a convenient chair. 'I'm afraid his livery was too badly stained and damaged, so it has been disposed of.'

Justin opened up the box. It contained Henry's personal grooming and cleaning items, a wig that was not part of his livery, and another pair of shoes; at the bottom was a smaller box decorated in an oriental style. There was no immediate sign of any way to open it.

He examined the decoration and said, 'I think this is a Chinese puzzle box, Clarkson. Do you remember my father having one?'

'Yes, M'lord., but its exact whereabouts today, I couldn't rightly say.'

'No matter; perhaps this works in the same way. It will open if you press something in the right way. However, there is no immediate necessity to do so now.'

'Is that everything, My Lord?'

'I have an errand for you, but I cannot tell you what it is, until I find a key. I hope it is not in here.' He gave the box a good shake, but there was no rattle of anything metallic. 'Let us examine the suit; it may contain what I am hoping for. Look in all the pockets, Clarkson.'

The butler made a methodical search of all the available pockets but only found a handkerchief, a small ivory notebook, and a pencil. 'I always encourage the staff to carry a means of writing orders down, in case their memory fails them, M'lord.'

'Very sensible, Clarkson, but these are not what I wanted. Where else can we look?'

'How about the shoes, sir?'

'An excellent suggestion. You take one, and give me the other.'

Simultaneously, they each drew out a rolled-up pair of white, cotton stockings, but as Clarkson tipped his shoe up, a key fell to the floor.

'Ah!' exclaimed the marquis. 'I believe you have found what we're looking for.' He held out his hand for the key. It appeared to be a room key, with a metal tag attached, on which was punched a number and the name of a street. He handed it back.

'Now, this is what I want you to do.' Justin went on to explain in detail exactly what he required, concluding, 'But first, you must go to Mrs Fletcher and obtain from her a likeness of Henry, which she has been executing for me. You will then have something to show for identification. I shall be at home; bring everything straight there. I shall take this.' He held up the Chinese box. 'Any questions?'

'No, M'lord."

'Better take this.' He handed Clarkson a purse of coins. 'Use hackney cabs; grease palms, if necessary.' He smiled. 'Please see that all these things, except Henry's personal items, are packed in a suitable container and sent to Mount Street, and of course everything that we have said and done here is just between ourselves.'

The butler gave his master an understanding look. 'Just like old times, M'lord. Will that be all?'

Clarkson had proved to be the perfect conveyor of covert messages when Justin ran a spy-ring on the Continent for the last five years of the war with Napoleon. This work was highly secret, sometimes dangerous personally, and always so for his agents, but it had been hugely successful in helping to defeat the enemy. Justin's present dilemma was not only secretive but personal, in a way that his previous work had rarely been.

'Yes, I forgot to ask you, what is Henry's surname?'

'Evans, M'lord.' The butler closed the door quietly.

Justin was beginning to believed that he would return with sufficient evidence that the quasi-footman, calling himself Henry Evans, was, in all probability, the son, legitimate or otherwise, of the late Sir Percy Abbot, and doubtless there was proof of this somewhere, possibly in the Chinese box. He was also in no doubt that he had come all the way from India to find the diamond, which he clearly believed did not belong to the Abbots. Did he have proof of that too? Only Henry could answer these questions, and at the present, he was far too ill to do anything of the sort. Justin collected his coat, hat, and gloves from a waiting footman and went out to his club.

He returned to Mount Street several hours later in a better frame of mind. It was clear to him that nothing could, or should, be said or done, until Henry was fit enough to be questioned, and that could only take place once everyone concerned was settled at Coverdale Hall.

CHAPTER 29

Coverdale Hall was situated in the Essex countryside, approximately fifty miles from London, and close to the town of Saffron Walden. The move took several days, with wagons carrying trunks, boxes, and certain items of furniture, followed by a coach loaded with servants. Finally, the marchioness's large travelling coach, with four horses, two coachmen, one with a blunderbuss at the ready, and two grooms, transported herself, Amanda, Rosalie, and their maids. The journey was easily accomplished in one day, with two changes of horses. The entourage stopped for a leisurely luncheon at Bishop's Stortford. Piers and Benedict had persuaded a somewhat reluctant Amanda and us tin, that they could drive themselves to Coverdale.

Amanda was very keen to see the house Lord Coverdale had described, when she had been looking at a painting of it in the grand saloon, but he had explained that it was an early one, and the house and grounds had been altered since. A coach gave little opportunity to see forwards through the narrow window, but a curving drive gave tantalising glimpses through trees. It seemed an age since passing through the impressive wrought-iron gates with coronets picked out in gold and flanked with stone pillars, bearing sculptures of rearing horses, but at last the edifice came into full view, and it was certainly a magnificent one. Built of dark red brick, between 1605 and 1609, it had originally been a four-square Jacobean mansion, with towers and domes at each corner. Later in the century, stone facings had been added to the facade, and later still, a large porte-cochère, in the neoclassical manner. The house stood three stories high, plus an attic with dormer windows; Amanda guessed it was nearly three hundred feet wide. It was certainly the largest private dwelling she had ever seem.

Inside, it was very much in contrast to Berkeley Square. The entrance hall, though roomy, was low-ceilinged and panelled in dark oak; on the right, a large, arched opening led into the Great Hall, which occupied the full height of two stories. A double row of windows faced the front, and a fireplace, large enough to stable a small horse, was situated on the opposite side, surrounded by ornate carving, and topped by a coat of arms.

The party was greeted by the ubiquitous Clarkson, who announced that tea had been laid out in the blue drawing room. Amanda was sure she'd seen him only that morning in London. A housekeeper, new to Amanda, and various other servants guided the parties to their respective apartments.

As soon as they reached their new rooms, Rosalie rushed over to the window. 'Look, Amanda, trees and grass, and there's a lake over there.' She gestured towards a sheet of water in the distance, glowing in the evening sun. 'I do like the countryside.'

'You were just as excited about coming to town, my dear,' Amanda pointed out, with a smile. She joined Rosalie at the window and was surprised to see that the fourth side of the building was missing, enabling the view Rosalie was rhapsodising about.

'Yes, I know, but this is more like home.' Rosalie looked round at the room, panelled once more in dark oak.

'So it may be, but it is much larger, and we had better find the blue drawing room, if we are not to keep your Godmama waiting. Jennie and Wilkins will unpack while we are at tea.'

Rosalie was disappointed, but hardly surprised, that only Piers and Lady Coverdale were present, but Piers explained that Benedict was feeling the effects of the long drive and had retired to his rooms.

'He told me he had been ill for a long time,' her brother added, 'and I can certainly sympathise with that.'

'Now, my dear, you must not think that you will be bored while we are here,' the marchioness said. 'We shall be giving dinner parties and small dances for the local people; they really look forward to it. And then, of course, there will be the grand harvest ball at the end of next month. I believe you have expressed a desire to ride while you are here, Rosalie.'

'Yes, Godmama, but I haven't got a riding habit with me. Amanda said it wasn't worth bringing one to London, as I wouldn't be riding there.'

'Quite so, Rosalie, but I am sure one can be found for you. My daughter, Hester, must have left at least one behind.' The marchioness looked Rosalie up and down in a critical manner. 'You are much smaller than Hester. However, we don't keep a sewing maid here for nothing. Mrs Anderson will see to it.' She waved an imperious hand as though the deed was already accomplished, and much to Rosalie's surprise, two days later, it was.

Piers, Rosalie, and Benedict were all assembled in the stable yard, eager with anticipation, but for different reasons. For Piers, to be allowed to ride again was like granting his greatest wish in the world, tinged with the concern that he might not be able to regain his former capability, although he knew that would still be a long way off. Rosalie, who considered riding only as a useful way of getting from A to B, when in the country, was unusually excited at the prospect, purely because Lord Benedict was present. What exactly Benedict was thinking, he kept to himself.

The head groom and two stable lads led out three horses. A rangy black gelding, whose loose lower lip betrayed his age, a small chestnut with white socks, that was a tad over fourteen hands, and a good-looking bay mare.

Benedict immediately went over to the black, smiling. 'Well, old-timer, I never thought I would ride you again.'

The stable lad who was holding him pulled a carrot from his pocket and gave it to Benedict, who patted his old friend and offered him the treat.

Meanwhile, the head groom was talking to Piers. 'I have strict instructions regarding you, Sir. His lordship tells me that you must take things very easy.'

Piers made a grimace; he had hoped that news of his injury might not have reached the Hall.

'So, Sir, we will go into the riding-house for your first ride; I need to see just how things are. Jim, Paddy, mount the lady and M'lord. in the yard, and escort them to the home paddock.' With that, he led the bay, followed by Piers, towards the stone riding-house that formed one side of the stable yard.

Amanda had found a room with a window partly overlooking the stable yard and was watching with interest. She was pleased that Piers' first ride would be away from prying eyes, not so pleased that Rosalie and Benedict were together. She worried about Rosalie; in her mind, there was no doubt that her ward was in love, or at least what she believed was love, but as to Benedict's feelings, she had no idea and just hoped that Rosalie wasn't going to have her heart broken.

She abandoned her watching post as the two riders left the yard. Afterwards, the two men reluctantly admitted that a very short time in the saddle was quite enough after such long absences. Rosalie, as was her wont, had already fallen in love with Socks, her little chestnut gelding, and couldn't wait to ride again, despite her general indifference to the exercise.

Benedict recovered his riding skills more quickly and was soon riding across the extensive grounds of Coverdale Hall. Piers was progressing more slowly; the groom advised an adjustment to his saddle to ease his damaged hip.

They had been there just over a week when Benedict made an announcement at breakfast.

'I am going to ride down to Longacre Farm this morning. Would you care to accompany me, Miss Rosalie?' He caught Amanda's questioning look and added hastily, 'I will ask Hawkins to come with us, of course.'

Amanda smiled at Rosalie's eager expression. 'I think that is an excellent plan,' she replied and could almost feel the relief issuing from the other two. 'What is so special about Longacre Farm, Lord Benedict?'

There was a note of pride in his voice, as he answered, 'At my request, Justin let me set up a place there, where wounded soldiers from Waterloo and other battles, and who are not able to earn a living or are homeless, can stay and be looked after. Those who are able, work the farm to provide food and an income; others do crafts and make things that can be sold at the local markets. There is no necessity for them to make a living, but all who can, take pride in what they are able to do.'

'That sounds like a wonderful scheme.'

'It is, Mrs Fletcher; the only sad thing is that it can only help so few, when there are so many needing it.'

As they rode side by side, with Hawkins, an under-groom, a discreet distance behind, Rosalie wanted to know more about the farm.

'How many residents are there, Benedict? I can't keep calling you "Lord Benedict,"' she said with a mischievous smile, 'especially since I stopped you falling off the curricle, and you must call me, Rosalie.'

Benedict said that it was not etiquette to do so—'

'Oh, fiddlesticks!' exclaimed Rosalie

He knew it was pointless to argue, so he agreed but added, 'only in private. Then continued his explanation of Long Acre. 'When I left, had my breakdown, there were twenty-seven men, but I have been reading the reports and accounts since we came back, and there are now thirty-two. Sadly, several have died. It is usually the ones whose wounds are not visible, injuries that have affected internal organs or damage to the mind.'

'Like yours, Benedict.'

Benedict turned in the saddle. 'What do you mean?'

'Something happened to you, something so overwhelming that you were unable to continue with your normal life, so you withdrew from it. The sergeant told me how it was—'

'He had no right to—'

'Fiddlesticks!' Rosalie used the expression he was becoming accustomed to. 'Of course he had. All he wanted was for you to get better, and he believed I could help. I had to know something about you.'

Benedict smiled and shook his head. 'There's no stopping you, is there?'

'Not when it's necessary to do something. She's not my mother, but Amanda has taught me that if something needs to be done, get on with it.'

'We're nearly there, Rosalie.' Benedict pointed to a cluster of farm buildings, with a well-kept track leading up to it.

They had hardly arrived at the farmhouse, when a plump, youngish woman, carrying a small child on her hip, opened the door, her face wreathed in smiles.

'Oh, sir ... Captain, I'm that glad ye've come. I was sure you would, one day. The men will be so pleased.'

Benedict smiled in return. 'Miss Rosalie, let me introduce Mrs Mary, the rock of this establishment, and little Arthur. How old is he now?'

'Just over two, sir.' The baby, who had a shock of red curls and bright blue eyes, waved a fat hand and said, 'Dada.'

'Please excuse him, My Lord; he calls all men that, just now.'

Rosalie covered any embarrassment. 'I do hope, Mrs Mary, that you will have time to show me round this place. Lord Benedict has been telling me of the good work that is done here.'

'Very pleased to do so, Miss.'

'I would like to have a word with the workshop manager,' Benedict said. 'Do you know where he is, Mary?'

'With the men in the new building; it weren't properly finished when you was last here, Sir.'

Benedict left, and Mary said, 'I need to go to the barn, Miss. It's where the more poorly of our men live, and those who cannot work, but I can find someone to stay with you till I come back. I need to be there for their dinner.'

'Why can't I come with you?'

The woman hesitated and then said, 'Some of them don't look or behave quite as a lady like you is accustomed to.' As she spoke, she was handing the baby over to a young girl. 'Don't let him get into any mischief, now.'

'I will be quite all right, Mrs Mary, I assure you.' Rosalie gathered her riding habit up. 'Now, if you're needed, let's go.'

The barn was large and airy, with lots of light coming through high windows. One end had been converted into about half a dozen curtained-off cubicles, and the other arranged as a sitting and dining area. A meal was in progress. 'We're a bit short-handed today, and some of these men in here need help with feeding, so I had to come; you understand, Miss?'

'Yes, of course I do; will you let me help?'

'That wouldn't be right, Miss, you being with the Captain, an' all.' She unhooked an apron from a peg and tied it round her ample waist.

'Nonsense, I am quite used to it. My brother was flat on his back for six months. Get me another apron.'

'All right, then, Miss, if you insists. You can help Davy,' she pointed, 'in the corner, there; 'is dinner's getting cold.'

As she approached the man looking forlornly at a rapidly cooling plate of stew, Rosalie could see what the problem was: Two empty sleeves told their own story.

'I'm Miss Rosalie, and you must tell me, Davy, exactly how you would like me to serve your dinner,' she said, pulling up a stool. 'My brother was most particular about his.'

Rosalie insisted on helping with the clearing up after the meal was finished. 'Tell me about your husband, Mrs Mary; Lord Benedict says he was killed at Waterloo.'

'Yes, I was told not long after. Arthur was born the next day, two weeks early; the shock, I expect.'

'You must miss him very much.'

'Every day, Miss, every day.' She sighed. 'I just wish ...' Rosalie waited patiently. Mrs Mary wiped her face with her apron. 'I just wish they had found his body, but Lord Benedict said there were lots like that.'

'What was his name, Mary?'

'Barker, Miss, sergeant Jack Barker. But that's all over now. I just wish little Arthur could have known his dad; he was a good man.'

On the way back, Benedict patted his horse and said, 'I think this old gentleman would like a little more strenuous exercise. Are you ready for a canter across that field, avoiding the corn stooks? There's a small jump across a stream, before we get to the trees; it's only about three feet.'

'Let's go.' Rosalie urged her horse into a canter, and they soon left the groom behind.

The jump accomplished without mishap, and the clump of trees reached, Benedict swung out of the saddle and helped Rosalie to dismount.

'I want to know what you thought about the Longacre establishment,' he said, 'and that sort of conversation is always difficult on horseback.'

'And I want to know about Mrs Mary. The men in her care seem so respectful, even fond of her. At least that's the impression I got from the man I gave dinner to, between mouthfuls, that is.'

'You did what?'

'She was short-handed, and Davy's dinner was getting cold; it was the least I could do.'

'Mrs Fletcher will never forgive me, if she finds out. Allowing you to do something like that,' he exclaimed.

'Fiddlesticks; she would do it herself, and you know it. The poor man had lost both his arms, above the elbow.'

'From the little I know about Mrs Fletcher, I would say you are probably right, but for goodness sake, don't say anything to my mother.'

'Doesn't she approve?'

'Oh, yes, she contributes financially and sends fruit down from the hot-houses, but she would consider any personal involvement beyond a lady's obligation.'

'But I still want to know about Mrs Mary, Benedict.'

She is the widow of a ... a gunner.'

Rosalie took immediate notice of Benedict's hesitation but said nothing.

'He was from my battery and killed at Waterloo. She and her husband were together, after we came back from America, for only a few months before Napoleon escaped from Elba, and we had to fight one of the bloodiest God damn battles in history. Sorry, I shouldn't say that in front of a lady.'

'No, perhaps not, but you can say it in front of *me*. Tell me more about Mrs Mary.'

'I needed someone to run the nursing side of Longacre, someone who understood the men there and what they had gone through. When I tracked her down, her son was nearly a year old; she was the ideal person for the job, and it gave her a real purpose in life.'

'I agree with you there, and little Arthur is a favourite too, I understand.'

'Yes, Rosalie; that is your great talent, as well as the music, of course.'

'What is?'

'Your ability to understand people, like the sergeant, Piers, the men at Longacre, my mother, me.' He paused. 'Me in particular. Oh, Rosalie, I don't want to be without you, ever.'

He turned away.

'Look at me, Benedict. You don't have to be without me, and I never want to be without you. Don't you understand that? And I mean forever, too, Benedict.'

He turned and put out a hand. 'Do you mean ...?'

'Of course, stupid.'

'But—'

'There are no "buts." What are you waiting for?'

Benedict didn't lose another second and swept her into his arms.

Hawkins, standing patiently beside his horse on the other side of the brook, turned his back.

CHAPTER 30

Later that evening, there was a wholly unexpected event. Justin arrived, having ridden from London that morning. After a quick change out of dusty riding clothes, and an equally quick greeting to his mother, he enquired of Clarkson where Mrs Fletcher might be found.

'I believe her to be in the parterre garden, M'lord.'

Amanda was sitting with needlework on her lap, but in truth she was more interested in the view vouchsafed by the absence of what had once been a fourth wing of the house; according to Lady Coverdale, it had burnt down in 1700 and was never replaced.

A voice behind her said, 'I agree, Mrs Fletcher, much better like this.'

Startled out of her reverie, she looked up to see the marquis's amber eyes smiling down at her.

'I hope I didn't scare you.'

'Not at all. Do you wish to see me, or to be alone?'

'I have sought you out particularly, as there are some important things I wish to tell you.' Amanda indicated he should be seated. 'I am only here on a fleeting visit, to make some arrangements. Firstly, Dr Pargeter has said, somewhat reluctantly, that Henry will be able to travel by the end of next week. I desire him to stay in the Dower House; he will still need a lot of care and rest. I shall be bringing him myself and staying there too, with my two servants from Mount Street.'

Amanda expressed pleasure that Henry had progressed so far.

'But,' Justin went on, 'I do not want anyone in the house to know who he is, only that I have an invalid guest, who is not well enough to socialise.'

'No one?'

'Well, obviously not quite no one. You, Clarkson of course, and I suppose Rosalie, because she has such an uncanny way of finding things out, and it is better you tell her and swear her to secrecy. But that is all. I have explained to Clarkson that no footman from Berkeley Square is to be allowed near the place.'

'What about your brother and the sergeant?'

'I'll have to think about that.'

'Where is the Dower House?' Amanda asked.

'You can't see it from here, but if you come with me, I can point it out to you.' He offered Amanda his arm, and they strolled to the edge of the parterre. 'If you look far to your left, there is a clump of trees; the house is just behind them.'

'Is it sort of cream-coloured?'

'Yes. It's modern; my father had the old one pulled down and that one built in the 1770s. It's much more convenient than this ancestral pile. I actually prefer it.'

'Why all the secrecy, sir?'

'I can't tell you that at the moment. I'm sorry, Mrs Fletcher, but I believe it to be necessary for now.' Amanda felt the pressure on her arm increase slightly, and before leaving, he said, 'I will see you at dinner.'

His absence seemed to be accompanied by a slight chill in the air, and Amanda shivered as she gathered up her sewing.

With Justin's presence, the dinner table seemed much more lively than of late. Piers was all enthusiastic about his new saddle, and there was definitely a light in Benedict's eyes that Amanda hadn't observed before.

The marchioness was as imperious as ever, announcing, 'Tomorrow, I shall go into Saffron Walden to buy a new bonnet. Rosalie, you will accompany me.'

'Yes, Godmama,' was all she replied.

Amanda was a little surprised; usually any sort of outing was enthusiastically embraced by her ward, but she realised Rosalie had been abnormally quiet during dinner. Not a good sign; it often meant she was hatching up some scheme or hiding something.

There was one particular incident that confirmed her suspicion. Lord Benedict, stretching to reach the salt, caught his sleeve on his wine glass, and some of the liquid slopped over onto the table. Benedict looked at the spreading stain, dark-red on the white cloth, and seemed to freeze. Rosalie immediately began to talk to her godmother about the new book they were about to start, covering the mishap. Lord Benedict gave a shudder and seemed to regain himself. To Amanda, there was no doubt that the look he gave Rosalie was more than one of gratitude.

With the ladies withdrawn, and Piers quickly excusing himself in order to check on his horse, which Hawkins had declared was showing a little heat in her off-fore, Justin and Benedict were left together.

'I need to talk to you, Benedict, so if we can retire from the drawing room as soon as is polite, we will go to my rooms.'

'I have things I want to discuss with you too, big brother.'

The marchioness, keen to be in top form for the next day's outing, retired early, giving the two men the opportunity they wanted.

Seated in Justin's comfortable sitting room, he said, 'You go first, Ben.'

'All right, Ju; it's quite simple. I want to marry Rosalie.'

'Yes,' replied his brother. 'I think I could see that coming.'

'Do you approve?'

'More to the point, does Rosalie approve?'

Benedict grinned. 'I think she must do. It was her idea.'

'Now why doesn't that surprise me? Do you really love her? After all, you haven't known her very long.'

'All my life, Justin. All my life. Who couldn't love a woman who, when I remonstrated about her helping out at Longacre, replied, "Fiddlesticks. Davy's dinner was getting cold. Of course I had to help him; he has no arms, you know." Rosalie's just wonderful, and she loves me. Of course, before I knew the truth about what happened at Waterloo, I couldn't even contemplate marrying Rosalie, or any other woman, for that matter, but now … One day, I hope you will find the right soulmate too.' He noticed Justin's knuckles whiten, as they gripped the arm of his chair. 'You have, haven't you, and it's my guess it isn't Miss Honoria Prideau is it?'

His brother dumbly shook his head.

'Is it Amanda Fletcher?' This time, a silent nod. 'You're not officially engaged to Honoria. You haven't asked her to marry you, have you?' Benedict asked.

'No.' Justin hitched in his chair and poured himself a brandy from the decanter by his side. 'No, Ben, I haven't, but it's the letter, you see.'

'No, I don't see; you'd better explain.'

'Before you had your illness, you remember I had been seen quite often with Honoria, and there was speculation.' Benedict nodded. 'After you collapsed, I don't know; I think my head must have been all over the place. Anyway, I wrote a letter to General Prideau, Honoria's father, asking permission to pay my respects to her. Then he was taken ill, and I never received a reply. Honoria cut short her season to look after him, and now I don't know if she knows about the letter or not, but either way, I feel committed, and honour bound, to fulfil my intention. I just can't bring myself to do it.'

He took a deep draught of his brandy.

'She might turn you down.'

'Slim chance of that; every time we are in company together, she keeps giving me hopeful looks.'

'Do you really dislike her, Justin?'

'No, of course not, but she seems so insipid after …, well, you know.'

'I can guess.'

'The only time I ever saw her really animated was when we were out driving, and she made me stop and reprimand a cabby who was driving with the martingales too short, and the poor horses couldn't get up the hill. She was very angry and made me wait until the cabby had loosened them. I was quite surprised. But no doubt she will soon be back at the Manor, and I will have to go and formally ask for her hand. At least one of us will be making a happy marriage. I congratulate you, Benedict.' He lifted his glass towards his brother. 'Although I have to say, you will need to get Mrs Fletcher's permission; she may say no.'

'If she does, I can wait. Rosalie is nineteen; two years is not such a very long time, although it would probably seem so,' he added rather dolefully.

'I really hope it goes well for you, Ben, but all this is not what I wanted to talk about. The matter concerns Henry.'

He went on to explain to his brother what he had already told Amanda and made him promise not to tell anyone else.

'It is very important; the fewer people who know that Henry is at the Dower House, the better. I shall be leaving early tomorrow, but back here in about ten days. You're in charge; good luck.'

Despite having to make an early start, the Justin found sleep difficult to come by. So many problems were bearing down on him. He still had no viable idea how to deal with the forthcoming meeting between Mrs Fletcher and her mother (or, indeed, if Amanda would even agree to it). He was worried about Benedict and Rosalie. He didn't want either of them to get hurt, but he could see there was great potential for just that, although he had not voiced this fear to Benedict. Most of all, he was concerned about Henry. That he was connected to the Abbots was, he felt, almost certain, but he had been unable to put together the pieces he did know about, in any coherent way. Only Henry could tell the whole story, and Justin hoped that when he did, it wouldn't do too much damage to the family he'd grown so fond of.

Benedict was also sleepless; the euphoria of the discovery of his and Rosalie's mutual love was tempered with fear. Fear that what had caused his collapse could recur. The incident at dinner had shaken him to the core. The sight of the red wine, staining the white cloth, had caused him to relive a field of battle. Not just as a memory, but he was there: the sound of guns, the screaming of men and horses, the smell of gunpowder, and the sight of the dead and wounded. How long it lasted for, he didn't know, but probably only a few seconds. Only his lovely Rosalie seemed to notice. He loved her far too much to put her through a lifetime punctuated by his nightmares and day-horrors. He'd have to tell her that the kiss was just a temporary aberration on his part. The engagement was at an end.

Rosalie had no problem getting to sleep, but she woke early; it was still dark. About Benedict, she was deliriously happy; at last, she had found someone who wanted her. Not for her pretty face, for her presumed fortune, or for an introduction to Piers, but just for herself.

Benedict might look like the epitome of the romantic hero, but she knew about his vulnerabilities, at least the effect they had, and was absolutely certain that even if her presence could do nothing to cure them, she would always be there to support him through them. She loved him in spite of them, and because of them. She knew from the look in his eyes, over the spilt wine incident, that there was mutual understanding.

There was something else on her mind too. She would have liked to get up and play her harp, but it had been placed in the long gallery, and she had no idea how to get there in the dark. It was a very complicated house to find one's way about in. So that problem would have to be solved without the aid of music, but somehow it wasn't, and she drifted off to sleep again.

Amanda's tossing and turning was caused by a problem entirely of her own making. No one had helped her to fall in love with a man who was promised elsewhere; she had managed that entirely on her own. There was no solution, no hope, no future. She decided she needed to pull herself together and engage in something to take her mind off such depressing thoughts, and work was the only answer. She had with her all the requirements to resume her botanical drawings. Essex had as many plants as Somerset, and although she had not been commissioned to draw them, the work would be interesting and require concentration. She would start in the morning.

CHAPTER 31

Breakfast the following day was a dour affair, not least because the marquis seemed to have taken the good weather with him, and everyone woke up to teeming rain. Piers and Benedict quickly drank up their coffee and departed, leaving Rosalie and Amanda to a more leisurely repast.

'I've decided to do some work while I'm here,' Amanda said. 'I meant to start this morning, but the weather seems to have thwarted me. I had been looking forward to exploring the local wildflower population.'

'There are plenty of flowers in the house, Amanda; why don't you make a start on some of them? I'm sure Godmama would like a nice flower painting, and it would be something different for you, too.'

Rosalie had been a little concerned recently about her guardian. She seemed out of sorts, and this was very unusual. It also meant that she was reluctant to tell her about Benedict. News like that needed the recipient to be in the best possible mood.

'You're right, Rosalie, lack of employment does not suit me. I shall start to look round the house for suitable subject matter.' So saying, she rose, threw her napkin on the table, and added, 'I shall start at once. What will you do on this wet morning, my dear?'

'I have sadly neglected my harp practice of late. It is time to put that right.'

She also wanted to seek out Benedict, as she had something in particular she wanted to ask him, but that plan was not for Amanda's ears. It was a little disappointing to find the long gallery, where her harp had been taken, already occupied by Piers and Benedict, indulging in fencing bouts. Not that there wasn't plenty of room for both activities in the gallery, being one of the longest in the country, but the two occupations really didn't mix. Instead, she took a seat to watch them and to admire the gallery itself.

It occupied the whole third floor at the front of the house and was completed at either end by the two towers, which created a pleasant sitting area. A further embrasure in the centre gave into the roof of the port-cochere, presumably added later. Two huge fireplaces with elaborately carved overmantles were built into the inner wall, which was lined with ancestral portraits. It was truly magnificent architectural space.

Piers *touched* Benedict three times in a row and put up his foil.

He said, 'I think you've lost your concentration, my friend, since my fair sister entered the gallery.' Piers was chaffing but had no idea how close to the truth he was. He went over to the window. 'It looks as if it might clear up, after all. Since it appears that you are not in the mood, I'll toddle off to the stables and see how my lovely Astarte is doing and leave you to the lovely Rosalie.' He grinned, put his foil into the rack, and waved a salute to the pair, as he left the gallery.

Benedict immediately went and sat beside Rosalie, taking one of her hands in his. He rushed into speech. 'It was terribly wrong of me to do what I did yesterday. I took advantage of you, no gentleman should; please forgive me.' He rattled on with broken sentences until his voice trailed off into silence.

Rosalie looked at him and said, 'Mmmm.'

'Is that all you've got to say? "Mmmm"?'

'There isn't much else to say to people who talk nonsense.'

'It is not nonsense, my love. I'm not the right man for you, or for anyone.' A little note of self-pity crept into his voice.

Rosalie paused before answering. 'For anyone? Certainly not, but for me, you are definitely the right one, and before you start on about what happened at dinner last night, which, I suppose, is what this is all about, I knew when you looked with such horror at the wine stain that it had triggered a terrible memory. I know I can't share such things, nor, I suspect, would you want me to, but I will always, always, always be there for you. I love you, Benedict; my life as well as my heart would be broken into pieces if you back out now.'

'My darling, my life has already been broken, and I know that only you can put it together, and … and there's another thing. I … I had an affair.'

'Of course you did,' said a completely unshocked Rosalie. 'Gentlemen always have affairs.'

'Only one, I assure you,' Benedict added hastily. 'I was twenty, and I'm afraid I made a bit of a fool of myself. It was when I was in America, during the War of 1812. We were stationed in York – a town in Canada, and there was a very beautiful woman—' He then realised what Rosalie had just said: What d'you mean, "gentlemen always have affairs"?'

'Piers told me. I admit that he was only fifteen at the time, so perhaps he didn't fully understand, nor did I then, but we both do now.' She laughed. 'And while we are in confessional mood, I admit to having had a terrible crush on my music master when I was fourteen. I'd have gone to the ends of the earth with him, but then his wife would probably have objected.'

'Oh Rosalie, my darling, what am I going to do with you? You are quite adorably impossible.'

'Marry me as soon as possible, don't you think?'

'That soon?'

'That soon. What is there to stop us?'

'Mrs Fletcher, Piers …'

'Fiddlesticks; if they object now, they'll have to come round eventually. So what's the point of objecting? Now I have something very important to ask you.'

Benedict looked puzzled. 'More important than our future?'

'That was settled yesterday; this is about someone else's future happiness.'

'Fingers in someone else's pie, my love?'

'Only if it's the right thing to do. I want you to tell me about the sergeant.'

'No, it's none of your business, Rosalie.'

'You're quite right, but let me ask you this: Is it right for someone to have the power to make three people very happy, to stand by and do nothing?

'And that's what you think I'm doing?'

'Yes, although I believe it may have been the right thing to do at the time. Two years ago, the sergeant's wounds must have indeed looked horrific, and his fear of disgusting his wife, a genuine one, and perhaps the maid who fainted at the sight of him confirmed his worst imaginings, but it is different now. There is no need for him to hide away.'

'When I was a boy, I used to hide here, in this very place.'

'This isn't much of a hiding place.'

Benedict stood up. 'Watch.' He reached over to the side of the tower without windows and pressed something, and a small concealed door sprang open. 'Look inside there. I wouldn't go in. It is probably very dusty.'

Rosalie peered through the opening and saw a wooden ladder leading to a platform.

'It goes to the very top of the tower; nobody ever found me. I don't suppose anyone knows the door is even there.'

'Don't change the subject,' Rosalie said sharply.

Benedict looked at her suspiciously. 'You were saying things are different for the sergeant, now. In what way?'

Rosalie closed the door and heard it click.

'Yes, he has lost an eye, but so have hundreds of ex-soldiers, and he has a scar, but it is fading, although he probably can't see the change. I have no doubt that every time he sees himself in a looking-glass, he sees what he first saw. His hair has grown long enough to cover the part where the sabre cut the top of his ear, and his slightly lopsided smile, if and when he chooses to use it, is lovely. Would you not agree that all I have said is right?'

'I don't think I have ever looked at it, or him, like that, but yes, you are right.'

'Well then, is it not time that a grieving widow and a little boy, who is the spitting image of his father, and who desperately wants his dada, to be reunited?'

'But if I say any of this to him, I know he will say no, and anyway, what if Mrs Mary, his wife, does reject him? I can't put him through that.'

'Of course you can't, but she won't.'

'How do you know that?'

'Think about what Mrs Mary does, day in and day out. She looks after men, many of whom are in a far worse case than the sergeant. To her, his scars will hardly register. Think of Davy, with no arms, or Sid, who she tells me sits in a rocking chair all day, unable to communicate, or, I don't know his name, who has lost both his eyes. The sergeant has all his faculties, all his senses, all his limbs, and a lovely little son into the bargain, but best of all, Mrs Mary loves him. She's desolated that she can't visit his grave. I know you owe the sergeant a great deal; without him, you might have ended up in an asylum. You need to do this for him.'

'What about his son? What if he cries at the sight of his father?'

'Why should he? He's lived all his life with maimed and disabled men.' Benedict looked dubious. 'I promise you, I will do nothing without telling you first, but you must see that the sergeant's family needs to be together, and I won't ask you to break your promise to him, either.'

'How do you know I made a promise to the sergeant?'

'I don't, but I can guess he made you say, on your honour, never to tell Mary that he was alive, or something like that. Yes?'

'You, my darling, may look like an angel, but you are the very devil when comes to finding out about people.'

'So I've been told, but now it is time for nuncheon, and since the sun has come out, to get ready for the great expedition to Saffron Walden with your mama.' She kissed Benedict on the cheek. 'I will let you know as soon as I've thought of a plan.'

She departed, leaving her fiancé amazed and bewildered, but all the more determined to make their engagement official. He found Piers just finishing his ride.

'Hey, Benedict; you just missed my first trotting session,' he exclaimed, sliding off the horse and throwing the reins to a waiting groom.

'Go well, did it?'

'Top hole.' He grimaced a little. 'I expect I'll feel it tomorrow, though. Going for a ride, now the weather's cleared?'

'No, I've come to find you. I have something important to say to you.'

They strolled across the yard an into a side entrance.

'We can go into Justin's study; he always keeps a spot of brandy there.'

Once they were settled, Piers said, 'You're making this all seem very serious, Benedict.'

'It is serious, Piers. I'll come straight to the point: I want to marry your sister.'

'Well, I'll be damned. I didn't even know she liked you.' Piers was not gifted with the same kind of instinctive insight vouchsafed to Rosalie.

'Well, she does, and I absolutely adore her.'

'Does she know that?'

'Of course, and I have every reason to believe she loves me too. Will you give your consent?'

'I'm not sure it's up to me; Amanda is her guardian.'

'I know, but you are the head of your family, so it is only right to ask you first, Piers.'

'What if I say no?'

Benedict took a sip of brandy before replying, 'One of four things will happen. One, we will elope; two, we will have to wait till Rosalie comes of age, to which she will not agree, so we will elope; three, you and Mrs Fletcher will not give your consent, so we will elope; or four, you both say yes, and we put the banns up on Sunday. If you want to know if I can support your sister in the way she has been accustomed to, the answer is yes. I have a regular and adequate income, from a small but well-run and profitable estate in Kent. I may be a younger son, but I come from an old and titled family; she will become Lady Benedict St Maure; anything else?'

Piers grinned. 'Can't think of a thing. Congratulations, brother-in-law.'

They drank a toast.

'You didn't put up much of a fight, though.' Benedict sounded almost disappointed.

'Never won an argument with Rosalie in my life. Not worth the effort.' He finished off his drink.

'I'm going to see if I can find Mrs Fletcher; no good putting it off. She may not be the pushover you were.'

'Give you a tip, Piers, brush your teeth before you see her; she might not appreciate the smell of brandy, despite it being Justin's finest.'

CHAPTER 32

Although the weather had cleared, Amanda felt that it would be too wet underfoot to revert to her original plan. So she set off exploring the nooks and crannies in the old house, where mahogany stands, marble columns, and jardinieres were crowned with arrangements of exotic hot-house blooms. She finally found what she wanted: a window embrasure with a bowl of roses on the sill. She selected one to draw. Sitting on her little folding stool, she set about the task, but somehow, she lost interest in the flower and began a meticulous portrait of the marquis. She drew the outline of his lean face, pencilled in the slight curve of his nose above the clean-cut shape of his mouth, and indicated the position of his golden eyes and dark brows. She was just starting on the elegantly tousled dark brown hair when she heard footsteps approaching on the wooden floor and hastily covered the sketch.

'Ah, Mrs Fletcher,' said the voice of Lord Benedict from behind her shoulder. 'I see you have not yet started.' He looked at the blank page., and the rose lying beside it. 'I would really like to speak to you, if you could spare the time.'

'I am at your service, My Lord, but I don't think this is the best place for a conversation. I believe the blue salon, or is the oak salon just along the passage from here?'

Amanda got to her feet, but before she could catch it, her sketchbook fell to the floor and skidded along the polished surface. Benedict picked it up and handed it back, but not before he had caught a glimpse of his brother's portrait.

'That is very good, Mrs Fletcher.' He quirked an eyebrow. 'Where were you going to put the rose, between his teeth?'

Without waiting for a reply, he ushered Amanda towards the blue salon.

'I will come straight to the point, Mrs Fletcher,' Lord Benedict said, when they were seated. 'I want to marry Rosalie.'

Amanda heaved a sigh. 'I've rather been expecting this, My Lord, and to be honest with you, I have been in two minds as to what to say, if and when you came to me. Your rank and station in life make you, without question, a suitable match, but there are other matters of greater importance to consider.'

'I am well aware of that, Mrs Fletcher, and as Rosalie's guardian, her welfare is your first duty. I can say little in defence of my suit, except that I love Rosalie with all my heart, and that we have an understanding between us that transcends anything that I, and I believe she, too, has ever felt for any other human being.'

'I think that is true, my Lord, but she is very young.'

'But perhaps, because of the music in her soul, she has a knowledge and understanding of what really matters in her life, and in the lives of other people, certainly in mine, beyond her years.'

Amanda looked at the young man, his dark eyes pleading for acceptance. 'Yes, Lord Benedict,' she said slowly. 'I really believe that you have understood my ward in a way I have never fully appreciated, and on those grounds, I would give my consent, but there is the issue of your health. It would be wrong of me not to be concerned.'

'You are right, and I can only say that I think my collapse was, in part, due to a belief that I had deserted my troops at the very height of battle; for a time, this belief destroyed my sanity, but I now know that it was quite untrue. I do not think it will happen again.'

'And Rosalie is aware of this?'

'Yes, and of the fact that I sometimes have episodes when I seem to be back on the battlefield. I can't explain it, I'm afraid, but Rosalie accepts that it can happen.'

'It goes without saying that Rosalie loves you and has told you so. In fact, she was probably the first to say so.' Amanda smiled. 'I would have preferred you to wait a bit longer, but I don't really think there is much point in doing so. So, Lord Benedict, you have my permission to marry my ward, Miss Rosalie Abbot.'

For a moment, Benedict was stunned; he hadn't expected such a rapid capitulation. He stood up to express his delight and happiness, but excitement and residual weakness from his long self-isolation made him feel faint, and he sat down again, leaning over to bow over Amanda's hand.

'Thank you, thank you, Mrs Fletcher; you have made me the happiest man in the world.'

Amanda saw the grey pallor fade from his face.

'I hope I have taught Rosalie enough about housekeeping to order you good nourishing meals when you are married.' She smiled. 'How many others of the interested parties in this engagement have been told of it? I imagine you kept the worst till last?'

Benedict looked a little sheepish, his plan having been so easily exposed. 'I have told Justin of my feelings for Rosalie, and I admit to asking Piers for his permission, being, as he is, the head of the family ...'

'Quite right, too,' interrupted Amanda. 'It is time I took a back seat, although there are still issues to be resolved, but now is not the time. Your mother and Rosalie will soon be back from their expedition to Saffron Walden and will expect me to join them at tea.'

She picked up her stool, and as Benedict held the door for her, he said, 'On my honour, and my life, Mrs Fletcher, I will do everything I possibly can to make Rosalie happy.'

'I know you will, My Lord.'

'Benedict, Mrs Fletcher; please call me Benedict.'

'Only if you will call me Amanda, Benedict.'

Although less than a mile from the town of Saffron Walden, the marchioness spared nothing in making a grand entrance. A coach-and-four in silver-mounted harness, complete with the head coachmen and two grooms in scarlet livery, together with an under-groom bearing a blunderbuss, stood under the port-cochere, awaiting the marchioness, Rosalie, and her ladyship's maid. It took some time for Lady Coverdale to be satisfied that everything was to her liking before the equipage set off.

On arrival in the town, it was not long before the news spread to the shopkeepers and members of the public, who were rarely treated to so grand a spectacle and gathered to watch. As regally as a queen, the marchioness visited the establishments of her choice and spent time examining in detail every proposed purchase. Eventually, she was satisfied with three bonnets, several yards of silk ribbon, and a paisley shawl. She also bought a pair of kid gloves and a quantity of blond lace for Rosalie. The largest of the emporia had laid on refreshments, which Lady Coverdale was pleased to accept, declaring that shopping was such a tiring affair. Rosalie excused herself, as she had a plan of her own to undertake.

After enquiring which was the largest apothecary's shop, she set off to find it. Her Godmama insisted that she was accompanied by one of the livered grooms, which, being recognised, had the added advantage of Rosalie being served by the apothecary himself.

'Do you do glass-blowing?' was Rosalie's unusual request.

'Yes, M'lady.' It was always best to be on the safe side. 'What do you require?'

She explained exactly what she wanted, and he agreed that doing it would present no problem. 'Can you make two for me now? One straight and one bent, like this,' she said, indicating an angle with her hand.

'Yes, M'lady, it will take about ten minutes.'

'I will wait.' Rosalie hoped that her godmama would take her time over the refreshments, but her request was quickly executed. 'Now if you will please make another half-dozen of each and send them to Mrs Mary Barker, at Longacre Farm, on the Coverdale estate. I will pay for them all now and will take these two with me.'

The man bowed her out of the shop, and she returned to her godmother just as she was ready to leave. Slightly more than halfway home, they reached the lane leading to Longacre Farm, and Rosalie requested to be let out. She was glad of the exercise and soon reached Mrs Mary's cottage, adjacent to the barn.

When the door was answered, Rosalie said, 'May I have a few minutes of your time, Mrs Mary?'

'Surely, Miss; the men could talk of nothing else after your visit yesterday.'

1. Rosalie drew a long thin package from her reticule and unwrapped two glass tubes about ten inches long, one bent at 45 degrees, four inches from one end.

'This for Davy; it will help him drink more easily. I noticed that the real straws he uses soon become soggy and don't work.'

'Why, Miss that's wonderful; he is always having to ask for a new straw. How could you think of such a thing?'

'I remembered it from the time my brother was not allowed to sit up, for more than six months; a very famous doctor said they were used in hospitals. I cannot stay long, but I have a very special request. Lord Benedict is coming here tomorrow; he will be leaving the hall at three o'clock and wishes to meet you and little Arthur outside. Will you do that, please, Mrs Mary? It's important; oh yes, the apothecary will be sending you some more drinking tubes for Davy, as soon as he has made them. I must go now, but don't forget: three o'clock. You don't want to keep his lordship waiting.'

'Thank you, Miss. I won't, I promise. Davy will be so pleased.'

Benedict was disappointed to find that Rosalie was not in the coach as it arrived back at the hall, and on being told she was walking back from Longacre, he set off to meet her, which he did only a short distance from the house.

He hurried towards her, picked her up in his arms, and said, 'My darling, darling Rosalie, they have all said yes; we can get married, whenever we like.'

Rosalie put her arms round Benedict's neck, kissed him, and said, 'That's all settled, then. I always knew they'd understand that we had to be together. Now to more important matters.'

'What could be more important than our marriage?'

'Nothing, of course, but it isn't going to happen tomorrow, and what I have planned is. I told you I'd have one.'

'One what?'

'A plan to get the sergeant and Mrs Mary and little Arthur together again.'

'Are you sure that's the right thing to do? It could all go terribly wrong, you know, my love.'

'I know one thing for certain: it would be terribly wrong not to try.'

'You're going to bully me into doing things against my better judgement for the rest of my life, aren't you?'

'Probably; now put me down and listen very carefully. You will leave the hall at precisely ten to three, tomorrow afternoon, accompanied by the sergeant. As soon as you see Mrs Mary come out of her cottage with Arthur, make some excuse to fall behind: a stone in your shoe or something. Tell the sergeant, you will catch him up. Love, and little Arthur, will do the rest.'

'What shall I tell the sergeant as to why we're going to the farm?'

'Oh, for goodness' sake! Use your imagination, Benedict. I just wish I could be there with you.'

That night, at dinner, toasts were drunk and decisions made to send notice of the engagement to the *London Gazette* and the *Times,* and an express letter to inform Lord Coverdale. One Sunday a month, Matins was conducted in the Coverdale's private chapel and would be the perfect opportunity for the first reading of the banns of marriage between Rosalie Abbot, spinster, and Benedict St Maure, bachelor.

That afternoon, Rosalie was on tenterhooks as she watched, from a discreet distance, Benedict and the sergeant walking towards Longacre Farm, until they were out of sight, sending up a little prayer for the success of what was really her responsibility.

'If I may be so bold, Captain,' the sergeant said, 'why do you want me to visit the farm?'

'The workshop manager can always do with some extra help, and you, not being disabled, as most of the men there are, could be a valuable asset.'

'I'm really not sure about that, Sir, but I'd like to offer my congratulations on your impending marriage to Miss Rosalie and wish you every happiness, Captain.'

'Thank you, Sergeant. I only wish everybody could be as happy as I feel.'

As they got closer, Benedict could just make out a figure emerging from the cottage. He began limping a little.

'Bother, I think I've got a stone or something in my shoe. You go on, Sergeant; I'll catch you up.' Even to himself, his voice sounded stilted and false, as he spoke the words Rosalie had suggested, but worse was to follow.

'No, Captain, I'd better wait; we should go together.'

This was something Rosalie had not prepared him for, and he was at a loss. He made a slow job of taking off a shoe, shaking it out, and replacing it, playing for time.

He murmured, 'That's better,' then standing up, he saw Mrs Mary, obviously wondering what the delay was, coming towards them.

About twenty yards away, she recognised who it was and froze, clutching Arthur tightly to her. The sergeant was also rooted to the spot, but Arthur wriggled vigorously in his mother's arms; he was big for his age, and she was forced to put him down.

Benedict laid a hand in the sergeant's shoulder and said, 'Go on, man.'

Freed from his mother's restraint, Arthur ran forward, tripping on the edge of a pothole as he reached the closest of the two men. Instinctively, the sergeant bent down and scooped the little boy into his arms.

'Dada,' said Arthur.

Benedict turned and walked quickly back towards the hall, but the surrounding countryside had suddenly become unaccountably blurred.

CHAPTER 33

J ustin and Roberts were riding behind the best-sprung post-chaise he could find, because travelling in it were Henry, Dr Pargeter, Mrs Clarkson, and Mrs Roberts. The doctor would only allow his patient to undertake the journey if he went with him. Henry had been up and about for the last week, being allowed to sit in the courtyard, but Pargeter was still concerned about the progress of his arm and insisted on the carriage being packed with numerous cushions and pillows to ameliorate jolting and jarring.

Normally, Justin looked forward to being at Coverdale, especially the Dower House, since it had been his childhood home, but now he felt weighed down with the problems that lay ahead. Benedict and Rosalie's engagement was the best bit of news in an otherwise worrying outlook, and he inwardly congratulated Mrs Fletcher on a wise but brave decision. Would she have the same courage and wisdom when it came to discovering that her mother was still alive? He sincerely hoped so.

After the second stop of their three-part journey, Justin decided to join the coach party, allowing his manservant to follow on, once the horses had been sufficiently rested. Everything inside seemed to have gone well, although Henry was looking decidedly pale, and the other occupants had little in common, except an interest in the invalid's comfort.

Once Justin had joined them, he and the Doctor discussed politics and current affairs until, as they neared their destination, Justin turned to Henry and said, 'I am going to ask you a question, but I do not want you to answer it at the moment. If you understand it, I want you to indicate that you do. Is that clear?' Henry nodded. 'This is the question: Why did you wait so long?'

The man sitting opposite the marquis took some time to make any sort of reply; at last, he said, 'Yes, My Lord, I understand the question.'

Ironically, at that moment, the carriage turned a corner, and the late afternoon sun shone through the window, directly onto Henry's face. Justin leaned forward and adjusted the blind.

'The light of the sun can be very worrying at this time of year, don't you think?'

'Indeed, My Lord, but I believe you may have solved the problem.'

After dinner at the Dower House, the marquis took Dr Pargeter into the drawing room. The public rooms in the house were attractive and well proportioned, and the six or so bedchambers adequate for a dowager to live comfortably. The aspect from the main rooms gave a view of the lake, and gardens were charmingly laid out. The doctor had taken a stroll to stretch his legs after the long drive and immediately remarked on the pleasant surroundings.

'Yes, Pargeter, I have always preferred this house to the Hall, but now we must discuss how best to introduce Mrs Fletcher to her mother, and if you think it would be wise to tell her before the de Vailleuxs arrive; they are due in a few days' time.'

'That, Coverdale is a tricky one, and I have been pondering over it myself.'

'And your conclusions?'

The doctor walked over to the window and gazed out at the still waters of the lake before answering. 'On balance, I think she should be told first that her mother is still alive. What her reactions are will govern the next move. If she is violently against a meeting, there will still be time to put the de Vailleuxs off. Do you agree?'

The marquis also gave pause before replying. 'Yes, I believe you are right, and I also think that it cannot be put off much longer. Tomorrow is as good a day as any. I shall be going over to the Hall this evening after dinner, and will ask her to wait upon you in the morning, Then you can break it to her.'

'I thought we had agreed that you should do it, Marquis.'

'We should both be present, don't you think, Pargeter?' Justin smiled. 'So she can be angry with us both at the same time.'

'Why?' asked the Doctor, 'should she be angry with you?'

'When she finds out that I have known for some time; after all, I am not a relation, and besides, you must be the one to tell her. I promised the de Vailleuxs that I would not.'

'And I promised her father that I would not.'

'I know,' said Justin, 'but the time has come, don't you think? Keeping your word now will cause more harm than good.'

'You're right, Coverdale; tomorrow, all will be revealed. Now I must go and see how my patient is faring, so I'll bid you good night.'

'Good night, Doctor, and please don't hesitate to make use of my staff for anything you may require.'

Justin's entry into the drawing room at the hall, just as tea was being taken, caused an outburst of simultaneous chatter. Everyone wanted to be the first with the latest news. He held up his hand to quell the noise and sauntered over to greet his mother first. She accepted his kiss.

'You've been away too long, Justin, and too much has been happening in your absence, but everything will be all right now,' she said with an air of complete confidence, holding out her cup to Rosalie for a refill.

Accepting a cup for himself from Mrs Fletcher, he said, 'I would beg a little of your time, Mrs Fletcher, after this conversation is over. May we meet in the green salon in about half an hour?'

'Certainly, Sir, but as you can see, for the moment, I am the officer-in-command of the teapot.' Amanda smiled and couldn't stop her heart beating a little faster in his presence.

'Now, I must go over and congratulate the happy couple on their forthcoming nuptials. You are pleased about the engagement, too, I imagine, since you must have given your consent.'

'Yes, I believe they are very well suited, and I also believe in bowing to the inevitable, Marquis.'

'Till later, then, Mrs Fletcher.' He smiled and drifted off in the direction of Rosalie and Benedict, where he offered his congratulations and was delighted to learn of the reunion of the sergeant and Mrs Mary.

'It was all due to my angel, her.' Benedict put his arm round Rosalie. 'She fixed it all without my having to break my promise to the sergeant,' he said enthusiastically. 'He has a son, too, you know.'

Piers joined the group. 'Oh, Coverdale, you'll never guess ...'

'Probably not, so you'd better tell me before you burst.'

'I've been cantering. What d'you think of that?'

'It's not what I think that matters, young Piers, but what Doctor Pargeter thinks, and it just so happens that he is currently a guest of mine at the Dower House.' Justin saw the young man's face fal,l and added, 'But I'm sure he'll be pleased, so long as the exercise hasn't caused you any problems.'

'No, indeed it hasn't; in fact, it is a lot more comfortable than trotting.'

'Good, now I see my mother has called for the card table to be put out; you had better go and do your duty, or I will give the good Doctor a shocking report.'

Recognising that his lordship was teasing, Piers joined the others, and Justin, seeing that the tea tray was being removed, ushered Amanda out of the room.

The small, or green, saloon, by most people's standards, would not qualify as small, but the low, heavily decorated and plastered ceiling, and dark oak panelling, made it seem smaller than its actual dimensions. A predominantly green Persian rug and green upholstery gave the room its other name. Justin went over to the fire and gave the logs a kick with the toe of his boot, creating a shower of sparks. 'I hope it is warm enough for you,' he said to Amanda, seated in an armchair.

'Perfectly, thank you; now what do you wish to say to me, Marquis?'

'There are several matters, but first I want to know what you really think about our young lovers; are you genuinely in favour of the match?'

'If I have any reservations, it's that Rosalie is very young, and perhaps I would have preferred her to have seen more of the world, before she made her choice, but on the other hand, Marquis, I had a very strong feeling that even if she had several seasons, and travelled to all four corners of the earth, the result would be the same. So what was the point of making two people very unhappy for no good reason, if I had forbidden the match, or made them wait?'

'I can't tell you how grateful I am for your decision; I know you must have had your doubts, especially about Benedict's health, but I know that Rosalie cares deeply for him. She is a very exceptional young lady. I have no doubt that the reuniting of the sergeant and his wife can be laid at her door, and I believe that your influence has played a great part in shaping Rosalie's character.'

Justin had a sudden urge to take Amanda in his arms and kiss her senseless, but of course, he could not. He turned away and gave the logs another dose of his toe.

'Thank you, Sir. I know you want Lord Benedict's happiness, as much as I want Rosalie's. However, I don't think that is what you really wanted to talk to me about, is it?'

'No; as usual, you are quite right. I have come on a mission on behalf of someone else.'

'I can't imagine who; I don't know anyone else.'

'You know this person really well; it is Dr Pargeter. He is staying with me at the Dower House and expects to see you tomorrow morning, if that is convenient.'

'This is a surprise; why is he here?'

'You won't be satisfied if I just say, because I invited him, will you?'

'No, certainly not; from what little I know of you, I believe you are the sort of person for whom human contact is a useful event that should benefit both parties, and not just for the pure pleasure of being together, unlike Rosalie and Benedict.'

Justin considered a further intrusion into the fire with his boot but instead came across the room towards Amanda.

'Is that a condemnation of my character, Mrs Fletcher?'

'Not at all; you are pragmatism personified, My Lord, but perhaps, one day, you will experience something in a human relationship more satisfying than the outcome of a successful plan.'

Taking the chair opposite her, he merely said, 'Humph.'

'Now you are going to tell me why the good doctor is paying you a visit?'

'He came with Henry; he wouldn't let him come otherwise, and I couldn't leave him at Berkeley Square.'

'How is Henry?'

'Improving, but a long way from fit, as yet. I'm sure you have had other thoughts about my mother's erstwhile footman, have you not, Mrs Fletcher?'

Amanda didn't really want to discuss her thoughts, or bring them to the forefront of her mind, but the events of the past weeks had certainly made her wonder.

'He certainly seems to be an unusual sort of footman.'

'After travelling part of the way in the coach with him today, I have reason to think that he … that he …' Justin's voice trailed off.

Amanda looked at him shrewdly and saw that his face was grey with tiredness, and the flickering candlelight emphasised the lines by his eyes.

'You know what I think, Marquis? I think you should go back to the Dower House, pour yourself a glass of brandy, and take yourself off to bed. We can talk things over in the morning. I shall wait upon you at eleven o'clock.'

'You are right, Mrs Fletcher. Shall I send a carriage?'

'No, thank you. I shall walk; someone will give me direction.' She stood up. 'Now take my advice. I bid you good night, Sir.'

As he left, Clarkson approached. 'There has been a message from the stables, My Lord. Roberts arrived safely, and your horse has been attended to. Roberts has returned to the Dower House.'

'Thank you, Clarkson; have you seen Mrs Clarkson, yet?'

'No, My Lord. I believe she would want to see to Henry's well-being first.'

'Well, come over tomorrow. I would like you to stay with her, but I cannot deprive the marchioness of your services, just now.'

'No, My Lord; good night, My Lord.'

The half-moon was high in the sky, casting a silver path across the lake; although it was the first of September, as yet there was no chill in the night air. The only chill was in his heart, as he walked the several hundred yards to the house. He knew his bed would be got ready, aired and warmed thanks to the efficient Roberts, but he also knew that the only real warmth in his bed, and in his heart, would be having Amanda sharing it with him.

CHAPTER 34

Promptly at eleven o'clock, Amanda was shown into the Dower House drawing room, a smaller, a simpler version of the one at Berkeley Square, decorated in the neoclassic style, in shades of pale green and gold.

Dr Pargeter was standing by the fire. He came forward to greet her. 'My dear Amanda, how delightful to see you again; it has been several weeks, I think.'

Amanda dropped a curtsey, and he bent forward to kiss her on the cheek.

A tray, with cups, a plate of biscuits, and a coffee pot, stood on a demilune side table. The Doctor walked over to it.

'May I pour you a coffee, Amanda?'

'If you please, Doctor.'

As he brought it over, the cup rattled against the saucer.

Surely he couldn't be nervous, Amanda thought, but he took a seat, and there was quite a long pause before he began to speak.

'What I am going to say, my dear, may shock and upset you, but the time has come, and it must be said. If you have questions, please ask them as I speak. It is essential that you understand everything I am going to say.'

Amanda already looked perplexed. 'I will try not to swoon, Doctor.'

Pargeter gave a slight smile and began. 'Do you remember your mother, Amanda?'

This was a question she had not expected. 'No, I was only just three when she died, but I have a miniature of her. It belonged to my father; he kept it with him always. His mother had painted it.'

'Yes, he showed it to me once. What do you know of your mother's family history?'

'Only that she and my father ran away together, because she was going to be forced into a marriage against her will. My father told me they were very much in love.'

'Certainly, he was, enough to throw away a potentially brilliant academic career. Your mother was only sixteen, not old enough to know her own mind, but desperate to take the only way she could to escape what I fear must have been a fate worse than death, and may even have resulted in her death.'

'I don't know what you mean, Doctor. What are you trying to say?'

'I'm saying that although your mother was both fond of, and grateful to, your father, she was not in love with him, and that is why, when she fell truly and deeply in love with someone else, she left him. Your mother, my very dear Amanda, is still alive.'

Pargeter leant forward and rescued her coffee cup before it crashed to the floor.

Amanda gasped. 'How can she be alive? My father told me ... I've seen her grave. She can't be ... What are you saying?' She clasped her hands together till the knuckles showed white. The doctor came over to her and covered them with his.

'It is true, my dear. When you were three years old, your mother ran off with the man she had fallen in love with. I'm so sorry to have to tell you something so hurtful, but it is time you knew the truth.'

'How do you know? How did you find out? I can't believe it.'

Pargeter sat down again. 'Amanda, my dear, I've always known, right from the day she left.'

'But why?' Amanda rubbed her hands up and down her skirt. 'Why would he tell me she was dead? I don't understand.'

On another table, there was a decanter and some glasses. Pargeter got up and poured Amanda a brandy.

'Drink this; it will steady your nerves, while I try to tell you what you want to know.'

Amanda accepted the drink, but it was her turn to have trembling hands.

'I believe,' he went on, 'there were two reasons why your father didn't tell you the truth. He wanted to protect you, and, quite understandably, he wanted to protect himself too. He didn't want you to think that your mother had just abandoned you—'

'Well, she did, didn't she? Amanda interrupted.

'Yes, I'm sorry, but that is the only answer to that. To the other question, I believe it was because he loved her that he couldn't bear to think of her with another man, and so he tried to convince himself that she really was dead; that is why, despite all my arguments to the contrary, he made me swear never to tell you. I always thought it was wrong, but until now, I have kept my word.'

'Why break it now?'

'Before I answer that, Amanda, I want to say that from now on, everything is entirely your choice. You have the absolute right to do whatever you want to do.'

Amanda looked puzzled. 'I'm not sure what you mean, Doctor.' She put her brandy glass down.

'You will when I tell you that your mother and her husband are back in London.'

Amanda jumped to her feet. 'Are you sure? Have you seen her, spoken to her?' She started to stride up and down the room in the way the marquis would have recognised.

'Please, Amanda, try to stay calm; be seated again, and I will tell you all I know. Take another sip of brandy.'

'Yes, I am being foolish; it's the shock.' She took the Doctor's advice and resumed her seat.

'The answers to your questions are, yes, I am sure. I would recognise her anywhere, but no, I have not spoken to her, but, and please don't be angry with him, Lord Coverdale has.'

'Has what?'

'Spoken to her and her husband.'

'This is intolerable. A complete stranger, well almost, knew about my mother before I did. Is this your doing?'

'I'm afraid it is; believe me, Amanda, it was for the best of reasons.'

'Really?' She was not mollified. 'I'd like to hear them.'

'Your mother's family history and behaviour at the time …' Pargeter held up his hand as Amanda was about to interrupt. 'Yes, I know it was a long time ago, but society's memory is a long one too. I was thinking of your wards. I know you would not want them to be involved in harmful gossip.'

Amanda's temper subsided. 'As usual, you are quite right. I apologise. So what should happen now?'

'As I said, that is up to you. The Marquis is waiting in the study, to tell you all he has learnt. Shall I ask him to come in?'

Amanda sighed heavily. 'I suppose so. Yes, please ask him.'

The moment Justin came through the door, the room seemed to shrink; it was not only his size, but his presence always made itself felt, and for Amanda, it made any burden she was carrying feel lighter. She had wanted to appear angry that he had known so much more about her family before she had, but instead, she could only feel relieved to see him.

'All this must have come as a terrible shock, Mrs Fletcher, and what you may see as my interference, as an impertinence, for which I apologise.'

'My Lord, I accept that you acted in the best interests of my wards, so no apologies are required, but now I want to know all you have found out, most especially, what is my mother like?' She indicated that he should be seated.

'To look at,' he began, 'she is very like an older version of you, and I believe that, like you, she is clever and spirited. She and her husband have had to face a great many challenges.'

'I don't even know her name.'

Justin turned to Pargeter. 'You didn't tell her?'

'No, I left that, and almost everything else, to you, Coverdale.'

'Well, you may have seen her in town, although they are now in Brighton. Her name is the Countess de Vailleux; her husband was a French émigré from the Terror, but at the time they met, he was your mother-in-law's gardener. She will have a great deal of interest to tell you; that is, if you want to meet her, and I can tell you now, and I must emphasise this, Mrs Fletcher, that if you say no, she will be very disappointed, but she's assured me that she will understand.'

'I need to think … my poor father; it is so sad.'

The marquis longed to comfort her, but instead, he said, 'Doctor Pargeter and I will leave you now. You have had shattering news.'

'No, I would rather take a walk outside. I always find I can think better that way. I will take a turn round the lake and let you know my decision. I won't be long.'

She returned about forty minutes later to find Justin and the doctor, still in the drawing room.

'I'm sorry to have kept you waiting.'

'You have every right to take as long as you wish, Mrs Fletcher.' Justin smiled.

'Have you come to a decision, Amanda? I know it must be very difficult for you,' said Pargeter.

'Yes, I have, and yes, it wasn't easy, largely because I had to reconcile my desire to see my mother, with how I felt about my father.'

The two men waited for her decision.

'I have decided that it would be extremely foolish to deny my mother's existence because of something that happened many years ago, which I cannot remember. My father was a good, kind man, if rather unworldly, and I don't think he would condemn me for wanting me to see my mother. So, yes, I would like to meet her.' Amanda looked first at the Pargeter, and then at the marquis to see their reaction and detected a degree of relief in both faces. 'How can it be arranged?

Justin spoke first. 'I think you have made a good decision, Mrs Fletcher, and as to future arrangements, I have taken the liberty of ordering a light repast in the dining room, where we can continue our discussions and assuage our appetites at the same time, if you are agreeable.'

Over luncheon, Justin explained that he planned to invite the Count and Countess to the Dower House, depending on Amanda's decision. He would now put that plan into action. 'They should be here by the middle of next week,' he concluded.

'I would ask one thing of you both,' Amanda said. 'That what has passed here this morning stays, for the time being, entirely between ourselves.'

'Naturally.' 'Of course.' Two voices spoke as one. If anyone asks why they are here,' Justin added, 'I will say they are old friends of Pargeter's.'

As Amanda was leaving, Doctor Pargeter took her arm. 'May I walk you back to the hall, my dear?' When they reached a seat overlooking the lake, he said, 'A moment more of your time, if you please.'

Amanda smiled. 'I always have time for you, Doctor; you know that.'

'Your mother will be so pleased with your decision, although I know she would have respected it, if you had refused. Before she left England, she sent me this.' He extracted a folded, sealed letter from an inside pocket and handed it to the woman beside him.

Amanda saw the familiar crest of a hand holding a star and clenched the paper tightly, as she recognised writing she had seen at home; it just said 'To my darling daughter, Amanda.' Pargeter could see from her expression that she wanted to be left alone.

'I will see you soon, child. I believe we are to dine at the hall tomorrow.' He rose and walked swiftly back to the Dower House.

Amanda broke open the seal and after a few moments began to read:

My Darling Amanda,

I do not know when or if you will ever read this, but I hope that someday, you will. I can offer you no excuses for what I did, and you will rightly say, how could any woman abandon her child, and the husband who loved her, and who had done so much for her? I can only say I did it for love.

When you are reading this, I will not know if you are sixteen or sixty. If the former, I hope you will experience, in the future, the kind of love that transcends everything; if the latter, I hope you already have, but if you are somewhere in between, and the opportunity has not yet come your way, when it does, grab it with both hands and bind it to your heart.

My only regret was leaving behind the little girl I also loved and hurting the man who had given up everything to save my life. Neither of you deserved the heartache I must have caused, and if you were brought up to hate me, that is no less than I deserve, but I will always be your mother. I will always love you, but I do not expect you to believe that.

*It is my most sincere hope that you have a wonderful life.
I know that between your father, and his good friend, Doctor
Pargeter, to whom I have entrusted this letter, your welfare
will always be secure.*

Goodbye, my darling daughter.

I love you. Georgina

Amanda sat motionless, her thoughts in turmoil. She had been the rock upon which other people had leant on in times of trouble, and now she longed for a support of her own, but there was no one. She laid the letter on the seat and buried her face in her hands, tears trickling through her fingers. She didn't see Justin approach.

A slight breeze lifted the paper off the bench, and it fluttered to the ground. Justin picked it up, seated himself at the far end, and waited. Amanda became aware of his presence and wiped her eyes with the back of her hand.

'Why are you here?'

'I was worried. You had taken the news about your mother too calmly; something had to give.' He was still holding the letter.

'Read it.'

'Are you sure?'

'Yes,' Amanda nodded. 'I would like someone else to understand why I don't seem able to think straight. Agnew was always a good listener, if not a particularly sympathetic one, but now there's no one.'

It only took Justin a few moments to read through the short letter. He handed it back to Amanda.

'I am here,' he said gently.

'Yes, but now I don't know what to say. Isn't that stupid?'

'No, it's not; we'll just sit.'

Amanda watched a pair of swans, followed by their half-grown brood of cygnets, sailing majestically past. 'I think it's because I have never known love; no, that's a foolish thing to say; lots of people have loved me, and I have loved them. Help me, My Lord.'

'You may not have experienced it personally, by which I mean the all-consuming passion, that according to your mother "transcends everything," but you have seen it. You see it every day.'

'I don't understand; what do you mean?'

'I mean Benedict and Rosalie. Their real life only began when they found each other. I don't think I fully understand it, either, but it exists, just as it did for your mother. I think you recognised it when you agreed to Rosalie's engagement, and perhaps that will help you to accept what your mother did.'

Amanda and Justin turned towards each other, and their eyes met in mutual understanding. Amanda quickly dropped her gaze.

The marquis stood up, saying a little gruffly, 'I hope I have been able to help.'

He bowed and walked swiftly back towards the Dower House. Amanda continued to sit for another few minutes, knowing there was only one person she wanted to love and be loved by.

Justin halted. The temptation to go back and take Amanda in his arms, was almost too great to be resisted; he half-turned, and the moment passed. Amanda had gone.

CHAPTER 35

When Justin returned to the Dower House, he poured himself a stiff drink. He needed what his mother called 'a little composer,' firstly because he had just avoided making an unpardonable mistake, and was still shaking inside; secondly, it was time to tackle the man upstairs, who called himself Henry Evans, and find out who he really was and what his intentions were.

'No, please don't get up,' Justin said as he entered the spacious bedchamber assigned to his guest and saw him struggle to do so. 'If you feel ready, I believe it is time we had a little talk.'

Sitting back again, Henry smiled. 'Yes, My Lord, I suppose it is, although I don't know how much you already know or have guessed.'

'From documents in Mrs Fletcher's possession, I know that the late Sir Percy Abbot went through a form of Church of England marriage to an Indian lady, about forty years ago, and I deduce from that, that you are the consequence of that so-called marriage, but of that, I have no definite proof.'

'You are correct, My Lord. I see that you have brought all my belongings here, from Berkeley Square and my lodgings in the city.' He pointed to two boxes in the corner of the room and smiled. 'I believe you are a man of great resource.'

'Yes, I took the liberty of doing so. And Clarkson arranged it. I have not opened either of them.'

'Ah, yes, the inimitable Mr Clarkson.'

'He spoke very highly of you, too, Henry;' his lordship smiled. 'But it is time I knew your real name. Is it Abbot?'

'No, my Indian name is Banerjee, and no doubt you will be very surprised to learn that my first name is, indeed, Henry.' He adjusted his position in the chair and winced.

Feeling that the erstwhile footman would not like this to be commented on, Justin said, 'Now perhaps it is time to begin at the beginning—'

'If you would open the larger box and bring me the decorated box from within it, I can show you some papers. It is a Chinese puzzle box. You will have to open it for me. I will tell you how, My Lord.'

Justin followed Henry's instructions, opened the box, and handed over the contents. Henry sorted through the papers, a little awkwardly with one hand, and held out a letter to the marquis. 'I think you should read this first, My Lord.'

Justin sat by the desk, situated in front of a window, smoothed out the tightly folded paper, and began to read. The letter was dated Abbots Court, 1782.

> *My very dear wife, Sunettra,*
>
> *I long for the day when we can be reunited, and I can hold you in my arms again, but matters here are much worse than I expected. My brother is dying and cannot last long, but the doctors are noncommittal. However, that is not the only reason that I cannot ask you to undertake the long voyage, only to arrive at a house that has been allowed to run to rack and ruin. He has been living in the only two habitable rooms. So a great deal will have to be done before the house is restored and suitable for my lady. While my brother is alive I can, of course, do nothing about repairs, but he has given me permission to deal with the estate, and that is what I shall be doing.*
>
> *I do hope you are well, my love. Please keep your spirits up. I know we shall be together one day, and I shall see your beautiful face once more.*
>
> *Your ever-loving husband,*
> *Percy.*

The marquis smoothed the paper over with his hand several times, before turning to face Henry.

'I believe that the content of this letter tells me that Sir Percy, as he became, had honourable intentions towards this woman, who married him in good faith in India, and I think Sir Piers and Miss Rosalie can but be glad of that. However, it is time to learn more about you, Henry, and your reasons for the worrying subterfuge you have been enacting recently, and to give an answer to the question I asked on the way here. Why have you waited so long?'

'My Lord, I am, as you have suspected for some time, the son of Sir Percy, but he never knew of my existence. A plague swept through the state shortly after I was born, and my mother died.'

'Did nobody communicate this to Sir Percy or tell him he had a son? I find that hard to believe.' His lordship frowned.

'It is because my mother made her father promise, on her deathbed, not to tell Sir Percy of my existence, although a letter was sent, informing him of my mother's death, soon after that event.'

'Why do you think she did this?' Justin asked.

'I believe she must have thought it best if I was brought up as an Indian, and in Hindu culture, although when I was old enough to understand, they told me I had an English father, and kept the papers you have on your desk as proof.'

The marquis's first feeling was that of relief. He could at least be sure now that Sir Percy had not been a bigamist, so Piers and Rosalie were not illegitimate, but a further worry was still unresolved. Was the man sitting opposite him, in effect, Sir Henry?

'I can see that you are worried, My Lord.' He leant forward, barely suppressing a moan of pain. Justin immediately jumped up and adjusted a pillow behind Henry's back. 'Thank you, My Lord; you are most kind.'

'Nonsense, Henry; you deserve every attention. You saved your half-sister's life, but you are right. I am concerned. As the eldest son of Sir Percy, you would have the right to the property and title. This would come as a terrible blow to Piers.'

Henry held out his right hand in a gesture of appeal. 'Please, Lord Coverdale, you have no need to worry on that score. Even if I were the rightful heir, I have no desire to displace Sir Piers or claim his property.

My English lineage would remain unknown. My home is in India, where my wife and children are patiently awaiting my return.'

Justin was taken aback; although his calculations had put Henry around forty years of age, he had never given any thought to his private life. 'You said even if, Henry?'

'Yes, My Lord; the answer concerns the reply to your very first question. Why did I wait so long? Briefly, the marriage ceremony conducted by the Reverend Agnew Fletcher was invalidated. Although,' he added, 'I sincerely believe that all parties believed it to be legal at the time, and no blame can be attached to any of them, but the consequence is that in the eyes of the Church of England, and therefore, also in English law, I am the illegitimate son of Sir Percy.'

Justin felt like cheering but didn't. 'So how did you find this out?'

'Not until two years ago, when the old so-called chapel was being pulled down, and it turned out that it was never more than an outhouse. It had never been designated as a religious building, nor had it ever been licensed for marriages, according to to English law.'

To give him time to absorb all this information, he asked Henry if he would like something to drink, and a flagon of ale was sent for.

'So, Henry, let me get this absolutely straight. You are saying that, although there is no doubt that your father was Sir Percy Abbot, and with this I concur, you are making no claim whatsoever to the title of baronet, or to the land and property known as Abbots Court.'

'That is correct, My Lord, but—'

'Yes, I know there is a "but"; however, in my opinion, that particular aspect, and the reason you have come all the way from India, is one that should not be resolved by me. It is the province of the family, and should you wish, I can arrange a family gathering here, perhaps tomorrow or the next day.'

'Yes, Your Lordship, I agree. I only hope they won't be too upset.'

'They are a very nice family, and I'm sure they won't be. So, in advance of the meeting, let me welcome you to the St Maure family, who are not such a bad lot, either.' He held out his hand.

Henry tentatively held out his, and Justin grasped it gently. 'Your family, My Lord?' exclaimed the astonished ex-footman.

'Yes, of course, I don't suppose you've heard yet, but your half-sister, Miss Rosalie, is engaged to my brother, Benedict. They will be married here, in less than three weeks' time, so we are going to be brothers-in-law.' Justin grinned. 'Now, if you are not too tired, perhaps you can tell me about our new relations.' Justin topped up their ale glasses.

'Gladly, My Lord,' Henry said, with a glimmer of a smile. 'It is always wise to know what you are getting into, even if it is too late. My mother was a princess, the granddaughter of the maharajah, whose son I now serve in the capacity of chief secretary. Her father was a son, by one of His Highness's many wives, not his number one wife, but a prince, nevertheless.'

'Becoming a footman was something of a comedown for you.' Justin couldn't suppress a smile.'

Henry smiled too. 'I learnt more about the English aristocracy than you can begin to imagine, both above and below stairs, My Lord.'

'No, I can't, but I *can* imagine that that was due to your excellent grasp of English. How did that come about?'

'I have a gift for languages, My Lord. I speak four Indian ones fluently and several dialects too. I was determined to speak good English; it is part of my heritage. So I took lessons from the many Englishmen in the East India Company compound, and my position with the maharajah gives me plenty of opportunity to exercise my abilities.'

'Just one more thing, Henry, and then I will leave you in peace. Tell me about your own family.'

Henry smiled. 'I have a lovely wife and three children, two sons and a daughter, My Lord.'

The marquis rose. 'You must miss them very much, and I'm afraid it will be some time before you see them again. Dr Pargeter is not to let you travel again until he considers you quite well enough to do so. I am due to dine at the hall tonight, my mother keeps country hours. I dare not be late. Thank you for all you have told me, and I will arrange a meeting for all interested parties concerning that other matter. Perhaps a small dinner, here, tomorrow?'

'I shall look forward to it, My Lord.'

On arrival at the hall, at the ridiculous hour of five o'clock, for dinner at six, Justin immediately sought out Amanda and found her descending the stairs.

'The very person,' he said, guiding her gently towards the library. 'I have news of a private nature to impart, before we tackle two hours of Antoine's excellent repast.'

'Good news, I hope, Marquis.'

'Indeed, it is. I had a long talk with Henry, and he has said something that will definitely put your mind at rest, at least on one point. So no need to stride up and down the room, as is your wont.' He smiled.

'You'd better tell me quickly, or I shall start striding, as you call it.'

'Firstly, as I have suspected, Henry is definitely a half-brother to Piers and Rosalie; there is no doubt about that.' Amanda gave a gasp. 'But,' went on the marquis, 'he is also illegitimate, according both to the liturgy of the Church of England and in English law.'

Amanda's gasp became a sigh of relief. 'So Piers' inheritance and title are safe?'

'Absolutely.'

'And what about the "you know what"?'

'Ah, now that is something I have not discussed with him, for two reasons; firstly, he is still very weak, and I had no wish to overtire him, and secondly, I think it is something the whole family should hear first hand. Would you not agree, Mrs Fletcher?'

'Yes, and since Rosalie is probably the one who is going to be most affected, Lord Benedict should also be present, don't you think, My Lord?'

'I will arrange a little informal dinner at the Dower House, tomorrow. We keep country hours; say six o'clock. We could have a meeting before that.'

'What about the marchioness? She will surely want to know why her entire house party is deserting her.'

'Leave that to me, Mrs Fletcher.'

'Willingly, but do tell me what else you did find out from Henry.'

Justin relayed what Henry had told him about his background and family history.

He laughed and added, 'I think they rank considerably higher than a mere Marquis, but now we had better join the others, or there will be footmen scurrying all over trying to find us, to tell us that dinner is served.'

CHAPTER 36

The drawing room of the Dower House was arranged with assorted chairs, in a semicircle around the fireplace, centred on a mahogany, piecrust breakfast table, on which rested some papers and a leather-bound book. Amanda and Rosalie entered, followed by Justin, Benedict, and Piers. When all were comfortably seated, an upholstered armchair remained unoccupied.

Justin began, 'Welcome to the Dower House, the scene of my youth and misdemeanours.' He smiled. 'This meeting is about Henry, and I have his full permission to say what I, and Mrs Fletcher, are about to tell you.' He turned to Amanda. 'Would you like to begin?'

'I must say it is difficult to know exactly *where* to begin, but I think I had better start with Sir Percy's will, the part that concerns Rosalie. The will was accompanied by a sealed letter, to be seen only by the trustees, in which he left a very valuable item, intended to form part of Rosalie's dowry, if and when she married.'

'What is it?' Piers and Rosalie both spoke at once.

'I will tell you that later, but first, I must explain how it came into Sir Percy's possession. As you know, he spent many years in India, and while there, he fell in love with a beautiful Indian princess, whom he married, in two separate ceremonies. One was conducted by my late husband, Agnew. And a second, Hindu ritual, was conducted by Brahmin priests. I have documentary evidence of this, which I will reveal later.'

'Was the marriage legal?' Piers interjected. 'I mean, all above board?'

'I know that is a very important question for you, Piers,' said Amanda, 'and I can say this: At the time, all the parties concerned believed that it was, and your father had every intention of bringing his wife back to England. There is a letter on the table that confirms this. When you read it, please treat it with the greatest care; it is very precious to its owner.'

'Who is its owner?' asked Lord Benedict.

Justin replied, 'I thought you would all have guessed by now, that it is Henry.'

'Henry?' exclaimed Piers. 'But he's only a foo—'

'Don't be so patronising, Piers,' Rosalie remarked sharply. 'Never forget, he saved my life.'

'I thought Lord Benedict did that.'

'Yes, but without Henry telling him what had happened, he couldn't have ridden to my rescue.' Rosalie gave her fiancé a dazzling smile.

Justin tapped the table. 'When you two have stopped bickering, perhaps we can get on. Please proceed, Mrs Fletcher.'

'It is just as his lordship says. Henry only took the position as a footman, in order to get closer to the family. He tried to do so while we were at the court and followed us to London.'

'Why would he do a thing like that?' Piers asked, puzzled.

Rosalie gave a sigh of impatience. 'Don't be so obtuse, Piers. If our father married this Indian princess, it's obvious that Henry is their son. I always felt there was something vaguely familiar about him. Despite being dark, there is a definite English look about his features.'

Piers leapt to his feet. 'That can't be true. Henry? My father's son? That makes him my brother. Half-brother. I don't believe it. It's all a trick.'

Amanda intervened. 'Sit down, Piers. I can assure you, and the Marquis will bear me out, Henry is your half-brother, but he poses no threat to you, your inheritance, or your title of baronet. He discovered, not long ago, that the marriage between your father and Princess Sunettra was not valid in English law, and Sir Percy had also been informed of his Indian wife's death before he married your mother. There may be a letter to that effect somewhere at the Court, so your only concern now, is whether or not to accept Henry as part of the family.'

Piers obeyed Amanda and sat down, folding his arms defensively. 'It's all a bit irregular, isn't it? What do you think, Rosie?'

'I think that if you don't accept him, I will never speak to you again. Without his courage and determination, I probably wouldn't be here today.'

'That's a bit harsh, my love,' said Benedict. 'After all, Piers has had a shock. It takes a bit of getting used to. But for my part, I will gladly acknowledge Henry as my brother-in-law. He can give me a few tips on how to keep the silver clean.'

Everybody laughed, and a tense moment was overcome.

'Now, if you would all like to look at the letter, and the other papers, I will go and see if Henry is ready to join us. There is still a lot more to this story, but it should be he who tells it.' The marquis went towards the door. 'However, I would remind you that he is still barely convalescent, and Dr Pargeter, who will join us for dinner later, has made me promise not to let him struggle to sit or stand, or to let you overtire him.'

The chatter that had ensued following Justin's departure quietened as he returned, supporting Henry on his arm. Before anyone spoke, Justin saw to it that his future brother-in-law was settled comfortably in the armchair.

Rosalie got up from her chair and was the first to speak. 'Oh, Henry, I'm so glad you're here; the last time I saw you, I … we… all thought you might die.' She knelt down by his chair and very gently took his right hand in hers.

Lord Benedict quickly added his own good wishes, and Piers mumbled something indistinct, but not overtly hostile.

'I thank you,' Henry began. 'I thank you all, from the very bottom of my heart, for looking after me so well. Especially you, Mrs Fletcher, who helped when I was so very ill. My memory is indistinct, but I do recall your presence. By now, you will all have been told of the circumstances of my parentage and birth. Sir Piers and Miss Rosalie, were you informed of my mother's last wish?' Justin shook his head. 'It was, I was told later, that your father should not be informed of my existence.'

'But why?' Lord Benedict asked. 'I don't understand.'

'My Lord, I was only two weeks old when my mother died, so all I know is what my grandparents, who brought me up, told me. She may have had many reasons, but whatever they were, my grandparents followed her wishes, but they never withheld from me the fact that my father was Percy Abbot, later, of course, Sir Percy.'

Piers, who had regained his composure, said brusquely, 'If you don't want my title, or my inheritance, what do you want?'

Amanda answered instead. 'Henry *wants The Light of the Sun;* he has come all the way from India in the hope that he will be given it, and is now relying on our, or most particularly, on Rosalie's, and perhaps I should add, Lord Benedict's, goodwill.'

'But what is it?' Several voices spoke at once.

Producing a small tattered book with a worn black cover from her unusual pocket, Amanda said, 'This is Agnew's diary of the time he was in India. Let me read the relevant passage. It follows a description of the marriage ceremony.' She turned over several pages and began to read:

> *As we left, a native dignitary of some sort, dressed in colourful robes, and accompanied by a liveried boy servant, came up to the couple and knelt down in front of them. The boy came forward bearing a cushion, upon which was a glistening yellow gemstone. The dignitary took it off the cushion and gave it to Percy. He then got up, and making the Indian sign of respect with his two hands together, as if in prayer, bowed and departed with the boy. Percy looked as if he didn't quite know what to do with it. The light was failing, but even as I approached, the jewel seemed to gather the last rays of the sun to itself.*

Amanda turned to the marquis. 'Will you do the honours, My Lord?'

Justin picked up the thick, leather-bound volume from the table. He carefully lifted out something from a concealed compartment, laying the yellow diamond on the table for all to see. A gasp went up all round, even the two people who had seen it before seemed overcome by its size and beauty.

'Behold!' Justin exclaimed dramatically: *'The Light of the Sun.'*

Piers and Rosalie leant forward eagerly to see it more closely, and Piers put out his hand.

'No,' said Justin. 'Let your sister pick it up.'

Rosalie lifted the jewel by the velvet ribbon, and immediately the last rays of a September evening sun caught the diamond as it revolved, casting its brilliant light to all corners of the room, just as it had done when Justin first saw it.

Rosalie carried it across to Henry, placed it in his hand, and said, 'Tell us about it.'

'I know little about its history, except that it has been in the maharajah's family for many generations, Miss Rosalie. It traditionally belongs to women, and is passed down as a dowry.'

'That's why my father meant it for Rosalie's dowry,' put in Piers, stating the obvious.

'Ah, yes, now I understand,' interrupted the marquis. 'D'you see, Mrs Fletcher? With the marriage not being legal, there should not have been a dowry at all.' He looked at Henry. 'Is that why you believe it does not belong to the Abbots?'

'Precisely that, Your Lordship, but I am asking for it back for a very special reason.'

'Of course you would,' Piers said. 'I've no doubt it is very valuable.'

'Be quiet, Piers.'

'Rosalie, really,' said Amanda.

Henry tried to lean forward to replace the jewel on the table, and Rosalie restrained him. 'Tell us your special reason, Henry.'

'The monetary value of the gem is of no interest to me. I have already explained to his lordship about my position at the maharajah's court, one which I am fortunate to have, since my heritage can sometimes make things awkward with the other courtiers. I have a daughter who is betrothed to one of the maharajah's grandsons. I cannot say that the marriage is conditional *upon The Light of the Sun* being part of her dowry, but the implication is there. It will be a very good marriage for her.'

'How old is your daughter?' asked Rosalie.

'She is twelve.'

'Isn't that much too young to be married?' Amanda asked, with a touch of disapproval in her voice.

'No, Mrs Fletcher, she is betrothed; it is a legal contract, but they will not marry until she is sixteen.'

Piers, who, having got hold of something, was loath to let it go, said, 'So you expect my sister to give up a fabulous diamond with nothing in exchange.'

This time, Amanda intervened, saying sternly, 'Piers, Henry all but gave up his life for your sister; no man can be expected to do more. The question of what happens next is entirely up to Rosalie and Lord Benedict. I'm sorry, Henry; Piers is entirely misguided and should apologise.'

'No apologies are necessary, Mrs Fletcher. Sir Piers is doing just what is expected of him as head of his family, looking after its interests, and he is right; to lose the diamond with nothing in return would also be morally wrong. My Lord, have you brought my box?'

The marquis rose and went over to a desk, bringing back Henry's Chinese puzzle box.

'You will have to open it for me; can you remember how?'

'I think so.' Justin twisted and turned the box for a few moments, and then the lid slid back, but the box was empty. A gasp went up all round.

Henry smiled. 'Search with your fingers along the side; you will feel some inlaid flowers. Press the second one on the right.' Justin did so, but nothing happened. 'Try the other side. Now turn it upside-down and push the base forward.'

The bottom of the box slid open and something wrapped in fine cotton fell out.

'Now please undo it, My Lord.'

A second jewel, quite unlike the yellow diamond, nestled in the white cloth. Nearly an inch square, glowed a fantastic, royal-blue sapphire.

'I hope Miss Rosalie and Lord Benedict will accept this as her dowry. It has no connection with any member of my family; I purchased the gem and had it cut to my design. It is a fine Kashmiri sapphire.' He turned to Rosalie. 'I hope you like it,' he said a little shyly.

Rosalie, who was still beside him, lifted Henry's hand and bestowed a kiss on the back of it.

'It's absolutely beautiful, Henry, and much more my colouring than the diamond.' She took the jewel from the table and went to Benedict. 'Can we have it made into a pendant, so I can wear it on our wedding day, my darling?'

Benedict looked over to his brother. 'Would that be possible, Ju?'

'I'm sure a simple setting could be achieved locally. I will look into it for you. Now everybody, I think we should make the formal return of the Light of the Sun to Henry. Rosalie, will you present the diamond to Benedict as your dowry for your forthcoming nuptials?' Rosalie did so. 'Benedict, will you return the gem to its rightful owner?'

'With all my heart and gratitude. Henry, all our good wishes are with you for your ultimate recovery and for the happiness of your daughter, when she marries.'

'Hear! Hear!' echoed the others, including Piers, whose voice was the loudest.

But Amanda still had a question. 'Why did you go about trying to get the diamond in such a strange way? I was really worried, you know.'

'I am very sorry about that, Mrs Fletcher. My original plan went wrong. I first tried to write to Sir Percy, explaining the situation, but after a year, I got no reply, so I decided to come myself, and as you know, My Lord,' he turned to the Marquis, 'I took a room in the city.'

'You could have gone to the authorities. Your claim was valid.'

'I did consult a lawyer and explained the circumstances, not giving him any names; he said my claim would have no chance of succeeding in a court of law and suggested I tried a personal approach.'

Amanda was not appeased. 'It still seems a very strange way of going about it.'

'My first note was intended for Sir Percy; at that time, I did not know he was dead. There was a sign on it that you probably did not notice, but he would have understood where it came from.' He paused. 'After that, I think I lost my head. I tried not to be menacing in my notes, but I can see now that it might have seemed that way, but what was I to do?'

'You could have called in person,' she said, a little tartly.

Henry gave a cynical smile. 'Imagine, Mrs Fletcher, what would have happened if I, an unknown half-caste Indian, arrived on your doorstep claiming to own a fabulous diamond currently in the possession of the Abbot family. I would probably not have seen the light of day, let alone the Light of the Sun, for years.' The others in the room murmured agreement. 'I then realised that I needed to get to know the family, before I tried another way, so I decided to join the Coverdale household, and in doing so discovered a lovely new family. I'm just sorry I caused you so much anxiety, Mrs Fletcher.'

To ease the slight tension, Rosalie turned to henry. 'it was you who danced with ne t the Alloa's masked ball. Wasn't it?'

'Yes, Miss Rosalie. I hope I didn't frighten you.'

'not at all, Henry, I enjoyed it, but I didn't understand what you were talking about. I didn't know of he diamond's existence hen—'

The Marquis observed the exhaustion in Henry's face. 'I think that's solved that puzzle,' he said. 'Now it's time we all adjourned for supper.'

CHAPTER 37

Two tall women, one dressed in the height of fashion, the other in a plain gown of green muslin, trimmed with an edging of lace, stood facing each other. Neither knew what to say. Neither knew what to do. Amanda was standing in front of her mother, unable to put two coherent thoughts together, never mind words.

Her mother's hair was white. *Would mine be like that in middle age?* The pale blue eyes she recognised from the miniature portrait, then she saw those eyes begin to glisten, and two tears welled out and ran down the older woman's face. Amanda realised that her mother must be hurting, while she was just being curious. She took two steps towards her, then held out her arms.

They held each other in a mutual embrace. 'I'm so sorry. I'm so sorry, my darling child; can you ever forgive me?'

Amanda produced a handkerchief from her unusual pocket, stood back, and gently wiped her mother's tears. 'I don't think forgiveness comes into it, Mo... Ma...'

'If that's too difficult for you, call me Georgina.'

'It's only difficult because I can't remember ever using it before.' This brought more tears to the Countess's eyes. 'Please don't. If forgiveness is due from anyone, it would be from my father. He gave me a happy life, and a good education, but he was not a man to speak about emotions.'

'I know; if he wasn't teaching, he was always reading or writing.'

'It was only when I saw other children with their mothers, that I wondered what I had missed. But many children lose their mothers from childbirth or disease; it didn't really make me different, not having one.'

Georgina managed a watery smile. 'I think you have your father's logical approach to life. That must stand you in good stead, as I have heard from Dr Pargeter that you have had many problems to overcome.'

And one I shall never overcome, thought Amanda, unable to dispel the image of the marquis that so often flashed before her eyes at inconvenient moments, however hard she tried to prevent it. 'Why don't we sit down and have some tea? I am sure that will make us both feel better. We will have plenty of time to get to know one another, and I have yet to meet your husband. Dr Pargeter thought it best for us to meet alone first.'

'Dr Pargeter is a very wise man. I was sorry we lost touch, after Étienne and I moved to Philadelphia. I sent you letters every birthday and Christmas.'

'I didn't know ...'

'Because your father told you I was dead, you could hardly receive letters from beyond the grave. So I expect he destroyed them. Amanda, my darling, I never, ever forgot you. You were in my prayers every single night.'

Amanda couldn't resist a smile. 'And mine were for your soul, in heaven.'

'Tell me about your two wards; you must have been quite young when you became their guardian. Was it difficult?'

'Not at all. I had known them since before Agnew became a trustee; he was a friend of Sir Percy's, and then when Agnew died, I had a ready-made home, just when I needed one.'

'I hope you will let me meet them.'

'Of course; perhaps you will stay for Rosalie's wedding later this month. She is marrying Lord Benedict St Maure, the marquis's brother.'

'She must be very young; do you approve?'

'Spoken like a mother.' Amanda smiled. 'Rosalie is an exceptional girl; they will make the perfect couple; besides,' Amanda added with a laugh, 'Rosalie was born knowing what her little finger was for. Shall we ask your husband and Dr Pargeter to come in?'

Amanda felt that it wouldn't be long before she grew to like her mother; whether she would ever love her was a different matter, but she could already sense a certain rapport, and was relieved that their first meeting had not become too emotional.

The Count entered, and his first glance was toward his wife, a degree of concern in his expression, which relaxed when he realised that the meeting had gone well.

'My dear,' he said, 'will you introduce me to your lovely daughter?'

Introductions concluded, Georgina said, 'Is Dr Pargeter not coming?'

'He will be along in a little while,' replied the count. 'He and the marquis have discovered something about each other that has left them deep in conversation.'

'Will you tell me something about your life together with my mother, Count?'

As he and his wife described some of the difficulties and hardships they had endured, before becoming successful in America, Amanda began to realise how their love for one another had sustained them through some terrible times, including, at one point, near-starvation. She also began to understand that Georgina's abandonment of her husband and child was not a whim of the moment, but indeed was a result of the deep abiding love she had described in her letter. It was what she herself longed for, but the man she wanted could never be there for her.

'Now that you have left America,' Amanda addressed them both, 'what are your plans?'

'Étienne wants to go to France, to see what has become of his home, but as he still has an interest in the business across the Atlantic, England might be a better place to live. For the moment, we are just enjoying being free to please ourselves. *C'est vrai, n'est pas, mon cher?* Tell Amanda about your escape from the Terror, Etienne; it's quite an amazing story.'

The count related his perilous journey, hidden in a turnip cart, sleeping in a hayloft, and disguised as a Belgian shoemaker, before reaching the French coast and being taken in a fishing boat and arriving at Weymouth.

'I suppose somebody must have organised all that. Do you know who?'

'No, but there was talk at the time about a mysterious character, known only as Le *Chat Noir*, the Black Cat.'

At that moment, Dr Pargeter came in, followed by Justin, who asked if he might join them, to which he received a chorus of assent.

'Did I hear you mention the Black Cat, as I came in?' the marquis asked. 'Because I just happen to know who that was; in fact, I have just this minute found out. Isn't that amazing?' He laughed, looking at the Doctor. 'Shall I tell them, or you?'

'Yes,' Pargeter admitted, with a little self-conscious smile, 'I was the man they called the Black Cat, but I was not alone,' he added hastily. 'There were others too. We called them all by that name, just to confuse the French. Every time we made a successful retrieval, a little picture of a black cat was left somewhere the French would find it. I was the organiser and stayed safely in England, although it was necessary for me to travel to France on more than one occasion.' He turned to the marquis. 'Is it not strange that nearly a generation apart, you were in charge of putting agents into France, and I was trying to get people out?'

Immediately, the Count jumped up. 'Let me shake you by the hand; it is something I never thought to do. Thank you with all my heart, *Monsieur le Docteur.*'

Pargeter turned to Amanda. 'There was always an escape that I regretted. I'm sorry, Count; if Weymouth had not been the only available place to land you, I would not have deprived Amanda of her mother, or William Kendal of his wife. It is something I always regretted, although I did what I could, in a small way, to make up for it.'

Amanda's eyes opened wide. 'All those books you lent my father and never seemed to ask for back, those parcels of expensive writing-paper, your visits, my work for Kew Gardens, my marriage to Agnew. All that was because you thought it was your fault?'

'Yes, because in a way it was. But there is one thing I should tell you. After Georgina left, your father wrote three of the best papers on philosophy that I have ever read, but because he had no degree, they could never be delivered under his name, so they went under mine, with an acknowledgement that Kendal as my assistant. I have left it in my will that the real author should be given the credit.'

'I don't think you should go on feeling guilty, Dr Pargeter,' said Georgina. 'I must thank you for looking after my daughter and husband, while I did not, and of course I, too, have felt … no, I have *been* guilty, but in an imperfect world, terrible decisions have to be made, and love can often mean loss too.'

Justin glanced at Amanda, but she was not facing him and did not see the look in his eyes.

CHAPTER 38

With ten days to go before her wedding, Rosalie was becoming increasingly anxious. Her godmother, no doubt with the best of intentions, was almost daily augmenting the plans for the occasion, and was now talking about holding it the parish church, instead of the private chapel at the hall. In desperation, Rosalie decided to talk to Lord Coverdale. She found him in the front hall of the Dower House, preparing to go fishing with Dr Pargeter.

'Please, Your Lordship, may I have a word with you?' Her cornflower blue eyes were dark with worry.

'Of course you may, Rosalie, my dear.' He turned to Pargeter. 'There are usually some good trout runs at the head of the lake, I'll join you there shortly.' When the doctor had gone, he said, 'Now Rosalie, what is troubling you?'

'It's ... it's the marchioness, my godmother, I don't know how to ...' her voice tailed off.

Just input down his fishing tackle. 'I think we'd better go into the drawing room, and you can tell me what my mother's been up to.'

'She ... she's very kind, I know, but now she's talking about having the wedding in the parish church, and having lots more people, and a wedding breakfast in the Great Hall. It's not for myself that I'm asking, but I know ... I just know that Benedict can't take it. He's still much too fragile for big social occasions. I'm so afraid for him, My Lord, and I don't know what to do. Can you help me?' her voice trembled on the brink of tears.

'Oh, Rosalie, that sounds like my mother all over. I'm afraid I have kept out of the arrangements for your wedding. You'd better put me in the picture.'

'It was all right at first. Well, you know it was going to be a private ceremony in the chapel, and then a small wedding breakfast, with just the family, and a few people the marchioness said would have to be asked, with a simple meal in the dining room, and a cake.'

'That sounds like an excellent plan and not too stressful for Benedict.'

'And it was, My Lord, and as you know, in the evening, it's the Harvest Feast, for all your workers and tenants, and you and your mother were going to host it, as usual. Benedict and I were just going to make an appearance, so everyone could drink a toast, and now she wants to hold it on another night, and everyone will have to be told, and Clarkson's tearing his hair out.'

'Rosalie, you did absolutely the right thing, in coming to tell me. Rest assured, my future sister-in-law, everything will go ahead as originally planned, and we certainly can't let Clarkson lose what little hair he has left, can we?' He smiled and received a reciprocal one from Rosalie, signifying both relief and amusement. 'By the way,' he added, 'how have you and Piers got on with the de Vailleuxs?'

'Very well. It is so nice for Amanda to have someone of her own, at last.'

'She told you?'

'No, I guessed that they must be related, and she admitted it. They are very alike, but Piers doesn't know yet.'

'I believe it is right that the relationship should remain a secret, at least for the time being; too many questions would be asked.'

'Thank you, Sir, for listening to me, I was getting really worried, you know…'

'I understand that, Rosalie, and you are the last person who should have that added anxiety. You've done so much for this family. I can never thank you enough.'

'I love Benedict, he is like my other half, and just now he needs very careful looking after. I think of him like an egg.'

'An egg?'

'Well. more like a newly hatched bird, perhaps; it needs lots of care until it can fly. I want him to fly; can you understand that, My Lord?'

'It's a strange way of thinking about it, but yes, I understand. You are a very remarkable young woman, Rosalie, and stop calling me "My Lord"; my name is Justin.'

'Well then, Justin, you'd better go and see what Dr Pargeter is up to. He'll have caught all the fish by now, or fallen in.'

Rosalie returned to the hall in better spirits, to be greeted with more good news. Amanda was holding a letter.

'This is from Lady Carstairs; she is going to allow Lady Sophia to come to the wedding and be your bridesmaid. I know that is what you wanted.'

Rosalie clapped her hands. 'That's wonderful; how did you manage that?'

'It was all arranged by your godmother, I asked her if it would be possible, and as luck would have it, Lady Denton, her eldest daughter, is staying in Berkeley Square and will chaperone Sophia. Hubert Dorsett is also coming. Piers needs someone to keep him out of the way and will escort them. I knew you'd be pleased.'

'Why didn't you tell me before?'

'I didn't want you to be disappointed if the plan didn't work out. Where have you been this afternoon?'

'I was worried about the wedding plans getting bigger and bigger, I went to see if the Marquis—Justin, he says I'm to call him that, as I'm going to be his sister-in-law—to see if he could help.'

'And can he?'

'Yes, he says he quite understands my concern and will sort it all out. I'm very relieved, Amanda. He's very nice, you know.'

'Yes, he is. Now your fiancé was looking for you; he said he'd be in the chapel, something about the organ and the music for the wedding.' Amanda looked at the gold fob-watch pinned to her dress. 'There's time to go there before dinner, if you hurry.'

The chapel was attached to the east wing of the hall. It protruded beyond the outer wall of the building, which area contained the altar and choir stall, behind which was a small, two-keyboard organ. The pipes were beautifully decorated, and as Rosalie entered, music was issuing from them. There were six rows of high-backed benches on either side of a narrow aisle, each bench with enough seating for four or five people, making room for a congregation of about sixty. The family pews were in a gallery overhanging the west end. The high windows in either side were of plain glass, but the east window was in the early Gothic style, with three pointed arches, each window depicting a different saint. The whitewashed walls bore many memorials to the St Maure family.

Rosalie stood for several minutes in the chancel, listening to Benedict playing, until something made him turn round, and the music died. He beckoned her to join him.

'Have you ever played an organ, Ros?' She shook her head. 'It's somewhat similar to the piano, but as you see, there are foot pedals, too, and the organ stops make groups of pipes play together, alter volume, and other things, depending on which ones you pull out. Like to try?'

'Yes.'

'Come and sit beside me.' Benedict slid along the bench. 'Take the treble end. The organ has to have wind, which is why young Jimmy pumps away like mad to keep the sound going.' He nodded in the lad's direction, and after a few seconds, Benedict began to play, using his left hand on the bass notes. Rosalie recognised a piece by Handel and picked up the tune on the treble notes. Hoping Jimmy wasn't looking, but not really caring if he was, they wrapped their spare arms around each other and kissed.

'Thank you, Jimmy,' Benedict said. 'That will do for today.'

He threw the boy a shilling, which was neatly caught. Jimmy grinned and touched his forelock before making good his escape. He usually only got sixpence.

'We'll have to sort out our music for the wedding, my love,' said Benedict, his arm still round Rosalie's waist. 'The church organist is quite good, but this organ is much smaller than the one in St Mary's.'

'I would like to enter the chapel to the sonatina you wrote for me,' she said. 'It is, after all, what brought us together. Can you write it for the organ?'

'Yes, that won't be a problem, and we must have something by Handel; he is supposed to have played on this very instrument. There is documentary evidence in the archives; at least there's a letter, thanking the then marchioness for his visit to Coverdale, so the family presumes he probably had a go at the organ too.'

'Really, Benedict, that's close to blasphemy, saying that one of England's greatest composers "had a go."' They both laughed as Benedict closed the organ doors. 'There's something you're not telling me, though, isn't there?'

'How do you know?' Benedict raised an eyebrow. 'I shouldn't need to ask that; you always know. I love you, my darling Rosalie.'

She looked up at him; he was a foot taller than she was. 'Well, what is it?'

'It's the sergeant. I've asked him to be my best man, and he's categorically refused; in fact, when I pressed him, he got quite angry and left the room.'

'What about Justin? Shouldn't he be your best man?'

'Yes, there is that too. I don't know what to do.'

Rosalie patted him on the chest. 'There's still over a week to the wedding; I'm sure things will all work out for the best. You'll see.'

CHAPTER 39

T he weather had turned blustery, with frequent squalls of rain and early falling leaves swirling in the wind, but Rosalie put on her strongest boots and cloak, tying the ribbons of the hood tightly together. No amount of inclement conditions were going to delay her mission. It didn't take long to reach Mrs Mary's cottage, and she wasted no time in knocking on the door.

The sergeant answered it, holding Arthur in his arms. 'Miss Rosalie,' he exclaimed. 'Mary is round at the barn.'

'I'll see her later. It is you I have come to see. May I come in?'

'Is your maid with you, Miss?'

'No, and if you're thinking I need a chaperone, Arthur will have to do.' She grinned, and the sergeant stood aside to let her enter. The small room he showed her into was cosy, with a fire burning in the grate.

Rosalie undid her cloak, and he helped her off with it. 'Turned nasty, today,' he observed.

'I haven't come here to talk about the weather, Sergeant.'

'No, Miss, I don't suppose you 'ave.'

'I will come straight to the point. You have upset the Captain by not agreeing to be his best man at our wedding, but I expect you already know that. Perhaps you could tell me why you have dug your heels in?'

'Not my place, Miss,' the sergeant mumbled. ''is lordship—'

'Not your place, Sergeant? Fiddlesticks!' Rosalie exclaimed. 'Who was beside him all through the American war? Who was beside him at Waterloo, until the guns could fire no more? Who carried you back to

235

the field hospital? And who has looked after him, day and night, when he could do nothing for himself, and would probably have died otherwise? And now you refuse to stand beside him while he gets married, to me. Not your place? *He* wants you to be his best man, you *are* his best man, and added to that, **I** want you to be his best man. Have I made myself clear, Sergeant?'

'Yes, Miss.'

'Now, I can understand why you have refused, and this is my suggestion: If you will agree to be his best man in the chapel, where he wants you most, during the ceremony, and holding the ring.' She smiled. 'And probably his hand, too, but once that part is over, his Lordship will take on all the other duties of a best man. You can then return to Mary, and in the evening, bring all those coming to the Harvest Feast from Longacre. Will you agree to that? Your captain needs moral support, from the man he has been closest to for at least five years, as well as someone to see that his neckcloth is properly tied.'

'Yes, Miss Rosalie.' The sergeant gave his lopsided grin, knowing that he had been rolled up, horse, foot, and guns!

'Good, that's settled, then. I knew you'd see sense. If you weren't a sensible man, you would never have helped me with the Captain in the first place.'

'This arrangement, does the Captain agree to it?'

'Rosalie smiled. 'He doesn't know yet, but I'm certain he'll be very pleased.'

'Oh, Miss Rosalie, you are a one-off, you really are. Pardon the expression.'

At that moment, Mrs Mary came in, surprised to see their guest, and immediately offered refreshment.

'No, thank you, Mary. I must be getting back, but I was just saying to your husband that you and he must bring as many of the men from the barn as are able, or want, to come to the harvest feast. I will arrange a special table for them.' She picked up her cloak, and the sergeant helped her on with it. 'No beating a retreat on our deal, now, Sergeant.'

'Much as my life's worth, Miss.'

'Very true.'

At the doorway, Mary said to Rosalie, 'It was your doing, bringing us together, wasn't it, Miss?'

'Let us just say that it seemed the right thing to do.'

Under the generalship of Clarkson, preparations for the wedding were well under way. The ceremony was scheduled for eleven o'clock, and following a brief respite, the wedding party would then be ready to receive guests in the front hall, to be ushered into the dining room for the wedding breakfast. This was intended to end by half past two, to give staff time to concentrate on the evening's harvest feast in the Great Hall.

In the tradition of the feast, the gardeners were responsible for the decoration of the hall, with fruit, flowers, and vegetables, and with the addition of sheaves of wheat, corn, and barley from the tenant farmers, and the estate workers with swags of greenery. The three huge, wrought iron chandeliers, that hung from the vaulted ceiling of the hall, were lowered and fitted with two tiers of wax candles, before being hoisted up again, to avoid risk of fire. Candelabra were arranged on the three long trestle tables that would be set up for the meal. A baron of beef would be placed at the end of each long table, and traditionally, the incumbent marquis, Justin, in this case, would carve the first slices for the hundred and fifty invited guests.

In contrast, the wedding-breakfast tables in the dining room, were arranged in the form of a horseshoe, with snow-white damask cloths, and an abundance of silverware. The meal would be restricted to six courses, including soup, fish, poultry, beef and lamb, and a large assortment of jellies, creams, syllabubs, pastries, and of course a wedding cake. The seating arrangements for this occasion occupied the marchioness to the exclusion of almost everything else, for which Clarkson was eternally grateful, since she had the habit, in the past, of wanting to make last minute, sometimes drastic changes, to already agreed arrangements.

Amanda, Rosalie, and Sophia Carstairs were fully occupied with styles, colours, and fabrics for their respective gowns. Wilkins and Jennie were co-operating in designing hairstyles. Extra seamstresses were drafted in from Saffron Walden, as time was short. Piers, delighted with the arrival of

Hubert Dorsett, spent most of the time well away from what he described as 'a lot of unnecessary fuss' over his sister's wedding, although he was quite proud to be the one to give her away, when the time came.

On the day of the wedding, the blustery weather had passed, and when Rosalie was woken by Jennie pulling back the curtains, the sun was shining.

'Oh, Miss,' she said, 'it's so exciting, you getting wed today, and Lord Benedict so handsome and all.'

'Yes, it is, Jennie, but I shall be glad when it's all over.' Rosalie was seriously concerned that the occasion might be too stressful for Benedict. 'What is the time, Jennie?'

'Just after eight, Miss.'

'I will have breakfast *en deshabille,* in our boudoir. Is Mrs Fletcher up yet?'

'I think so, Miss; Miss Wilkins is with 'er, and Lady Sophia too.'

'Good. We can all discuss in what order we should prepare. I want you to do my hair, Jennie. We can decide who does Lady Sophia's, but of course, Wilkins will do Mrs Fletcher's.'

'Oh, Miss, can I really? I thought Miss Wilk—'

'I was going to ask you, Jennie. After I'm married, would you like to be my maid and come to Kent with his lordship and me, or would you rather go back to London? Have you got family there?'

'Only me bruvver, Miss, an' 'e don't much want me around. Can I really come wiv you?'

'Yes, of course, now I'll go and have my breakfast, then I shall take a little walk, only about half an hour, while you lay out all my wedding clothes. I expect Wilkins will want to supervise; don't upset her.' Rosalie smiled. 'After all, when Mrs Fletcher comes to stay with us in Kent, you will take precedence over Wilkins in the servants' hall.'

Rosalie returned from her walk, feeling refreshed and eager to start the lengthy preparations required for a wedding. She found Sophia's hair arrangement almost complete. Her dark hair was piled into a chignon, with ringlets framing her face, and tiny curls drawn across her forehead, only the coronet of small blue and white flowers was yet to be put in place. After her bridesmaid's dress had been put on, Jennie immediately started on Rosalie's hair style, which was similar, but longer at the back, and instead of flowers, which she would have preferred, one of the smaller Coverdale tiaras was glittering on the dressing table, waiting to secure a veil of Honiton lace.

Three quarters of an hour before the ceremony was due to take place, Sophia was already fully dressed, and Jennie had just finished tying Rosalie's stays, there came a gentle tap on the door.

'See who that is, Jennie; Sophy, you can help me on with my petticoat.'

Jennie came back and whispered in her mistress's ear, 'It's the sergeant, Miss; he says it's urgent.'

Rosalie's heart sank; she was sure it was news that she had been half-expecting. 'Quick, Sophy, tie the petticoat. Jennie, give me my robe. I must go; quickly, girl.' She shrugged into the silk dressing gown and whisked out of the room. The sergeant was standing a little way beyond the door.

'It's the Captain, Miss; 'e's gone.'

Rosalie had never seen the sergeant look so worried. 'What do you mean, gone? Gone where?'

''e was just a-tying of 'is neckcloth, when 'e all of a sudden like, tore it off, an' throws it on the floor, an' rushes out of the room, saying, "I can't … it's not fair," an' I don't know where to look. What shall I do, Miss?'

Rosalie saw that the sergeant at a complete loss. 'Don't worry, Sergeant. I'll find him; I sort of expected this.'

'You did, Miss?'

'Yes. Lord Benedict is not yet fully recovered; he's bound to feel the stress of the occasion. Besides, weren't you nervous before your wedding?' Rosalie knew that the sergeant needed reassurance too, although she didn't feel all that reassured herself.

'But where is 'e, Miss? This is such a great barrack of a 'ouse, an' I ain't been 'ere afore, like. 'E could be anywhere.'

'I think I know; leave that to me, but I want you to do something too, Sergeant.'

'Anything that'll 'elf, Miss.'

'Good, then find Clarkson, tell him you need to speak to his lordship urgently, but privately. Let's hope that doesn't take too long, and when you speak to his lordship, tell him what happened and have him take control of things, if we're late, which we may be. He will know what to do. Tell him also that I am dealing with the situation. After that, come up to the west door of the long gallery and wait. Have you got that?'

'Yes, Miss.'

'This is the moment to be the best of best men; now go.'

Rosalie went back into her room and beckoned to Sophy. 'Find Amanda, and tell her that I have had to go and sort out a little problem.'

'What's the matter? You're not dressed yet.'

'Never mind that; just do as I ask, please. That's what bridesmaids are for.' She hesitated for a moment. 'Tell her that the marquis knows about it; that should ease her mind. Please hurry, Sophy,; there's not much time.'

Rosalie picked up her petticoat and dashed along corridors, round corners, and up the stairs, finally arriving at the long gallery, entering by the east door. Immediately in front of her was the tower alcove and her harp. She tiptoed towards it, turned the little gilt knob, and eased open the door to the tower, leaving it just ajar. Then she sat on the window seat and began to play her harp. Just soothing cords at first, then gradually segueing into the melody of her sonatina. She ignored a slight sound coming from the tower and started to play the variations she and Benedict had worked on together in Berkeley Square. There was a shuffling sound, followed by creaks. The door opened a little more. Ignoring it, Rosalie played on.

After about five minutes, the door opened wide, and Benedict, almost bent double, covered in dust and in shirtsleeves, came out. Rosalie didn't say a word, just smiled, and indicated that he should sit beside her. He put his arm around her.

She stopped playing and kissed his cheek, whispering, 'You silly old thing,' then added, 'we can stay here as long as you like, until you're ready.'

The sergeant was waiting for them exactly as Rosalie had requested. 'The Captain could do with a bit of a dusting down, don't you think, sergeant?'

CHAPTER 40

The wedding went superbly well. The blue and white theme was carried out in the chapel, with flowers in the windows and ribbons at the end of each pew. In front, on the right, stood Benedict and Justin, each attired in black swallow-tail coats, satin knee-breeches, white silk stockings, and silver-buckled shoes. The marquis wore the red ribbon of a Knight Commander of the Bath across his chest, and Benedict's waistcoat had been fashioned from a fine eighteenth-century Spitalfields silk one, embroidered with flowers. Between the two brothers, the sergeant stood resplendent in the uniform of the Royal Horse Artillery. Behind them sat the marchioness, her daughter, and an elderly uncle. On the other side, Amanda, wearing her favourite pale amber, trimmed and flounced in creamy Valenciennes lace, sat in front. The de Vailleuxs were behind her and Henry and Dr Pargeter behind them. The front row of the balcony was occupied by senior members of the household.

Rosalie, in a gown of white satin, with a demi-train edged in lace, and a fine veil of silk muslin, entered on the arm of her brother. The gown had a heart-shaped décolletage and long sleeves, puffed at the shoulder. She carried a posy of white roses, tied with long blue ribbons; suspended round her neck was the magnificent sapphire, which ustin had had set in a simple white gold surround, and matching chain.

The bride and groom made their responses, the sergeant placed the ring on the Bible, and the ceremony ended with a bridal kiss. There being no vestry in the chapel, the book was signed and witnessed in the library. Those concerned with the formal reception and wedding breakfast departed to the front hall, to receive guests. Henry, Dr Pargeter, the de Vailleuxs, and Hubert Dorsett went back to the Dower House, for their own luncheon.

To Rosalie, the six-course meal seemed interminable, but speeches mercifully were kept short, a factor that had much to do with the Justin's intervention, who understood the strain Benedict must be under. After the cake was cut and distributed, the couple stayed no longer than was polite.

By mutual consent, Rosalie and Benedict went to their respective apartments to rest before the evening's entertainment. As Jennie had unlaced Rosalie's stays, after carefully laying the wedding dress and petticoat in the press, Amanda came in.

'Thank you, Jennie. I want to speak to Lady Benedict.'

The little maid made a curtsey. 'Yes, Mrs Fletcher, My Lady.'

'Now, Rosalie, was that, as the Duke of Wellington once said, "a damn close-run thing"?'

Rosalie laughed. 'Not really, although we might have been a bit late.'

'I nearly had a fit when I was summoned to see the marquis and told that Benedict had disappeared. When you got back, there was no time to talk, only to get your dress on. Can you tell me what happened?'

'I told Justin that Benedict was still like a bird that had not yet learned to fly. He just got a bit too far out on a branch and didn't know how to get back; that's all.'

Amanda gave Rosalie a long look but said nothing.

'I expect the sergeant was still wielding a clothes brush at the chapel door, but everything was beautiful in the end, wasn't it, Amanda?'

Amanda put her arms round Rosalie. 'Oh, my darling, I'm going to miss you so much.' Her eyes glistened with tears.

'And I will miss you too, and Piers, but you can come and stay, once we're settled. I want my darling Benedict to have peace and quiet, and for us to enjoy being really together, at least until after Christmas.'

'Of course you do, and my mother and Etienne are also coming to Abbots Court, and Henry, too, when he's fit enough for such a long journey. Piers is talking about setting up a stud farm.' She pressed her eyes to keep the tears from falling. 'Now, you have a good rest; there's plenty more excitement to come.'

When Benedict and Rosalie entered the Great Hall, the feasting was already over. The marquis had done the honours of carving the beef, and the tables groaned with tureens of vegetables, jugs of gravy, and tankards of the best ale and beer, which were constantly being replenished. There were also gammons of fine ham and raised game pies. As was traditional, Justin and his mother sat at a table on a raised dais, in front of the fireplace, to have their meal with the heads of all the departments, responsible for the smooth running of the large estate.

When the dinner was over, the minstrels, situated in the gallery, struck a loud chord; two footmen entered, bearing a second wedding cake, immediately followed by Rosalie and Benedict. The tumultuous applause was deafening. His lordship held up his hand for quiet and made a speech, thanking everyone for all their hard work during the year.

He ended by saying, 'And now I want to introduce two people, one you know well, my brother, Lord Benedict, and the other, his lovely new wife, Lady Rosalie, whom I know some of you have already met.' There were more cheers and the sound of tankards being thumped on the table. 'Now, please, Rosalie, Benedict, will you cut the cake?'

After the first ceremonial cut, the cake was whisked away, to return, sliced and ready to be given to each person, with both Justin and Benedict helping in the distribution, but Rosalie took a large plate, piled with cake, to a special table at the end of the hall. There were seven or eight people seated there, and Rosalie was delighted to see that Davy was amongst them. The men rose at her approach.

'Sergeant, Mary, I hope you've all had a really good feast.' To Rory, who was blind, she said, 'I've brought you all some cake. May I sit down? I want to enjoy it with you.'

The chairs were shoved round, and the sergeant went off to assist Benedict. Rosalie sat down beside Davy. 'Will you allow me to give you some of my cake?'

'I dunno, Miss, it's not for the likes …' Rory nudged him in the ribs, and he realised his mistake. 'My Lady.'

'Fiddlesticks!' said her newly entitled ladyship. 'It is everyone's place to help men like you, who have given so much for their country.' She picked up a spare fork and gently offered him a piece of cake. She also heard him say to Rory, 'Some of your cake has fallen off your plate, on the right.'

Perhaps a mutual aid partnership was developing. She sincerely hoped so. Benedict joined them. 'I'm so glad you could come; enjoy the rest of the evening,' he said, 'but now I must take my wife away so they can clear the hall, ready for the dance.'

All the rest of the party, except Henry and Dr Pargeter, came in for the dancing. The bride and groom led out the first waltz but were not seen much after that; Justin invited Amanda, but was almost silent throughout, and she felt it was very much as etiquette demanded, rather than any desire on his part to do so. Piers, Sophia, and Hubert had a grand time, under the watchful eye of Lady Denton. The marchioness retired early, fatigued after all the excitement of the day.

Rosalie and Benedict departed the next morning for his estate in Kent, and over the next few days, Coverdale Hall would empty of guests, and it would go back to sleep, until Christmas.

While preparing to leave, Wilkins came to Amanda, complaining that one of her bandboxes was missing.

'Don't worry about it; it must just have got overlooked when they were getting luggage out. I'll see if I can find a footman to look for it.'

She walked down a particularly dark corridor, thinking that no matter how many footmen there were, one could never find one when one actually needed one. A square of light filtered onto the floor as a door was opened, and within seconds, she was nearly knocked over by the solid figure of the marquis. He put his arm out to steady the person he had bumped into.

'Oh!' Amanda let out a cry.

At the sound of her voice, his grip changed to an embrace. His head lowered, and his mouth met hers. She made no attempt to escape, and for a few blissful seconds, she could taste his lips, teasing hers, then becoming demanding. Her hand came up to feel the texture of his hair, smell the fragrance of his skin. Earth was turned to heaven, as her entire body was filled with an exquisite, and hitherto unknown, sensation.

Then he pushed her towards the wall and squeezed past, muttering, 'I'm sorry, Amanda, I'm so sorry,' and hastened down the passage.

As she caught her breath and regained her composure, Amanda heard a door slamming shut.

CHAPTER 41

Hubert and Piers had left for the Dorsett's country seat in Warwickshire; the Marchioness, Amanda, Sophia, and Lady Denton set off for Berkeley Square. The Dower House party, including Henry, departed two days later and would eventually journey on to Abbots Court, with Amanda. For several days, Justin had estate business to attend to, but when that was completed, he mooched about the grounds, knowing he could no longer put off the moment he had dreaded for so long. He knew, also, that he should never have kissed Amanda, but he didn't regret a second of it. It was a guilty pleasure he would never forget, especially as her response told him everything he wanted to know, but could never have. The sooner he made it beyond his reach forever, the better.

The next day, Justin ordered his horse; riding was quicker than driving, as he could go cross-country. In half an hour, he was at the gates of the manor. He trotted towards the square-built, pink-brick house that held his future and halted before the porticoed front door. He tied his horse to the ring-post and raised his hand, but before he could grasp the knocker, the door opened, and he was immediately surrounded by a stream of assorted dogs, including a small terrier with only three legs. Amongst them stood Honoria Prideau, who, for a moment, he mistook for a maid or housekeeper. Over a plain blue dress, she was wearing a calico bib-and-apron with two large pockets stitched onto the front.

'I saw you coming, Justin. Come in.' She called to someone in the back, 'Eddie, put the dogs in the kitchen.' A female voice called to them, then a manservant appeared and helped the marquis divest himself of his greatcoat, gloves, and hat.

The three-legged terrier remained at the feet of its mistress, who scooped it up. 'Bloody snares,' she said, adding, 'come this way.'

Justin was stunned into silence. All he had managed to accomplish on arrival, so far, was to raise his hat and bow, his opening remarks sticking in his throat. Honoria led the way into a pleasant, comfortable, but slightly shabbily furnished room, shedding the hideous apron as she went, revealing that the navy-blue gown was exceedingly plain, with long sleeves and a high neckline, no lace, trimmings, or jewellery, nothing to take the eye from an undoubtedly flat chest. Justin almost wished the apron was back.

'I hope I find you well, Honoria, and the general.' Justin at last found his voice.

'I am as fit as a fiddle, I thank you, but my father is dying.'

Justin, knowing this to be the case, muttered his sympathies.

'I'll take you in to see him when this is over, Justin. You'd better get on with it. I haven't got all day.'

The Marquis felt he had been carried into some sort of back-to-front dream world. What was Honoria saying? Was she mad, or was he? This was not the Honoria Prideau he knew in society London.

'I'm sorry, Justin, that was rude of me, but I've had to wait for this for so long.' She looked alarmed. 'Don't tell me you've come for some other reason, broken fences, straying cattle?'

'No, indeed, not.' He took a deep breath, but before he could get any words out, Honoria turned away to open an adjoining door.

'Eddie, you'd better come and hear this. I don't want any misunderstandings later on.'

The person Honoria called Eddie was small, round, rosy-cheeked woman of thirty-plus years of age, wearing a simple but fashionable gown and a mob cap.

'May I introduce my somewhat distant cousin, Miss Editha Dearing? Eddie, the Marquis of Coverdale.' Thus presented, the two parties curtsied and bowed, respectively. 'Go back into the other room, Eddie,' Honoria ordered. 'I don't suppose his lordship wants to say what he has to say with others present, but leave the door open so you can hear.' She turned to face Justin. 'Eddie goes into society sometimes and often corresponds with her brother's wife, Agatha Dearing, a great gossip, and a friend of your mother's, I believe. Anything said in this room today will be all over town in no time. Well, best get it over with, My Lord.'

Justin had had to let go the deep breath he'd started with previously, so he went down on one knee and took another. 'Miss Prideau, Honoria, will you do me the greatest honour of becoming my wife?'

'No, My Lord, I will not.'

'I'm sorry I kept you waiting for so long.'

'Didn't you hear me, Justin? I said, no. I do not wish to marry you, although I am conscious of the honour you do me, in asking, despite the fact that you didn't want to, but I have no intention of being a wife, yours or anyone else's. Now that's settled, do get up; you look very uncomfortable down there. You'll find the sofa more to your taste. Eddie,' she called out, 'come back and pour us some of that fine claret. Lord Coverdale looks as though he could do with it. We should drink a toast. My father, when he was able, always kept an excellent cellar.'

Every conceivable thought was galloping through Justin's mind. He was free. She had refused. Had he really heard right? Was he dreaming? Should he ask again?

He felt a glass being pressed into his nerveless hand and a voice saying, 'It's all right, Justin; your months of agony are over, and so are mine. Let us drink to a happier future for all of us. Eddie, go and tell Brogan to rug up his lordship's horse.'

Wanting to confirm that it was all true, Justin said, 'You're absolutely sure, Honoria?'

'Yes, of course I am. If only you'd asked me a year ago, I could have refused you then.'

'Would you have?'

'Yes, but then you wrote that stupid letter to my father, and I just had to wait. I must say you took your time. I tried flirting with you, but I'm no good at it, and then you had to go and fall for that Mrs Fletcher.'

'Just a minute, Honoria, what are you saying?'

'You can't fool me, Justin; it's written all over you, but perhaps it's in a code that only women, or perhaps only people who have known you for a long time, could decipher.'

247

'I don't think I know you at all, Honoria.'

'Perhaps not; the person you see in society is not the real me, and you've probably forgotten what I was like when we were younger: no interest in girlish pursuits.'

'I'm beginning to realise that. So what does the real you want to do with your life?'

'When the General dies, I expect it any moment now, Eddie and I are going to have a sanctuary here for sick, injured, and unwanted animals.' She patted the three-legged terrier, snuggled in beside her. 'We've already collected quite a few, but we need money to do it properly, and Father threatened to disinherit me if I didn't marry. Now I can tell him that you've proposed, or rather you can. He won't believe *me.*'

'But you turned me down.'

'Yes, but he won't know that. Since his second stroke, he is almost completely paralysed and has lost the power of speech, except for two words: "marmalade," which means "yes" and all things good, and "dog," which means "no" and all things bad. Sad, but there it is, although he can understand everything that's being said, so mind your manners.'

'That's awful, Honoria. I'm so sorry.'

'Don't be. He's very well looked after. One more thing before we go in and see him. If you want to use any of the land which borders yours, there is more than I need for my project; I will lease it to you at a very reasonable rent, with one proviso: No hunting or shooting over it. I do my best to stop the poachers, but, as you see …' She patted the terrier again.

For the second time, the marquis was almost speechless. 'I'll think about it,' he croaked.

'Bring your drink with you, Justin; it's time to tell my father the good news.'

Honoria led the way across the hall to a large front room, that had once been the main saloon, but was now furnished with a large half-tester bed, and all the accoutrements required for nursing the very sick patient, who was propped up on many pillows, eyes closed.

'Someone to see you, Father. He has something to tell you.'

The eyes opened, and the left hand raised about two inches from the covers. A barely audible voice quavered the word, 'Marmalade.'

Justin cleared his throat. 'General, sir, I have just asked your daughter for her hand in marriage, and ...' He almost stumbled over the words: '... and she has made me the happiest man in England.'

Honoria smiled; the General said, 'Marmalade,' and pointed feebly to a table arranged with multiple medicine bottles and a carafe of water. Honoria went over to pour some out.

'Dog, dog, dog,' came a stronger voice, that passed for a shout.

'He wants some wine,' Honoria explained and disappeared to get the decanter, returning with it and a wine glass. A small amount was dispensed into it, and a large refill for the marquis. Honoria raised the glass to her father's colourless lips, and Justin took a large swallow of his. He didn't think he'd ever needed one more.

'Marmalade,' the General said and fell back exhausted, onto the pillows.

'Time to go,' said Honoria.

'How long has he got?' asked Justin.

'Difficult to say; the doctor reckons no more than a week, probably less, but you never know. I will keep him comfortable for as long as it takes. I think he'll be quite happy now.'

They were in the hall, and Justin picked up his outer garments. 'It's true what I said to your father, Honoria; you have made me the happiest man in England. Thank you.' He raised her hand to his lips.

'I know.' She picked up her hideous apron. 'I must go and feed my animals. Just leave the rug on the post, and don't keep Mrs Fletcher waiting.' She opened the door.

The combination of elation and too much claret on an empty stomach caused the marquis to vault too quickly into the saddle, and he fell off the other side. He could hear Honoria laughing as he remounted and cantered away, waving his hat.

CHAPTER 42

J ustin was driving a sad jade of a horse, pulling a gig that had seen better days, an equipage that he wouldn't be seen dead in, in London, but because he was driving towards the greatest happiness of his life, he couldn't care less. Abbots Court soon came into view, the October afternoon sun lightening its grey stones, and glinting off the narrow lattice windows, just as Amanda had described it. He drew up at the iron-studded door and jumped down, throwing the reins to the groom who had been sitting behind him. He yanked on the massive handle and could hear the bell jangling, somewhere deep inside the building.

Less than a minute passed, but to Justin, it seemed like an eternity, before the heavy door creaked open, and a black-clad servant said, 'Yes, Sir?'

'I have come to see Mrs Fletcher.'

The butler looked the marquis up and down with a critical eye and, recognising a person of quality, said, 'Who shall I say is calling, Sir?'

'My card.' The Justin extracted a white card, engraved with the words, 'The Most Noble, The Marquis of Coverdale,' and bearing a marquis's coronet.

The butler bowed deeply. 'My Lord,' he intoned, slightly overcome by such an exalted presence.

'Mrs Fletcher?' said the marquis. 'Perhaps you could convey to her my compliments, and my desire to see her.'

'Mrs Fletcher is not currently in the house, My Lord.'

'Will she be home soon?'

'I cannot say, My Lord; she has gone out in the … er, trap.'

'With Duncan, no doubt, so she cannot be far; do you know where?'

The servant gave the glimmer of a smile at the mention of Amanda's donkey. 'I believe she mentioned Jeffries' Field, My Lord.'

'Can you direct me? Is it far?'

'By foot, it is but a quarter of a mile, but if you wished to drive,' the butler looked critically at the vehicle, 'it is nearly two miles, My Lord.'

'I shall walk; please direct me, and please will you inform Sir Piers of my arrival, and arrange some refreshment for the driver and horse.'

'It shall all be as you wish, My Lord, but Sir Piers is not currently in residence; the Count and Countess de Vailleux, and Mr Henry, are staying here. I shall give orders for your groom and horse.' He bowed.

The butler's directions proved accurate, and most of the way was through woodland with a well-cared-for path, for which Justin was thankful. Believing that it was only right and proper to come courting in his best, he was attired in a bottle-green, superfine, swallow-tail coat, pale yellow pantaloons, and Hessians, which Roberts had spent hours bringing to their height of glossy perfection. The walk through the autumn-tinted woodland was a pleasant one, and the wicket gate that led onto the field where Amanda was said to be working soon came into view, as the trees thinned, Justin could see her, seated on her folding stool, bent over her work, oblivious to everything else.

As he was about to stride towards her, in joyous anticipation, two other things caught his eye and turned the moment of joy into one of absolute terror. In the next field, there was a very large bull, and the gate between the fields was wide open. While every instinct cried out for instant action, a cool head and a careful plan were what he needed now. The bull was not grazing peacefully, but standing still, moving his huge, horned head from side to side. The knew that bulls were short-sighted and reacted to movement, more than to anything else. Returning officers from the peninsula had told him of bullfights in Spain, and how matadors deliberately made the animals charge by flourishing a cape (and also that not all matadors survived).

Justin stood stock-still, while he did some calculations. Amanda was seated closer to a gate in the hedge, which he presumed led on to a lane, than she was to him. The bull was standing rather more than twice the distance from Amanda than she was from the gate, but then, he knew that a bull can run at least twice the speed of a man. A deadly triangle, indeed. To reach her, he would have to run about thirty yards at top speed. If the beast decided to charge, the odds would be even, at best. The slightest error of judgement on his part would be fatal, probably for both of them.

While this was going on in his head, he was, with the minimum of movement, shedding his coat, unbuttoning his waistcoat, and removing the cravat that had taken him half an hour to tie to his satisfaction, all the while keeping an eye on the bull. On balance, he decided to keep his boots on, being more likely to stumble in stocking feet. Discarding the idea of crawling or running, until he had to, Justin began to walk steadily towards Amanda, who was still quite unaware of the terrible danger she was in. He was almost halfway to his goal when a fourth party entered the fray. Whether to warn his mistress of her danger, or just because he wanted to, Duncan gave a loud bray. Justin's heart, already beating like a trip-hammer, seemed to leap out of his chest. The bull pawed the ground a couple of times and started his charge. Justin ran, the bull galloped; there was no doubt who was the faster.

Amanda heard the sound of thundering hooves, looked up, and let out a scream; a split-second later, the marquis reached her; put his arms round her waist, snatching her off the stool. The bull was almost upon them, but Justins's action had thrown Amanda's sketchbook high into the air, and the fluttering paper distracted the enraged beast, who spent precious seconds reducing her table and stool to matchwood.

It gave Justin just enough time to reach the gate and throw Amanda bodily over it. She landed with a thump on the other side. He vaulted the gate after her, but not before the bull, now hell-bent on bigger prey, caught his trailing leg with one horn, ripping his pantaloons from ankle to hip, fortunately leaving only a deep, but bloody, scratch on his thigh.

Amanda, gasping, still partly winded, was attempting to get up, but Justin pushed her down again, dragging her into the drainage ditch that ran beside the hedge, landing almost on top of her.

'Keep still,' he ordered, and Amanda realised that the bull had not finished with them yet. She could hear the beast roaring and snorting, butting the gate with mighty force, and the frightening sound of splintering wood. Lying full in the ditch, the noise seemed to go on forever.

'Keep still, 'he reiterated. 'If he brute breaks out, I don't think he'll find us.'

'Duncan,' squeaked' Amanda, through a mouthful of mud.

'Sorry, sweetheart,' Justin mumbled into her hair. 'Are you hurt?'

'Just a bit bruised, I expect. You?'

'Only a scratch, but mostly it's my pantaloons that suffered, and I daresay Roberts will kill me when he sees my Hessians.'

It hadn't rained recently, so the ditch had no water running in it, but the bottom was wet, muddy, and smelly. Even when the noise ceased and presumably the bull had become bored, Justin wouldn't let them move. Amanda's hair had become completely undone, and somewhere in the field, there lay a widow's cap.

Justin pushed some damp locks aside with a muddy finger and whispered in her ear, 'My darling Amanda, will you marry me?'

He could feel her body stiffen under his.

Amanda spluttered and wiped some evil-tasting mud from her lips, muttering one word: 'Honoria.'

'She turned me down flat, totally refused my offer.'

'Refused?'

'Yes, I begged, I pleaded, I went down on one knee, I went down on both knees, I grovelled, all to no avail. She was adamant.'

Amanda wriggled into a more comfortable position so she could look at him. 'So you've come hot-foot for second best?'

For a moment, the Marquis thought she was being serious, then, despite the mud on her face, he saw the laughter in her eyes.

'Second to none, my darling. Come on, minx, I think it's safe to get up now.' Carefully, to avoid crushing her, he climbed out of the ditch, then pulled Amanda to her feet and held her close. 'You haven't answered my question.'

'What question was that?'

'You know perfectly well. Will you, Amanda Fletcher, do me the greatest honour in the world, of becoming my wife? There, is that clear enough for you?'

'Yes, yes. yes. Is that clear enough for—?'

She hadn't finished the sentence before, muddied and bloodied, he kissed her. After a long time, he murmured, 'Oh, my darling Amanda, I thought I was going to lose you.'

'That, My Lord,' Amanda smiled up at him, still cradled in his arms, 'is something you're going to find very difficult to do.'

THE END

Readers: *If you enjoyed meeting the Abbot and Coverdale families, meet the again, and many new characters in* **Staplewood Park***. Here is a short excerpt to whet your appetite:-*

Mairsford Manor in the County of Kent: July 1838.

Eight-year-old Bethany St Maure jumped down from the window seat. 'Mama! Mama,' she exclaimed excitedly. 'Aunt Amanda's carriage is coming up the drive. I'm going to meet her.'

Before her mother, Rosalie, Lady Benedict St Maure, could remonstrate about unladylike behaviour, her daughter had fled the room, tugged open one half of the massive front door, and was running across the wooden bridge that spanned the moat surrounding the mediaeval manor house, arriving on the other side, just as the vehicle pulled up. She was followed by a butler, who managed to squeeze past, and open the carriage door. The occupant, a tall, middle-aged lady, of athletic build and smiling brown eyes, descended without assistance, and immediately bent down to kiss her eager niece.

'Oh, Aunt Amanda, what was it like? Did the Queen wear her crown all day? Did Uncle Justin kneel down before her? Did…?' The Questions tumbled out one after another. 'Will you draw me some pictures….please Aunt Amanda.'

'My darling Beth, I will tell you all about the Coronation later, but first I must say hello to your mother, and shake some of this travel dust off.' They crossed the bridge together, and Amanda embraced Rosalie. 'I'm so glad to be here. Peace and quiet at last. London's been quite impossible for weeks.'

'I'm just as keen to hear all about the Coronation as Beth is, after, that is, Mrs Soames has shown you and your maid to your rooms.'

Settled comfortably around a table, laden with refreshments, Rosalie and her daughter were eager to hear all about the crowning of the young Queen Victoria. An event in which Amanda, as the wife of the Marquis of Coverdale, had an excellent view of the entire proceedings.

'It was a very long service, over four and three quarters of an hour, and none of us could move. I was so stiff I could hardly walk to our carriage, and then there was a long procession all through London. The crowds were amazing. We were cheered all along the way.'

'Did you wear a crown, too, Aunt Amanda?'

'Yes, but it's called a coronet – not quite so grand – or so heavy,' laughed Beth's aunt. 'The little Queen bore up really well, even when poor old Lord Rolle fell down the steps. She actually got up and helped him. She is only nineteen, the same age as Julia, and you, when you married Benedict, so I hope we are in for a long and happy reign. At least, God willing, I shall never have to go through another Coronation. Three in one life-time is quite enough.'

Rosalie agreed, 'But you didn't actually go to George the Fourth's one, did you? If I remember correctly, you gave birth to James the very next day.'

Amanda gave a sigh. 'Yes, I can hardly believe he goes up to Oxford next year, it makes me feel old.'

'Nonsense, Amanda!' exclaimed her sister-in-law. 'You're not yet fifty.'

'Next year, my dear, next year,' she replied with a rueful expression, 'but I want to hear what has been happening here, Ros, since my last visit?'

Before her mother could answer, Bethany said: 'Mama has found a man…' Amanda's eyebrows rose questioningly.

'Not the sort of "found", you're thinking, Amanda, but Bethany's right, I did find a man.' Rosalie pointed through the window. 'He was lying right there, in the drive, in the middle of a thunderstorm.'

'My goodness! What did you do? Who is he? Where is he now?' Amanda exclaimed, in a flurry of questions.

AUTHOR'S NOTES

In using the alternative spelling of "marquis", which I prefer, I am following the doyenne of Regency Romance: Gergette Heyer, who first stimulated my interest in the period, many years ago. The events depicted at the Battle of Waterloo The successful defence of the Chateau Hougment, albeit with great loss of life, was a crucial to winning the battle. The aftermath forms an important part of the story of The yellow diamond.

ACKNOWLEDGEMENTS

I would like to offer my sincerest thanks to all those who have been helpful in bringing The yellow diamond to fruition. My very special thanks to Roger Woodward, who not only sorted out my technical difficulties, but also for his invaluable advice: also to Joyce Rawlings, whose encouragement has been inspiring. Author House personnel have demonstrated amazing patience, especially my first Publishing consultant, Dexter Lopez.

Printed in the United States
by Baker & Taylor Publisher Services